A haunting journey into the dark depths of Niagara Falls. This is the side of the Falls they don't want you to see.

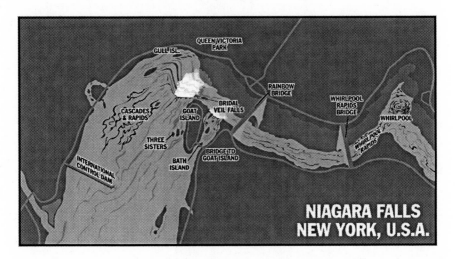

Amusement parks, video games, virtual reality. Forget'em. What if you could take a real life ride down a turbulent river through raging rapids and over the most famous waterfall in the world in the tradition of the turn of the century barrel-jumpers? And survive. *Maybe.* Would the thrill and the rush of adrenaline be worth the danger of such a risky adventure? The Ultimate Thrill Corporation is betting that you would be willing to take just such a risk. And they believe their high-tech passenger craft can endure the rigors of just such a journey. What no one can foresee is how mysterious events in the plunge basin – a void at the base of the Falls so deep that it has never been surveyed, will forever change the lives of all who dare to enter into it.

Then there is the mystique of the Falls itself, with its deadly history and the haunting psychological shadow that it casts over its denizens and all who dare to challenge it. Let Ro Patric, a self proclaimed river rat who knows just about all there is to know about the Falls and whose job is to fish its victims out once they resurface-if they resurface, be your guide, as you discover the dark secrets that are hidden underneath the Niagara façade. Will Patric be able to battle the demons that plague him – past, personal and otherwise. And as the stakes escalate will the Falls become the battleground between good and evil for the new millennium – the modern day Armageddon? In any event you'll never look at Niagara Falls in quite the same way again.

Iroquois symbol for "rising mist."

Other books by Robyrt Snyder

THE FALLS II: IN THE CROSSFIRE OF MIST AND
MADNESS

Visit us at our web site www.robyrtsnyder.com
Or www.trafford.com or www.thefalls1.com
Phone orders 1 866 752 6820 fax 250 383 6804
Or write Trafford Publishing 2333 Government St. Suite 6E
Victoria B.C. Canada V8V 4K5
Cover Design and Layout by Grinning Moon Creative,
www.grinningmoon.com
Lyrics by Farrenheit, www.charliefarren.com

This book is dedicated to all who have lost
their lives looking into the eye of the beast.

Also to R and J.

Thanks to my teenage son Ryan.
Thank God one of us is not afraid of computers.

THE FALLS

DESCENT INTO THE MAELSTROM

A TALE OF INDELIBLE HORROR BY

ROBYRT SNYDER

Valkyrie Productions

Note for Librarians: A cataloguing record for this book is available from Library and Archives Canada at www.collectionscanada.ca/amicus/index-e.html
ISBN 1-4122-0128-4

Printed on paper with minimum 30% recycled fibre. Trafford's print shop runs on "green energy" from solar, wind and other environmentally-friendly power sources.

TRAFFORD
PUBLISHING™

Offices in Canada, USA, Ireland and UK
This book was published *on-demand* in cooperation with Trafford Publishing. On-demand publishing is a unique process and service of making a book available for retail sale to the public taking advantage of on-demand manufacturing and Internet marketing. On-demand publishing includes promotions, retail sales, manufacturing, order fulfilment, accounting and collecting royalties on behalf of the author.

Book sales for North America and international:
Trafford Publishing, 6E–2333 Government St.,
Victoria, BC v8t 4p4 CANADA
phone 250 383 6864 (toll-free 1 888 232 4444)
fax 250 383 6804; email to orders@trafford.com
Book sales in Europe:
Trafford Publishing (uk) Limited, 9 Park End Street, 2nd Floor
Oxford, UK ox1 1hh UNITED KINGDOM
phone 44 (0)1865 722 113 (local rate 0845 230 9601)
facsimile 44 (0)1865 722 868; info.uk@trafford.com
Order online at:
trafford.com/03-2039

10 9 8 7 6

Go to a place of falling water and listen to the vibrations
of mother earth; look deep into its glistening pool: if you
listen well and look deep enough only then will its rhythms
and reflections help you discover answers to the mysteries
of life.
– Anonymous

We must see the earth around us again the way it was meant
to be seen; we must recognize the spiritual meanings of the
sky and earth and waters, of mountains, rivers and rocks.
We must again become grounded on this earth. It is time.
Arthur Versluis – Sacred Earth

BOOK I

PROLOGUE
THE CATHEDRAL AND WEDDED BLISS
Niagara Falls, Autumn 1675

IT was a time when the moon marked the seasons for man
to reap and nature to die. A harvest moon hung blood red in
the fall twilight sky and would bear witness to all that was to
follow this night. A night when man and nature would trade
places. In the effervescent hierarchy of the natural world then,
roles could be reversed with the frequency of the waxings and
wanings of an orb.

She stood on the rocky precipice, her image silhouetted
against the gray rising mist, almost *too* beautiful for such
a fate, but also the perfect choice. It was a marriage for all
intents and purposes, therefore it was her beauty as well as
her blood that had sealed her destiny. It was this dowry that
had been deemed acceptable by the powers that decided such
things and so it had been ordained. The fruits of the year's
harvest had been exceedingly bountiful and homage was
due. Mother Nature thirsted for the taste of a woman. Or at
least something did. Something in the deep dark. Something
in the recesses where the water falls, then spins and weaves,
crafting a cyclic undertow that sucks man, beast or thing to its
vortex. That something thirsted for the taste of a woman.

She was known by the name Naomi which meant pleasing
to the eyes and her selection was a great honor, which had
made her family very proud. Unfortunately this was also a
union that demanded it be consummated on a pyre of wet
granite, sandstone and shale.

Thick torrents of water rushed furiously to the edge of the
escarpment next to her, charging the brink before catapulting
into space, then plummeting into a roaring miasma on the
craggy rocks below. This constant pulverization of water
created a spiraling vapor, like the boiling steam of a hot spring.

The woman could feel the vibration from the thundering hydraulics, and despite her fear, she embraced it as the most powerful entity in her life. To it, she would betroth her wedding vows. It was their way. It was the way things were done in the valley of the river of the snake.

Audible through all the sound and fury of the waterfall was the steady thump, thump, thump on primitive leather stretched over bone. A multitude of bronze-skinned, loin-clothed men had assembled on the shore bank. A relentless drizzle drenched everything between sky and ground, hanging shrouds of cold and gray like curtains on this early autumn day. The air was heavy with condensation and difficult to breathe. It also rendered any manner of clothing translucent if not completely transparent. Time was rolled back to its most innocent and natural of states, forced to its knees before the power of the heavens.

Darkening clouds foretold the coming of a much heavier deluge. It was as if mother nature were planning to wash the land of its transgressions in an epic baptism. Or perhaps in her infinite wisdom she had just decided to show her grief and shed some tears for one of her innocent creatures.

The pounding dirge of the drums gained in tempo and the black-haired maiden stiffened. She edged closer to the brink of the mist-drenched granite and, with her toes, felt for the stone-etched markings that had guided others before her. Not even her preoccupation with ritual could anesthetize the pain coming from her leg. A spiral brand had been seared into the flesh of her thigh just hours ago and the throb had grown painful and unrelenting. Spots of red had leached through the fabric of her garment where it touched the wound.

She wore a long white tunic that clung to her body like moist gauze, sculpting her strong supple figure. Fawn-like, her beauty induced a mood of great reverence and offering among her tribe. Her hair was parted in the middle and banded by two strings of colored beads holding two white lilies. In contrast to the flowers, her dark eyes were sharp and

clear. Her fear of a moment ago had turned to eagerness. She
looked toward the sky and the mist funneling into the clouds
as though it were a stairway to the heavens.

Even if she had been inclined to do so, she could not have
ignored a smell that seemed to permeate all that was around
her. It was the smell of salt-water. She had been told to expect
it even though there wasn't an ocean for at least five hundred
miles in any direction. Long ago her ancestors had known
what it meant and its decree had been passed down through
the generations as if it were a torch in the night.

Now she knew the significance of that covenant.

She was in the regal presence of the hunter.

The time was at hand.

The groom had arrived. Vows could be exchanged.

The nuptial ceremony could proceed.

The prophesy would be fulfilled.

Lightening shattered the darkening terrain and froze
the scene for an instant, capturing it in a display of divine
pyrotechnics. A long rolling crack of thunder boomed and
the high priests intensified the cacophony of drumming,
dancing, chanting and canting to crescendo-like proportions.
Clouds crashed and clanged against each other like bells in a
panoramic belfry. Another barrage of lightning and the horses
reared wildly, their nostrils flaring from fear and expectation.
The vaporous plumes of their hot breath on the cold air made
it appear as if they were snorting fire. The Falls roared, its
powerful ancient engine bent on destruction. Man and nature
melded in a maniacal concert of sight and sound. The world
suddenly seemed on the edge of an apocalypse.

By contrast the woman remained insulated and oblivious
to the madness that enveloped her, as if in a catatonic state. She
appeared hypnotized by the omnipresent and engulfing mist.
Not always so dominant, on some days the mist was thin and
wispy. Yet on others, the mist was as thick as fog supported
by the humid nature of the air. But regardless of its volume, its
form always suggested smoke. The stream of smoke oozing

out of the plunge basin could feign one into thinking that the water itself was on fire. To others it suggested an altar in a perpetual state of offering.

In sunnier times, a rainbow with its bouquet of color would hang like a ornament on the drab mist.

A rainbow was tangible evidence of a spiritual presence-at least in the minds of the Iroquois. It was one of many reasons why the Iroquois regarded Niagara as its most vaunted and hallowed of cathedrals. For them it was an intersection of their spiritual and material worlds and the perfect altar for human tithing.

Calm and serene, as if stepping into a warm, shallow pond, the young maiden walked off the rock ledge. However in this last instant she had caught a glimpse something out of the corner of her eye. A thickening somewhere in the mist. Then, in that moment she knew this place was not what it seemed. It was all a LIE. The men on the banks who had whipped themselves into such a feverish pitch were either complete fools or the most devious of blasphemers. Either way she knew her life had been given in vain. She had seen the face of the hunter. Looked in its eyes. Sensed its soul.

For her the truth had come too late.

She tumbled and twisted, head over heels, to a scream-less, unspeakable mutilation on the wet granite far below, never reaching the roiling pool of water at the base of the Falls. It had to be like falling off the edge of the earth for what else could it be compared to. Her destruction was absolute-her life ended in a terrible rending of flesh from bone- her head wrenched at an impossible angle-twisted completely backwards on her neck – the last visage of her horror and disbelief seared onto a face that was still trained skyward. Only now it was a visage battered and glazed over with eternal void. And then there was a torso splayed and laid open like the gutted carcass of a fish. Just the way the gods liked it.

Innocent blood had been splashed about.

Her spirit had been joined; made whole.

Now she was one with the ages.

A wedding. A funeral. A beginning. An end.

What did it matter? It was all the same to her now.

The spirit, essence and blood of a virtuous woman was considered the most sacred of provenances and holiest of tonics. Powerful medicine indeed. More powerful than any of the shaman's potions.

As for her tribe, the Iroquois, they had sacrificed the most precious of their daughters in a gift of homage to the gods.

The moon held its solemn vigil as now it was the river's province to glaze red as blood.

ANCIENT IROQUOIS PROPHESY:
(translated)
On a day when salt air swallows the fresh air
The god of thunder will rise from its lair
A mortal soul on such a day in such a place
Will become one with the hunter and touch its face

Indians first began appearing on the North American continent between 20,000 and 30,000 years B.C.

The Iroquois Indians began immigrating to the valley of the river of the snake between the years 800 and 1300 A.D.

The translation for the word Iroquois is snake or rattlesnake.

No one knows when the hunter first appeared.

The hunter was just always there – as far back as anyone can remember.

FOREWORD

The tale is ended now. Yet I was to think of these days many times over. Looking back it's hard to believe it happened the way it did. The lights are dark now and the players have left the stage. And a grand stage it was. At times the whole world had a spotlight on it. When the curtain came down I was still in character, my lungs still drawing air. Not all the players who acted on that stage could say as much. At the time I would've chalked up my good fortune to an alignment of the stars or a deal of the cards. Now I know better. Some might say I saw the error of my ways, others might say I finally saw the light.

In retrospect it's hard to know if I was in any real danger. Who knows, a twist here or a turn there and I might have found myself in the path of a more deadly current. Whatever the true latitude of my peril, it doesn't really matter because I felt as if I were swimming in a dangerous riptide the whole time and I was struggling just to keep my head above water. I was in uncharted territory and the dangers were unfathomable. Though I never asked for any of it I just couldn't seem to duck out of the way of even one wave of the flood. It just kind of came at me and before I knew it I was caught in the maelstrom. All I was really looking for was just some peace and quiet.

Well it's quiet now. As I said the tale is done. The lights are down. My candle and my candle alone burns brightly enough to light the page to record the legacy of what happened here. And so I do this thing, as best as I can, always your dutiful servant so that you will know what went on in this place.

But before we embark on our journey I just want to plant a couple of seeds of thought for germination in your collective stream of consciousness. Did you know that scientists are just now discovering that our planet may have undergone a world-wide mass extinction of life hundreds of millions of years before the meteor or comet that hit the earth and wiped out the dinosaurs? Evidence is showing that a period of violent volcanoes and earthquakes may have released high concentrations of sulphur into our oceans to produce toxic chemicals and gases that killed not only all life in the water but on land as well. And that there are still bodies of water even today that at certain depths are highly toxic. By the way the smell associated with these black holes of toxicity is one of rotten eggs. Did you also know that just recently scientists are uncovering vast stretches of the ocean bottom that are completely covered with dead plant and animal remains? In these "dead zones" as they are referred to, every form of sea-life from plankton to algae to fish, have mysteriously died. There is no smell or toxicity present and although the cause is still unknown, the theory is that it is related to global warming. I can attest that the sickening sight of such absolute destruction of life is one of the most bizarre and grotesque images you will ever witness on the face of this planet. I only say these things now so that later when your mind screams for a breath of the oxygen of logic-for a scrap of something-a twig of anything to make some sense of this affair-desperately seeking an island of intelligentsia in a sea of insanity, then thou will have been forearmed.

And forewarned.

Now we begin.

I was present for most of it and when I was, I speak to you directly. For the other parts that I learned about, I can only tell you what I know. Here's what I know.

Shaking the chains
Shaking the chains
We got to shake it
If you want to break away
Shake the chains
By Farrenheit

CHAPTER ONE
THE SMELL OF BLOOD IN THE WATER
Niagara Falls, Sunday June 24th 2007

A storm was coming.

Traffic was jammed.

Cars were piled up from Canadian customs all the way across the Rainbow Bridge and into the side streets of Niagara Falls, New York.

The spring of '07 in the Falls had been extraordinarily warm. In fact, the entire winter had been so mild that even some of the old-timers had trouble remembering one quite like it. Naturally the doomsday experts said global warming was the culprit and were quick to point out that it was more evidence to support their edict, that at least environmentally, we were all headed to hell in a hand-basket. A moral direction that many men of the cloth had been forecasting since the expulsion of man from Eden.

Nevertheless there had been some snow. This finger of the land pinched between Lakes Erie and Ontario never escaped its share of lake-effect snow; in fact, in this region you could never be sure when one season ended and the next began. Temperature like time always seemed to be a relative kind of thing. Seventy degrees in the fall after a long hot summer seemed a lot colder than the same seventy degrees in the spring after a cold winter. Yet it was the same seventy degrees. Time had been known to operate on a similar template. Summers raced by, winters crawled. And any clock-watching school kid worth his hall pass knew that an hour of summer vacation dissolved a lot faster than that same sixty minutes when school was in session.

But spring had come suddenly and early this year, and any theories the locals offered about a temporary thaw were dispelled as the clement weather Marched, then Apriled into May. At this juncture of the calendar it was too late for a storm even this far north, and the townspeople and visitors embraced the reprieve from winter and the coming glory of summer days.

However it wasn't just the mild weather nor the upcoming holidays that drew the endless line of automobiles to the small Canadian tourist town of Niagara Falls.

"Have you ever, I mean ever, seen anything like this?" asked Derek Cope, more to his cigar, a perpetual fixture clamped between his teeth, than to anyone else. He was getting on in years and it seemed that with age came the uncanny ability to mumble at inanimate objects. Cope, a short squat fireplug of a man, owned and operated the American Motel on Lundy's Lane the four lane main drag in the Falls. He had been in the motel business here most of his life, having taken it over completely when his father retired.

"This is just damn unbelievable!" he said as the spectacle of bumper to bumper traffic inched its way up Clifton Hill. "Ever since that announcement from those Thrill folks, this town has exploded. I hear there isn't a room left from here to Hamilton, and that's fifty miles away. And people are still flocking in! I do believe this is the biggest thing this town will ever see! Not that it hasn't already seen its fair share."

A monstrous trailer truck with the letters ABC emblazoned on the side of its expansive panel turtled into sight. Jake, who was Cope's front desk clerk, dug fingers through a shock of yellow-white hair that was older than icebergs and said,

"Well, that means all three of the major American networks are here. Now who could have predicted that? We've all turned into a bunch of sheeple, if you want my opinion."

Age and prolonged exposure to human nature had jaded

old Jake to the point of cantankerous. And with the passing of his wife a few years ago there weren't many people left who Jake would consider worthy of keeping company with, Derek Cope being one of the few exceptions.. The two had been together for a long time and had seen a lot of life come through this town. The flotsam as well as the jetsam. Jake had always been a loyal and hardworking employee and for his part Cope knew how to be tolerant of Jake's less-than-optimistic but otherwise harmless ramblings on the state of the world. Now their relationship was less employer-employee and more 'odd couple'.

"What tongue are you babbling in now?" asked Cope.

"Sheeple. It's what you get when you cross sheep and people. It's what we're all becoming. Everyone plays follow the leader."

"Well, it's a good thing they do. Because these sheeple as you call them, are here in droves and they are what pay the bills around here, in case you forgot."

"Yea, yea, it's just that no one has an original idea in their heads any more. Just ask the bloody movie industry. Everything's a damn remake. "

"What about the people responsible for the Thrill expedition. Now that's pretty original. I understand that what they're attempting to do has never been done before."

"Sounds to me like another bunch of charlatans who've worked up their own variation on the original barrel jump. Why don't they just leave the Falls alone. It doesn't seem right to be always challenging a creation of nature. It's like waving a red flag in the face of God. Besides hasn't there been enough death over there already and still we don't learn our lessons. It's almost a desecration to allow it to continue as a tourist attraction. It should be declared hallowed ground, like a Gettysburg or something." Then Jake's voice trailed off into some indistinguishable train of thought.

"Stop mumbling will you. You know how I hate it when you do that," said Cope forgetting that he had a similar propensity for talking under his breath.

Jake in a louder than usual voice, an obvious display of overcompensation, "That's the trouble with this society, where are the men like Abraham Lincoln when you need them? They just don't make leaders like they used to. By God, I'll bet there's been enough blood spilled over there to consecrate it three times over."

"Gettysburg and Abraham Lincoln, for bloody heaven's sake. The trouble with you is you're still living in the dark ages. Well anyway, I happen to think what they're trying to do is downright ingenious."

"Bah, those Thrill people probably think they know it all. I'll bet they think they have it all figured out. But a little knowledge applied the wrong way will end up being their downfall, mark my words."

"It sure does have a way of filling hotel rooms."

Undaunted Jake continued," But there's one thing that never fails to amaze me, no matter how much people around here try to deny it. And Niagara is one place that continually lays it bare for everyone to see. It's so much a part of this place I think the talking heads who fancy themselves in charge should probably write it up and include it in the city charter."

"Okay, I'll bite. What's that?" inquired a curious Cope intrigued by Jake's flair for the dramatic even though after all these years he'd have thought he would have been immune to it.

"Niagara Falls proclamation number one...thou shalt never underestimate the capacity of human beings to be attracted by the smell of blood nor the depths they will sink to seek it out. In that respect they are just like sharks, if you want my honest opinion."

"When have you ever refrained from offering us all your 'honest opinion'.You sound more like Moses coming down from the mountain with the eleventh commandment. I am amazed that you can hold human-kind in such low regard and still give it permission to live on the same planet with you."

Jake, grumbled unintelligibly as he shook a canister with a perforated top and held it over the gurgling expanse of a fish tank that was the centerpiece of one wall in the motel lobby. That was all the Pavlovian substitution it took to draw a dozen angel-fish of all colors to the surface. It was as if the fish were spit out from every nook and cranny of aquatic paraphernalia on the bottom of the fish tank – trappings all arrayed to look like a Disneyland – for fish. An orange and a black one conjured itself out of the hold of Captain Kidd's sunken pirate ship and a yellow one woke from a snooze in a open treasure chest labeled Davy Jones' locker. Three more squirted out of the windows of a gray castle from Camelot. Once at the surface the 12 denizens of the artificial deep sucked hungrily with toothless mouths for food that wasn't even in the water yet.

"Patience my little ones. Patience is a virtue you know," as the golden flakes of wafer-like sustenance salted the surface. At first the fish crowded in a group, taking in what they could, but when that wasn't enough to slake their thirst some began to thrash with tail fins in order to muscle their way into a more favorable position in the queue. The water at the top of the tank began to froth, bubble and stipple with white. The noise of agitated water seemed to trigger an urgency among the fish and even though by now Jake had shaken out more than enough food for all, a feeding frenzy developed. The combative angelfish were lashing out and biting each other and anything else they touched. A piece of meat in piranha-infested waters did not vanish so voraciously. The surface of the water boiled for almost a full minute until every morsel had been consumed and only then did the fish drift back to the corners of their domain; exhausted.

"Now is that any way for you little devils to behave? Shame on you. That display of manners is something I'd expect from that crowd out there." scolded Jake.

"Sometimes I think you care more about those fish than you do about the guests that stay here. What do you expect from primitive animals?" said Cope. "All they know is brute force and violence. Survival of the fittest is the law of their world."

"Fish only do what comes natural to them. They don't know any better. People do."

A wind from the west had sprung up, cold and untamed, riding herd on black woolly clouds.

And the cars still kept coming.

The smell of blood in the water was beckoning.

The sharks were not about to be denied their fix of blood-lust. The approaching weather was proving to be little deterrent as the heavens got ready to express their displeasure.

Three miles upstream, in the usually peaceful village of Chippewa, Ontario, Charlie Knowales placed the phone receiver on its cradle and began to drain what was left of a now cold cup of Dunkin' Donuts coffee. He looked over at his pilot, Judd Blackadder, who was leaning on the back of a wooden swivel chair with his feet up, uncharacteristically, on the only desk in the small cluttered office. Knowales cleared his throat and said, "That's it. The Washington Post has just confirmed Sara Wilson. We're a go for Fourth of July week."

Knowales struggled to his feet with the help of a black-shafted wooden cane, then in passing by Blackadder, he employed it like a riding crop to deliver a sharp rap to Blackadder's leg-in a fashion similar to the way a herd tender might apply it to a goat or donkey to spur them to action. The blow struck Blackadder on the ball of his ankle bone in just the precise manner as to cause it to go numb. Was it the target of intent or just a lucky strike? One never really knew with Knowales. Knowales was the kind of man that if it suited his purposes he was not above studying the human anatomy so that he was apprised of all its pressure points and then committing this knowledge to memory to be dispensed in some future instance.

Blackadder made no sound unless one counted the hiss of air escaping his lungs like a leaking tire. He removed his limbs from the desk but the look of resentment that flooded his face was nevertheless undeniable even as he tried to shield it from Knowales. The mood inside the room-or at least in Blackadder's corner of it-matched the darkening condition of the skies outside.

"We have to look lively now", pontificated Knowales. "These will be busy times for us. There can be no tolerance of slackers. Idleness is the work of the devil."

Blackadder rubbed his wounded ankle in silence but knew better than to retaliate or argue.

Most people would concede that they found it hard to go up against the nature of this man. It was how Knowales got things done. This was Knowales' way, crude as it was but you couldn't argue with results and Blackadder was smart enough to recognize that it was Knowales who had gotten them this far. But he also knew that change was coming.

Big change. And soon.

In fact it was just on the horizon. He could wait. After all he had waited this long. He could wait a little longer for he was nothing if not patient. And after all, he was a Wellander and Wellanders were known for their patience. But for now it was better to bite one's tongue. For now it was better to focus on the moment at hand.

The man had earned it so let the man wallow in his glory, thought Blackadder.

The two men looked at each other for a moment. Nothing else needed to be said between them. The significance of the silence was not lost on either one of them. They were savoring the moment as people do when a dream becomes a reality. This was it. They sat alone in the darkness of their tiny shack/office in a secluded cove off the Niagara River.

Blackadder got up and both men limped over to the expansive front window of the building, standing below a sign that read, Ultimate Thrill Company. At least Blackadder could take some satisfaction in knowing that one of the limps was only temporary and it happened to be his. Looking out at the river to where a mysterious, sleek craft lay moored, they could just see it shrouded in the dusky shadows of the tree-lined river bank, since the sky was now as black as some men's souls. They savored the peace and quiet of this moment as much as the satisfaction of it. Clearly, this last moment of tranquility would soon be supplanted by the most tumultuous days of their lives.

They were going to make history and capture the imagination of the world.

They were going over Niagara Falls.

A low, ominous growl of thunder rumbled in the distance.

The storm was getting closer.

LOOKOUT POINT GOLF CLUB-FONTHILL AND THE KILLING MACHINE

Twenty miles away a white sphere soared in an arc that was easy to follow against a backdrop of dark threatening clouds. The rumble of thunder accompanied the flight of the golf ball as it traced a path long and true, temporarily unfettered from earthly bonds.

I knew that I was in trouble.

"Let's see you get out of this mess, buddy." Michael Napper exclaimed unable to contain the glee from dripping onto his words..

Napper, my golfing partner for the last ten years had just nailed a perfect drive on the 18th and last hole of our golf match on a summer day that up to now had been so beautiful we should have had to pay someone just for the privilege of being alive to breathe it.

"Well, you know what they say, it's not over till it's over.

Especially in a game as unpredictable as golf. Always be prepared for the unexpected."

"You can spare me the preaching. We're not down on the river now."

I stepped up to the tee and proceeded to slice my ball dramatically right, into the woods and down into a gully.

"I see exactly what you mean." This time the words were lacquered in sarcasm. "You know Ro, I've been waiting for ten years for this day. I'm finally going to beat the great Ro Patric on his home course. And don't be looking to that sky to save you. That rain's still at least a half an hour away. Plenty of time to finish this last hole."

Even with the rumblers rolling in, the day had been a winner. The summer sun had been warming and even though it was early in the season the grass had been laid out like a lush green carpet and all of it had been orchestrated to the song of birds foraging for their young. The melody of new life had serenaded us all during our sojourn-a constant declaration of how good it felt to be alive on such a glorious day.

"You know what your problem is, Mike. You get too wound up in the logistics of the game. You need to relax a little. Patience is the watchword, my friend. Have a little patience."

"I might remind you once again that we're not down on the river. *That*, I might concede is your domain but you're never gonna convince me that Indians have any special affinity when it comes to a golf course. So please, you can get down from your pulpit or your totem pole or whatever."

"But what you fail to see Mike is that the lessons that you learn from the river can be applied to all aspects of life, golf notwithstanding."

" Spare me the sermon on enlightenment and don't you try and weasel out of this. This is gonna be one sweet day when you finally have to cough up a c-note to me. Let's go finish this before you pull one of your Indian tricks. Like maybe a rain dance or two."

"Yes, my ancestors always looked to the sky as well as the river for answers. I won't deny that. But if more people treated nature with the respect my ancestors did perhaps the world would be in a better condition. That's the problem- we have become so disconnected from the land-the land that only wants to nurture us and so it means nothing to us to abuse it."

"And I didn't forget your Irish half. See this," he pulled out a coin with a leprechaun stamped on it. "This is to counteract any of that four leaf clover Irish luck you might try to pull out of your hat."

"You are too much, my friend. Next you will be pulling out a black cat out of your golf bag," I said shaking my head in disbelief.

We piled into the golf cart and zipped down the fairway to the one white speck floating on a sea of green.

"I feel your pain as they say, so I'm even gonna go get your ball for you. But as you well know, you're outta bounds. It's gonna cost you another stroke if you play it from here in the fairway." Napper offered.

"You're too kind," I replied in a tone of sarcasm but also resigned to the fact that my defeat was almost assured now.

As Mike left the cart and melted into the woods to retrieve my ball, I heard more rumbling from the sky, but there was a discernible difference between this noise and the rumblings of the last fifteen minutes. I glanced at the sky as the pounding in the air grew all around me as if a giant mutant dragonfly was approaching. Out of the clouds, a Sikorsky Skycrane S-64 helicopter hovered, then landed on the fairway of the golf course.

Phil Stinson in the pilot seat opened a window and yelled above the din of the rotors,

"Ro, it's an emergency! They need you at the Falls."

I knew Phil Stinson to be a man of few words and not one apt to be flying aimlessly around on a whim in a piece of million dollar machinery. It must be serious. I pulled on the passenger door, threw my golf clubs in, climbed in after them and we lifted off – no questions asked.

About 100 yards up I could see Mike Napper emerge from the woods with a look of astonishment on his face that, for a minute you'd have thought he'd seen a purple deer with two heads-both reciting Shakespeare. Through my window I held my hands out, palms up.

"What can I say", I yelled not without some hidden zeal leaking through onto the words, "Unfortunately duty calls."

I saw him whip the golf ball he had just retrieved hard into the ground, where it plugged. Then he went over to the cart, grabbed one of his clubs and began smashing the roof of the golf cart.

"I always thought that he was a little too tight in the knickers for a game that requires as much patience as golf does. He really does need to learn to relax," I said to Stinson as rain began to fall.

"Looks like I came at a bad time," remarked Stinson.

"*That*, my friend, is a purely relative observation based solely on the reactions of only one of the parties involved."

Even Hoover Dam couldn't have kept a smile from spreading across my face.

"And I'll be damned to hellfire if Mike wasn't right. We *would* have been able to finish that last hole just in the nick of time."

For the moment, it was one streak that would remain intact and I wasn't even sure which side-the Irish or the Indian-to give credit to. In retrospect my escape from defeat at golf would prove miniscule on the scale of life's tribulations when measured against the horror that I was now being drawn into.

And so it began. On the wings of this mechanized beast we were borne out of the lush greenery of a virtual Eden-like garden into an odyssey that would lead us to our destination-the valley of the river of the snake. This was a journey that would leave indelible scars on all of us until we reached the cold and hollow vaults of our graves and for some of us that would come sooner rather than later.

Unaware for the moment of the danger that lay ahead, we tilted rotor towards Niagara Falls.

That's when the sky really opened up and buried us in a deluge every bit as fierce as the one that must have lashed at Noah's gunwales.

It was about 20 miles to the Falls on the tailfeathers of undistracted crows and we got there by early evening. The rain had spent itself during the trip over. The cloud cover had broken and to the Falls we towed behind us a red sun bobbing on the horizon. Blackness followed in our wake.

A huge crowd had gathered around the railing that protected tourists from falling into the river from Goat Island on the American side of Niagara Falls.

Back in the 1830's someone had the incandescent idea that this would make a good spot to build a tower to get a closer view of the Falls. So they built what was then called Terrapin Tower right out in the river. From Goat Island one traversed wooden planks to the tower built on rocks out in the middle of the river. I mean how close did one have to get? This wooden path had no rails. You couldn't even call it a sidewalk. It was the first tourist viewing structure built at the Falls. It was a miracle that no one ever got killed in that scheme but I don't recall reading that anyone ever did. Thank God they finally came to their senses and ripped the monstrosity down. Incredibly the reason for tearing it down had nothing to do with safety. Some preservationist society had complained that it destroyed the aesthetics of the waterfalls. Such insanity was the norm at Niagara.

As we descended to Goat Island I remarked to Stinson, "Looks like we're not too late."

"Yea, I can see her standing on the outside of the railing," he confirmed.

"I still don't know if I can help her. There's usually nothing you can say. They've already made up their mind," I resigned myself to the reality, "I don't know why they called me? Since when did anyone think that I was good at saving anybody?"

As far as I knew I had never been able to save anybody. Sometimes it was all I could do to keep my own head above water. I had found myself in this position a couple of times before over the years and in both those instances it had turned out badly. I wasn't sure I could handle another failure. I needed to change tactics. That or get really lucky.

Just the thought of it spurred me to desperation, "Don't they have anybody else they can get to do this?"

"Maybe they couldn't get anybody else here in time and besides,...well, you're the expert on the river."

"Wait a minute, what'd you just say?" I asked, ready to grasp at any straw.

"Don't let it go to your head but no one knows more about the river than you do. Everyone knows that. Maybe that's why they requested that you be here."

"Thanks Phil. You just gave me an idea that I can use. Just maybe....."

We pushed our way through the crowd over to an area that had been set up as a makeshift NFPD, command center. Everyone was on edge. Three detectives were cupping their hands against the wind trying to shield the flame of a match in order to light their cigarettes. Just before the third one was lit I reached in and snuffed the flame between my thumb and forefinger. The sizzle and smell of burnt flesh tinged the air and punctuated their looks of astonishment. It wasn't the first time my flesh had been seared.

"Don't you guys know it's bad luck to light three on the same match."

The detective who had to refire to light his cigarette, was especially irritated and barked out, "You know Patric, maybe not everyone believes in that superstitious gobbledygook like you do."

"Maybe you should. My horoscope for today said I was going to have to work with three jerks and it looks like that came true."

The three detectives growled something intelligible as the captain came over to brief me on the situation at hand.

I was instructed that the woman on the other side of the railing had recently lost her teenage daughter to a drug overdose, her husband was out of town, and that she had made no specific demands; she was just depressed. Was there anything that I could say that would help until they could get trained personnel here?

"I can give it a try," I offered less than enthusiastically.

"Hey Patric", one of the detectives called out. "don't overwhelm her with your sense of optimism."

He was right, I thought. I was going to have to shift attitude gears. And quick. This was not a situation in which you could stay neutral-you had to put yourself out there. Phoniness was something they could smell on you quicker than a cheap cologne. This was going to take more than a good luck charm.

As I drew near to the railing I could see that the woman was fairly young . That was a good sign and I was hoping to use that to my advantage. After all, I was up against a foe that demanded that I use any edge I could get. For this woman to have had a teen-aged daughter meant that she had gotten married at an early age.

The wind from upriver whipped at her red hair clearing it from her face. I couldn't help but noticing that her hair and the hue of the setting sun were a perfect marriage of red.

She was troubled, there was no doubt about that, but even though she held her head down I could see that she was very pretty. That was even better and another point in our favor. I didn't even need to see the daughter or look at her rap sheet to know that she had probably been a hard core user. The pain and worry of such a life was written in the premature lines of her young mother's face and told me all I needed to know. The rest of the story was easy to guess. The agony of her daughter's death was mirrored in this woman's eyes. I had witnessed that kind of agony in lots of faces before, but they were usually down in the river and already dead.

The story on the face did not indicate a quick paragraph down at juvy hall. Each chapter and verse was punctuated with suffering. The lines of worry in the woman's face translated into countless hours in detention halls, police stations and rehab clinics.

There was poetry as well. The sad poetry of a broken heart. In between the sagas of desperate lives were the etchings of loving someone so much and not being able to help them no matter how hard you tried. The sonnets and iambic pentameters cried out in measured strokes of the pain of watching someone die slowly before your eyes and then having that pain come back on you and slowly start to kill you in the process.

It was a tale of couplets that neither rhymed nor a plot that made sense. Certainly the ending was not gilded with glass slippers and handsome princes. The reflections in her eyes represented a recent stint at a morgue and a cemetery. In the epilogue, all that was left were the tear-spattered pages of a mother's struggle to save her child, a sad chronicle awash in the tears of a desperate fight. A fight she had lost and in its course it had taken from her, her youth and now her will to live. Only a parent who had gone through as much could understand the similes and metaphors of such an experience.

A mother. A woman. A child. All three stood perched before me now. Which one was the key that would allow me to save all three? I couldn't afford the luxury of unlocking the wrong door. There would be no consolation prize. Death would claim its trophy and the rest of us-especially me would try to forget it and go on with our lives. But it was not that easy for me to forget-to live with the consequences of yet another failure-of committing your emotions to someone you didn't even know and letting them suck you dry and then it was all for naught. No, for me it was not that easy and I didn't want to dwell on that thought.

I'd already decided on an approach thanks to an idea germinated by Phil Stinson back in the copter. It was risky but

I was going with an instinct. In my other two previous cases, preaching and sweet talk had proven to be faulty scripts.

What if I could scare her? I wasn't sure that I could. Maybe it was going to take something more. Whatever it took, I just wanted her off the ledge, most preferably on the land side – not the water side. Maybe what she needed was a dose of reality. Maybe the prescription here called for a bottle of Falls 101. But I was going to have to be careful. This was a medicine that was best administered one teaspoon at a time. If it was meted out too fast or too much at a time it could throw the patient into shock. Quickly I tried to muster up my best bedside manner.

"Hello,..ma'am. Would you mind if I called you Marie?... they told me that was your name."

No answer.

"If you don't mind then, Marie it is. Anybody that knows me knows that I'm not much on formalities."

Still no response.

"Listen,....I know you don't know me but my name's Ro Patric. I also know better than to pretend that I'm going to be your savior. I'm not anybody's savior. I'm a river rat. That is I'm just a guy who works down there...(for some strange reason, I felt that that could have been taken to mean some other nether region from below so I specified)... on the Niagara River. Some say that I know the river better than anyone. Maybe that's true but don't tell anyone you heard it from me. Even though I'm proud of it and my Irish side wants to brag about it, my Iroquois heritage requires that I be humble about such things."

The distraught woman gave no indication that she was aware of my presence.

My impression of the young woman at this point was one of overwhelming despair – it had a grip on her that was so deep down that I had to concede that her future was already a forgone conclusion-that is she had no future. Knowing that, depression was beginning to descend on me as well – but I was determined not to let her know that or sense it. Of course I would never give up.

"Listen ma'am, I don't know you or what you've been through and so I can't tell you not to do this because I don't know what you have in your life to live for. But I'm not going to give you the standard crap that life can't be all that bad. Maybe in your case, it is."

I could *feel* the detectives of the NFPD behind me rolling their eyes at that one.

"But what I do know is this river and what will happen to you if you let go of that railing. You see all that water next to you, falling. It almost looks soft and pillowy, like a wet cloud, doesn't it?" And the mist. It's all sweet and lacy and you just want to let it kiss you with it's coolness.

That's what this place does. It beckons. Believe me I know. Many a sane person less troubled than you, myself included, has stood at this very railing and felt that very enticement to become one with that web of water. Sometimes it only lasts for the flicker of a flame. Other times it can be relentless. I know of people who can't come here to view the Falls unless they are in the company of someone with a strong grip. It's an urging that tugs on primal roots, that's for sure. For my money, ma'am, this whole place is like a giant spider web."

For the first, time since I started talking, I saw her stir. She lifted her tear streamed face a little to look out at the Falls.

I continued, "Even with your feet planted on dry land the Falls will try to hypnotize you . It will seem as if it's message is for you personally. It likes to make you think that it speaks to you alone. But once it gets you in its grasp it rarely lets go. The lives saved from Niagara could be tallied on the digits of a three-toed sloth, the souls lost; uncounted.. That's because only when it's too late will you realize how diabolical, how demonically apocalyptic it all is. It does not care for you at all. It sucks you into its teeth and whatever is left is spit out the other side. You may have felt that its invitation was highly personal but when it's too late to escape only then will it let you know that you are merely more fodder for the shredding mill. It is a glorified killing machine."

The woman seemed to be staring with unseeing eyes straight into the mist, while everything else around us seemed to be bathed in the red communion of setting sun and sky. The handle of a rainbow was visible protruding out of the far side of the mist but that wasn't what seemed to have her attention. I thought I detected a flash of fear creep into her eyes overriding the reflections of pain and despair . That expression of fear was not a stranger to me but I say again that it was usually implanted on visages that had ridden the Falls to its natural conclusion.

"Believe me when I say that its mystique will fade faster than a cheap card trick. There is nothing glamorous about dead flies in a spider web or stuck to a strip of fly paper. Don't let the illusion fool you ma'am. It's the biggest infernal lie that this place can perpetrate. I make my living down there. I battle this monster every day of my life and also many a night when I've had to relive its horror from my bed. I've seen just about everything there is to see and it won't be like what you think it will be. It will not be gentle. Your best hope is that the inevitable will be relatively quick. I can tell you that there is no guarantee on the quickness but the pain... the pain comes with an iron-clad, money-back-if-you-are-not-satisfied warranty."

The detectives behind me were about to have a conniption.

She had still not uttered a word but I saw her seriously studying the grayness that was close to swallowing her. At the time, I thought she was giving my words the weight they deserved.

I felt as if I was getting to her and now was the time to strike deep while the iron was hot. I had presented the reality and now it was time to hook it into the vanity. Despite all her troubles she was still a woman, after all.

I showed her the back of my hand. My voice took on the

added conviction of personal experience.

"Do you see these scars, Marie? They form letters that I had burned onto my hand. CYFIC. Those letters were inspired by this river on the day a couple of guys from our crew made a rare rescue. It stands for Can You Feel It Coming. I was a young man then and the guy they pulled out of the water said it to me and I've never forgotten it. I don't have time to go into all the details now but it means to never underestimate this river because it will COME at you. I screamed when they seared those letters into my skin because I wanted the pain to never let me forget. It's what's kept me alive all these years.

You're still a young woman ma'am. Very pretty if you don't mind me saying, but if you let go of that railing you will experience a side of Niagara that very few get to feel. And when its over I'm afraid your own husband will not be able to recognize, let alone identify, what will be left down there when this river is done with you. You will know firsthand the real "glory" of Niagara. Marie, I would suggest that if you are really intent on going through with this, that you take your wedding ring off of your hand and SWALLOW it. You heard me right, I said swallow it. At least that will give them something to go on at the autopsy."

There, I had done it. Administered a full measure of defribrillation. Could she absorb it? Only time would be the judge.

The woman started to sob. Softly at first, then more deeply. I could feel the emotion unleashing inside of her and it made me feel connected to her despite my best efforts to prevent that from happening. I already knew deep down that if I lost this woman, it was going to be a tough road to come back from. It was my guess that it was probably a road I would never venture to go down again.

The red sun was about to dip below the horizon.

Long, menacing shadows lunged at us from everywhere.

She gathered herself, turned to face the water, took a deep breath and held it while her body tensed, like a coiled spring.

The mist seemed to have her in its trance.

My God, I thought, *she was going to do it anyway. What did it take to get the message through?* Now I was the one with breath and heartbeat on hold. My whole world was hanging on life support waiting to see how the drama would play out its next card. Time itself was entombed in purgatory. There it was. That time-is-relative-thing again. I felt the desperation of a ship out in the ocean caught in a monstrous storm. For some reason, all I could think of was a line from a Gordon Lightfoot song, "when the waves turn the minutes to hours."

A gust of river-sent wind blew on her as if she were a tattered sail, seemingly in a last ditch effort to make her decision for her. It also blew some of that grayish mist that she seemed so preoccupied with, towards her and now threatened to devour her as completely as the whale that mouthed Jonah.

My natural inclination was to make a grab for her but I resisted the temptation. I was too far away and with the addition of the iron railing in between us, it would prove an awkward maneuver at best. Any movement on my part would be telegraphed. She would see it coming and would have plenty of time to avoid it if she so chose. I had no intention of seeing my calculations borne out. Our training had taught us not to make up their minds for them with rash moves. So even though, up to this point, I had pretty much thrown the book away, now I went with it.

It was with some surprise that the young woman held fast in the face of all of this elemental coercion. She let out a gasp, exorcising her lungs of all the pent up air and leaned forward.

Then suddenly it was as if she had broken the spell.

She turned back to face us and cried, "Please help me," and stretched out a trembling hand. The detectives practically fell over themselves to get to her and pulled her to salvation. *Hallelujah, it was over!*

I remembered saying to Phil Stinson as we packed up our gear, that if this was any indication of how the rest of the week was going to go, we were all in for one helluva ride. Today we had been lucky. But I knew Niagara had a long memory and she would make someone pay for interfering in her business. Vengeance would be put on account for now but make no mistake it would be extracted. This was a club whose membership did not tolerate uncollected dues for very long. That's just how it was-business as usual in the valley of the river of the snake.

And even though I was given credit for getting the woman off of the ledge- one truth still remained unchanged. I still hadn't saved anybody-although it would have been impossible for me to know it at the time.

A CONJURING OF THE FORCES OF NATURE

That spring and into early summer a series of events had occurred, not all of which were known to each other at the time and not all of which could be adequately explained.

On March 15th a total eclipse of the sun was visible only in the Northern Hemisphere. Even within that realm, viewing was limited to certain places – the western end of New York State that included Niagara Falls – being one of them. At the height of the eclipse – with the moon blocking the path of all the sun's light to the earth except for an outer halo, observers in the Falls area saw this corona turn from white to a deep purplish-red for no apparent reason. This phenomenon was not evident anywhere else. The official scientific explanation was an irregularity in the ozone layer. The Amerindian culture would have interpreted this to be a sign that their creator was displeased and that the inhabitants of this region were being put on notice.

In June, in the lush fruit belt of the Niagara Peninsula Adam Wright was engaged in a battle. His north field of blueberries, strawberries and raspberries which usually produced the first yields of the growing season followed later by the tree grown harvest of apples, peaches, cherries and pears., was under siege. This year his north field had been plagued by a heavier than normal influx of crows. Not only were their numbers greater but their demeanor was much more brazen than in past years.

Of course Wright had set out the obligatory scarecrows and wind mobiles but these had been ignored by the marauding birds right from the outset. Next he tried a couple of sound cannons(devices that emit a blast resembling a shotgun.) These contraptions had initial success but the crows soon caught on to the ploy . Before long they were back scavenging in the fields.

In danger of losing his crop Wright was forced to resort to the real thing. He and his sons patrolled the fields with loaded shotguns. This tactic again produced initial results but the aggressive nature of these crows was not anything he had seen in 35 years of farming. They were not to be denied. And they were not afraid to die.

In the time it took to shoot one crow scores of others could be filling their bellies. To Wright it seemed as if they knew how to fan out so that only one crow was sacrificed by each blast from the gun.. If Wright didn't know any better he would have sworn that they were organized to *sacrifice* individuals for the good of the whole flock. In a manner that could only be likened to warriors of the Divine Wind or kamikaze.

It all came to a head one day when the crows attacked Wright as he was reloading his shotgun. They descended on him with such fury that they plucked out an eye before his sons could intervene. Reporters searching the annals of their newspapers could find nothing of this nature having been recorded before. Wright surrendered his north field to the crows and when they had plundered that, other farmers in the area reported isolated incidents of similar circumstances.

Back at the turn of the century when electricity was being coaxed out of its cradle and most of it was just an untested idea, Niagara Falls, and its endless supply of natural energy, was considered a prime location to build the turbines necessary to produce this new phenomenon. Oddly enough it was not the water already going over the waterfalls that interested these pioneers but the water from up river. This, they could divert from the main flow and channel it down the escarpment into the ravenous maws of their generators. Tunnels were built to achieve this. Over the ensuing years, many of these individual enterprises foundered as the technology advanced and most of these obsolete tunnels were abandoned. Some of them made excellent observatories for geologists.

It was for this reason that Jon Bertrand from the physical science department of Niagara College came to find himself ensconced in the 1912 excavations of the Toronto Power Company, during the last week of June. This was not his first excursion into this tunnel (in fact he had been here only about a month ago) and as his light played over an inscription on the wall he wondered how it was possible that he could have missed its existence before. The Lord's prayer had been scratched into the rock with a blackened stick.

Backwards.

That spring there were happenings of an unprecedented nature taking place on the Niagara River as well. Frogs! A proliferation of frogs had descended on the river in numbers never seen before, especially in the plunge basin area adjacent to the Falls. In the past, the violent nature of the water in this section of the river had discouraged most species of aquatic life from establishing any sort of a foothold, not to mention a domain. And the frogs certainly paid the price for their efforts at cohabitation with the turbulent water.

Hundreds of bruised and battered corpses floated on the surface-so thick that at first glance it was mistaken for seaweed. Tourists on the Maid of the Mist thought that the greenish hue on the rocks surrounding the Falls was moss, until upon closer inspection, movement could be detected. The men who worked on the river were baffled. Then as quickly as the frogs had appeared, they vanished.

The men operating the tour boats started to notice another uninvited visitor that was not indigenous to these waters. Black snakes were spotted in the waters near both shores of the river. It was noted that some had horns. A couple of the more curious ones even accompanied the tour boats on parts of their journey. Wasn't it cats that were supposed to be curious? When contacted, two local biologists agreed that this phenomenon was probably a result of the abundant food supply caused by the frogs, and as they had dissipated, so too would the snakes. And indeed, this hypothesis was eventually borne out but not before an incident occurred that shook the tight-knit community of men who worked on the river to its core.

A young boy of no more than twelve, David Slinger from Nazareth, Pennsylvania, was at the side of the boat, pointing out the Falls to his mother when a black snake as thick as a man's arm, sprung at least four feet from the depths of the water and wrapped itself around the boy's outstretched arm. I happened to be on the Mist that day and everyone was galvanized to the deck with shock at the sight. The boy let out a curdling scream with about as much fear as could be stuffed into a single vocal expression.

The snake had used this precious time to twist its wet coils around the boy's throat. I tried to pry a fire axe from the wall of the aft deck cabin but the metal clasps that held it in place had rusted because of inactivity and the damp river air. It slipped from my grasp and as the snake began to tighten its coils around the young boy's neck, his screams were choked down to a sickening gurgle. That's when a curly-haired fellow by the name of Randall Sampson, who came with hands as big as hams, ripped the axe from its rusted moorings, pinned the head of the snake to the gunwale of the boat and struck a blow that cleaved the snarling, spitting, wide-eyed head of the reptile from its coils.

The head plopped into the water even as the coils were releasing their grip around the young boy's neck. The horned head of the snake was still snarling and flicking its forked tongue before it sank from view-an image not many of us would soon erase from our memory. Some who were there still maintain to this day that they noticed scaly knobs manifested on each side of its head. A greenish vile smelling liquid gushed from the remains of the snake. Sampson unraveled the limp snake like it was a wet scarf and flung it far out into the current.

Hardly a mention was made of the incident in the local paper, which was not surprising as there was a deliberate and concerted effort to underscore anything that might upset the tourists. Horned snakes were a bad omen in Indian culture. Sampson, the hero of the day, would die years later when a load-bearing column of a building collapsed on him and many others. David Slinger would later return to his hometown and develop a carbonated juice drink and become so popular that he would earn the moniker, "king of juice".

I went back to my job on the river.

Also in June, a man with a peculiar condition that produced growths of bone on the sides of his head exclaimed to his brother-a brother who prior to this had hack-sawed these abnormalities off, when they had become too prominent,

"Just let them grow."

CHAPTER TWO
A LESSON IN CHEMISTRY AND SCHOOLING IN THE
SMILE OF DEATH
Niagara River Gorge, Thursday night, June 28th

Even if I hadn't read my horoscope that predicted that
I was going to have a crazy week I would have sensed it
anyway. Although we had yet to enter July's house of the
thunder moon, as the Indians referred to it, we were well in
the midst of the rose moon and since full moons were known
to be harbingers of such things, I knew that it was going to get
crazy. Real crazy.

All signs pointed in that direction. Helicopters buzzing
overhead, hellish traffic tie-ups on every side street, throngs of
people milling about on anorexic sidewalks. All the ingredients
were there: one part full moon, one part Niagara, and one
part media circus. Voila. It was a high octane concoction for
craziness squared, if ever there was one. Underlying it all,
was the magnetism radiated by the spectre of death-a recipe
no one should underestimate.

I was twenty stories below the surface of all that madness,
waiting for a floater and glad to have gotten the call – morbid
as that may seem. It was a lot more peaceful down here in the
gorge, with the Falls doing its watery symphony a mile and a
half upriver, it's orchestration translated into a muted roar in
the background of my thoughts.

The big show was upstream; here under the shadow of
the Rainbow Bridge, the perpetual drone was lulling. The
foaming, bubbling rhythm of the river passed by the safety
and solitude of my little hut, soothing my senses.

A link seemed to forge between my nerves and the war
torn water as they both tried to convalesce before the next
battle. And there was always another battle. The very nature
of the Falls perpetuated the endlessness of such a cycle. As
long as it flowed there would be life and death. And life again.
A river like the Niagara is a lot like life, at least that was what

my grandfather had always maintained.

"Learn the lessons the river can teach you and you will have a blueprint for life. Take what it gives you, no more, no less," he would say.

Indians from their earliest presence had fostered a special connection with nature and my Iroquois ancestors had always been drawn here to this place by Niagara's sacred siren call. I was a fourth generation river rat and believed it was my Indian blood that allowed me to "understand" the moods of the river. These instincts had been passed down in my genes in a manner no different than my black hair or brown eyes; instincts that I had relied on for almost thirty years to make my living. I took what the river would give me. Right now it gave me the peace and quiet that I needed. But not for long.

A woman, escorted by two men, was slowly picking her way down the rocky goat path that led from The Maid of the Mist dock to my hut down in the gorge. It was a sight so alien that my mind had to sift through the denser rings of memory wood to recall if it had ever happened before. Didn't I say things were about to get nutty? In all the years that I had been doing this, I'd never had reporters come right down into the gorge while I waited for a floater. Thursday night, and I could feel that my peace and quiet was about to be sucked down river along with everything else in the Niagara.

As they continued to wend their way down toward me, I was reminded of ants on an alligators hide, trying to find the path of least resistance. I was pretty sure that I had seen the two men around before. They looked to me like a couple of reporters from the *Niagara Falls Gazette*, which figured. Only a couple of local guys would have been able to find me down in the gorge. I'd never seen the woman before. My occasions for dealing with women reporters if that's in fact what she was, were as numerous as the times I'd spoken Farsi to bespectacled kangaroos. I racked my brain but in my wildest dreams I couldn't imagine who else would have business down here.

This one appeared to be on the cradle side of thirty and

unless I was being misled by a baby-face, it made me wonder how much of life she had really seen.

Probably right out of journalism school and now she's gonna go out and write about the big bad world. Well she'll find something along those lines to write about down here. If she's got the mettle to handle it. One thing about this place, it'll make you grow up fast.

She wore boots, not hiking boots but street boots with heels, rugged enough to accommodate a hike in the downhill terrain of the gorge and yet still be considered stylish on the sidewalk.

Now there was a feat that not too many people could pull off.

The rest of her dress followed suit. She wore jeans but not the cheap ones like the ones from around here; expensive maybe even designer and they ran for miles down long legs. A black short leather jacket over a white blouse and pony-tailed blonde hair completed the ensemble giving the entourage the look of a young English lady with her grooms on the way to the stable to select a mount.

Definitely not one of the local yokels with that kind of style. Probably never even went to a real school. Probably one of them women's schools like Vassar or Radcliffe with mommy and daddy picking up the tab. Probably been spoiled from day one. What Suzie wants Suzie gets. And now Suzie wants to play reporter in the grown-up world.

As an Indian I prided myself on being able to read the river and I liked to think that sometimes those skills extended to people as well, or maybe that was a trait that resided in my Irish half. Regardless, it was my prediction that this woman appeared to be a element that would not fare well in these circumstances. Some substances just didn't mix well with the H2O of the Falls.

It's always been my opinion that the Niagara and its environs just instinctively seemed to be more suited to a man's game. However don't tell Annie Taylor that I said that. For the record, in 1901 Annie Taylor was the first person ever to go over Niagara Falls and live to tell about it. Other than that women and Niagara never seemed to be a good mix. And it certainly wasn't a place for a school girl.

That's when I remembered that Charlie Knowales had informed me that a woman reporter from the *Washington Post* was booked for the maiden trip. At the time I remembered having doubts about the wisdom of such a choice. I also wondered how she rated. I mean, what made her so special? I was beginning to think that I knew the reason why Knowales had selected her and my guess was that it probably had something to do with money. I decided to apply my own litmus test.

Despite all the negativity I had conjured up about the woman there was something about her gait, her demeanor, that even from a distance seemed to belie a sense of purpose and even determination. At least she deserved some credit for coming down here at all. That alone meant she had more ambition than most. The national press people that I'd dealt with before were too arrogant to have wasted their precious time. I wondered if she'd have the guts for what else she might find down here.

"Sara Wilson?" I asked as I nodded at the two men.

"Yes. How did you know? I don't believe we've ever met before."

She was a little surprised, but not caught off guard. In fact, she seemed to possess what I can only describe as an overwhelming sense of calm. If the world was a hurricane she was the eye. To a man like me who was in constant search of peace and quiet wherever it could be found-this was like water in the desert.

Sometimes when you meet someone for the first time you sense something. I detected a weird kind of bond with her almost immediately. It didn't seem possible but it was like some part of us came from the same place. However this initial instance of connectivity wasn't about to excuse her from her freshman test on Weird Science of The Falls. However that was for later.

It had been my experience that the laws of attraction work almost the same with people as they do with magnets. Isn't that really the way it is with us human beings anyway? We mingle and migrate around and about each other like magnetically charged bits of steel. And every once in a while we find ourselves in an alignment that produces either intense repulsion of an unknown origin or- in fulfillment of the adage that opposites attract-an extreme synchronicity. Either oil and water or peanut butter and jelly'

"No, we haven't met," I said. "It was just an educated guess steeped in a little Indian intuition. Ro Patric, at your service."

We shook hands. She had a firm grip, but soft and soothing too, like she'd just rubbed lotion into her hands. I could imagine such a touch stroking the fear out of the feathers of an injured bird. Ogling the canyon-like walls as if she were stuck in the parting of the Red Sea, "Oh oh. Something tells me we're not in Kansas anymore, Toto."

The remark caught me off guard in a manner that forced me to chuckling and exposed a sense of humor in her that I found pleasant to be around. It was not what I would have expected from her. I expected her to be more serious. More into her. If indeed self-deprecation was her way, than if nothing else, at least we would have that in common.

"H'mmm," she said. "Patric. That doesn't sound particularly Indian."

"It's not. It's Irish. The Indian's on my mother's side."

"Didn't a Patrick have something to do with chasing all the snakes out of Ireland?

"That would be Saint Patrick and the snake part is probably an Irish myth. Doesn't really matter because I ain't no saint and I'm surely not likely to be ever confused with one."

"And Ro. That's very unusual, what is that ?"

She pulled out a pen and a small, leather-bound pad of paper. Already going to work. I offered her a chair, and we all sat down.

Just like in school, I thought. *I bet she's real good at taking notes. That's good, because Falls 101 is about to begin.*

She perched on the edge of her chair, leaning toward me as I spoke, her active listening skills plainly lubricated by practice.

"My first name is Robert. Ro is just a nickname the river rats gave to me."

"And what are the river rats? Almost sounds like you are a group in need of a good exterminator."

"Not exactly," I replied, although I could appreciate her attempts at humor in order to keep things loose-she was more on target than she knew. "If anything we're a dying breed, dictated by the very nature of our profession. There is no river rat academy. It's either in your blood or it isn't. It takes a special kind of person to cope with the things that happen on this river on a day-to-day basis.

Water is such a dichotomous substance. It is essential for life and yet it also has the ability to take life. We live on the dark side of that dichotomous relationship every day.

River rats are anyone who make their living down here at the river. My family has been employed at the Niagara for four generations. My great grandfather was here in 1850 when the original Table Rock collapsed into the Falls. It was his job to make sure that no one was near when it happened. And a Patric has been here ever since. Today, I'm a fourth generation river rat and proud to be one. It must be keeping this old hide busy 'cause I haven't noticed any flies on it yet. Ain't never gonna get rich, but the river's in my blood and I love coming to work everyday. Not everyone can say that."

"Now how in heaven's name does one come upon the decision that they want to become a professional river rat? I don't imagine you'd see too many advertisements in the want ad section."

"That's funny you should ask that question. I remember the first time I ever saw Niagara Falls, I guess I was about six or seven years old. What I remember most was the natural beauty of the area then; none of these towers were here and Clifton Hill was nothing like it is today. Sure, there were shops and quaint places to eat, but the neon commercialism and horror house stuff had not yet arrived. There was a real innocence back then, but then I guess you could say that about anything. I remember seeing the Falls from a distance and I was exhilarated. I wanted to get closer, so my father took me to the Table Rock House. As we got closer to the railing, I can still recall the sun shining, reflecting on the river as it flowed to the brink. I remember the clearness of everything; the sunlight, the sky, the water, everything was crystal clear and bright.

"When the people in front of us had left, we stepped up to the railing right at the brink of the Falls. I remember looking over and I couldn't see the bottom. I mean, it just disappeared into the mist and tons of falling water, into who knows where, another world. That's when I became terrified, when the real horror of this thing struck me full force. Even on a day so clear with the sun shining brightly – a joyous day when life was meant to be celebrated – this thing could take me down there somewhere in the darkness, and no one would ever see me. I wouldn't even know where I was or how to get back. I would just be gone in the gray rising mist. I was a little old for that sort of thing, but I remember grabbing onto my father so tightly that I could have crawled inside of his skin. Anything to get away from that *thing*. I was crying when my father finally took me away. But even then somehow I knew that I was inexplicably tied to this place."

"That's rather interesting. As a kid you are deathly afraid of the Falls and yet you make a career out of working on that very river."

'Now that you put it to me in that way it does sound a little strange. I can't explain it except to say that perhaps in some cases we are drawn to the thing that we fear most like a moth is to a flame. I'm not sure what takes precedence in my case- the need to overcome my fears or just plain stupidity."

"Sounds a little strange to hear someone refer to themselves as rats and be so proud of it. What exactly does a river rat do?"

"Anything to do with the river, but most of the action is concentrated from the Falls through the rapids and down further to the whirlpool. There are twelve of us and its like a brotherhood that can't be put into words. In this fraternity any one of the others would be willing to put their lives on the line for you. It really is quite an indescribable feeling. Some rats work on the boats that go near the base of the Falls. Others are involved in river conservation and public safety. My particular field of expertise is rescue and recovery."

"What part of your job are you performing tonight, the rescue or the recovery?"

"Strictly the recovery, ma'am. Rescues are few and far between in this neck of the woods, unless my man has a skin made of steel and lungs that could hold air for three days. Police reported a white male, middle-aged about 190 pounds, went off the Horseshoe Falls about 10 PM Monday night."

Here was yet another reason to think we were all being drawn into a realm of madness. The guy had jumped into the Falls on a Monday. Monday had never been a popular jump night in the past. Friday and Saturday nights, on the other hand, were prime nights for your average leaper-inclined. Then again we were on the heels of a full moon and they didn't get the term lunacy for nothing.

"When the weather turns we average about one to two jumpers a week. Some psychologists say that it has to do with the negative ions created by falling water. It makes you feel good and perhaps it has a lot to do with Niagara Falls' association with romance and being named the honeymoon capital. According to them the effect is hypnotic and especially seductive on the weaker minded. I knew a man that had recently moved into the city. He would never let his wife come here to have a look at the Falls unless he was with her, and even then he would walk on the water-side of her to keep her from throwing herself in if she should happen to catch the impulse."

"I was there for your heroics earlier this week. Congratulations, the whole town is talking about it."

"Prevention is mostly out of my hands," I told her. "That day was a rare exception . That woman out there just wanted her pain to end and she wasn't thinking about the consequences. She was still young and pretty and I was banking on that. In general, stopping them on that end of the rink is someone else's game. The other end of things, down by the goal line. That's my zone and really all I can do is pick up the pieces.

You know it's funny how some people fight so hard to stay in this life and others want to give it up so easily. Then of course there's always the revenge factor. You know the guy who puts the shotgun in his mouth and pulls both barrels. That's staged for the "see what you made me do, I bet you're sorry now" effect. Victims who jump over the Falls can achieve that same effect without the use of a gun. The legacy of tissue destruction may even be more dramatic than in most self-inflicted means of demise. Certainly it's borne out by the fact that no one is allowed in the identification room of a Falls victim without at least two attendants accompanying them. About 90 percent faint at the sight of Niagara's handiwork and that includes men as well."

"Sounds like when our visitor does arrive I'm in for a real treat."

More than you can ever know.

"Believe me when I tell you, that luck plays more of a part in getting someone out of that situation than anything that I do."

"And modest too. A modest hero. Now that's something I never would have expected. I figured that for someone who had worked on the river as long as you have and had finally been credited with their first rescue, they would be crowing about it to anyone who came within shouting distance. At the very least, I thought you'd be out on the town celebrating."

Well, well. Another surprise. It appears Miss Vassar was not above doing some homework although I'm not sure I appreciated the way she framed it. So she wanted to fence a little, did she?

"If you really knew me and you knew this place you'd realize it's not that way. In this job you have to learn not to let it get you too high or too low. This river never lets up. So you can never let your guard down. Not if you want to live. It has a way of keeping you humble in its presence. If nothing else you'll learn that tonight."

"Should I write that down?" she parried.

I hadn't known her long enough to tell if she was being facetious or not, so I decided to give her the benefit of the doubt, " Anyone can take down notes. The trick is to know the meaning behind the words. I'm just saying that the river can tell you things and if you listen and learn those lessons you have a better chance of surviving."

I should have left well enough alone but I couldn't help getting in another little chop, "The things you'll see down here just don't show up in a Vassar classroom on daddy's dime."

"Is that what you think....you... you... what was it they call you?...river rat. Well I think in your case they got the "rat" part right!"

This was a woman who was not caught at a loss for words for very long and I suddenly got the feeling that I was going to be getting a lesson on judging a book by its cover. I also got the feeling that even though I had upset her enough to warrant the likes of much stronger language she was above it. Such restraint was a strange quality to find in a person who made their living in the rough and tumble world of journalism but it was not about to stop her from setting me straight.

"I...I... didn't mean..." I tried to eke out in my defense, but she was having none of it. She had given me enough slack in my rope to form my opinions and now it was her turn. Now she was going to hang me with it.

"I get it now. I'm young, I'm a woman and now you think I come from privilege. What could I know, right? She probably never earned her way in anything. Right. What did I know of life compared to the great river rat Ro Patric, who battles the river and faces life and death everyday? Well. Let me tell you Mr. Patric what little I do know of life. And what its taught me..

When I was sixteen years old my middle class parents went to a Christmas eve party. They took a cab because they were very conscious of drinking and driving. That was my stupid parents for you, always playing by the rules. There was a man at the party-a friend of my father who had a problem with alcohol and it got out of hand that night. My father and mother offered to drive the man home in his car and take a cab from there. Again how stupid of them to try and help someone out. Anyway, they never made it. Their car was hit head on by another car driven by some important government official. My mother and father were killed instantly. The other two people survived. Because there were bottles and cans of liquor littered throughout my father's friend's vehicle the police assumed that my father had been intoxicated.

Reporters with cameras and lights knocked on our door at 4 am and shoved microphones in front of my face to ask me what I thought about my alcoholic father. That's how I found out my parents were dead. It was New Year's Day I was sixteen years old. Is that old enough to learn about life Mr. Patric? It was in the midst of all this tragedy that I felt a divine presence. Something beckoned to me and gave me the strength to go on. And I've been listening to that voice ever since. I don't think it was a coincidence that I chose this profession.

As it turns out the government bigwig was the one who was drunk and had caused the accident, but there was a cover-up and he paid very little penalty. That's when I decided to become a reporter. The first reason was not to jump at conclusions but to try and learn the truth before I went public with anything. And the second reason was to try to show victims a little sensitivity and compassion, not like the jerks who showed up at my door that night. And for your information there was insurance money but I needed that for my younger brother and myself to live on. To pay for college I had to wait tables and anything else to earn money. And it wasn't Vassar but journalism courses at Georgetown weren't cheap either, especially on a waitresses' tips. But you know what, I earned my tuition, I earned my marks, and I earned my job and I earn it every day by doing the best job I know how."

"I'm sorry. You're right, I was out of line. I apologize. I didn't know."

"Apology accepted. Now can we get on with this?"

I couldn't help but think that this was the kind of feistiness that might come out of Annie Taylor- another woman to whom I probably owed an apology.

"That man who jumped. This is Thursday. That was three days ago," she said.

From the perspective of my newly gained respect I would have to concede to Knowales that Sara Wilson knew how to ask the right questions. But she was a reporter after all, and that was her job, even though her age (I'd guessed late twenties or early thirties) meant that she was not that many years out of school. And I still had to wonder how much of life could she really have seen. However I had to admit that maybe I needed to take a second look at this woman. She'd already surprised me on a couple of counts. She intrigued me with her friendly, unwavering interest, but that's how she got me talking. Or was there more to it? She acted as if I was the only person worth talking to on the planet, and everything I said was of the utmost importance. I have to admit she completely disarmed me with her intelligence and professionalism.

Don't get me wrong. She was pretty as well. Her blonde hair was done up, business-like yet still feminine. She had a trim figure, athletic with long legs decked in tailored dark jeans. Not tight enough to show every line but not loose enough to hide every curve either. The way she moved, the word "coltish" came to mind.

While there were others more beautiful she was good-looking enough. Yet she didn't hit you over the head with it and I appreciated that she wasn't playing up her looks, but then with me, she didn't need to. Hell, I was pushing 50, had arthritis in both hands and one foot, and my days of chasing anything were long over. At least that's what my wife Susan kept telling me. She had put up with me for 30 years and now that she had just gotten me broken in she was not about to let anybody else reap the benefits. It's just my clumsy way of saying that we were happily in it for the duration. Besides, Sara was young enough to be the daughter that I never had. Now that I think about it, Sara would be just about the same age,…but I won't get into that.

My mind went on like that, pursuing its own avenues as I fielded her questions. I brought myself back around to her last one. I realized school was still in session.

"Yes, that was three days ago. That's the funny thing about Niagara. It's my experience that when it comes to a floater, you've really got three types. The first is that the body comes up to the surface almost immediately. I mean within minutes, the body is up. Those are the easiest ones to handle. The tissue is firm and allows for a reasonably efficient extraction. Also, there's no waiting around.

"The second one is what I like to call the Three Day Dipper. If a body does not surface within the first fifteen minutes, it will invariably come up exactly three days after it hits that plunge basin."

I pointed in the general direction of the Falls.

"Give or take an hour. I am not really sure what the mechanics of such a timetable are, but I can tell you, after having discussed it with countless coroners and forensic scientists, that a body submerged in water for a period of time does have a natural tendency to resurface, as long as it's not physically restricted from doing so.

"Everybody's read Tom Sawyer. When Tom and Huck were

feared drowned, a cannon was fired in the belief that it would help the drowned bodies to rise. That practice arose from a theory that bodies came to the surface during thunderstorms. Anyway that's what they practiced along the Mississippi, in Mark Twain's time. Here at Niagara; we just wait.

"I can also tell you, from all the documentation I've seen, nowhere else in the world does a body resurface with such precision. Seventy-two hours and bingo! Only here at Niagara."

"That's amazing," Sara said. "But wouldn't you guess that the precision of the seventy-two hour timetable, being unique to Niagara as you say, would have something to do with a quirk in the falls or the river itself?"

"It's more than just a quirk of the river," I said. "The key to the whole matter is over there, in my opinion."

Again I pointed in the direction of the Falls and, as I did, I noticed the gathering darkness. "I surmise that the key to everything that happens here at Niagara lies in the plunge basin."

"Explain that," Sara said.

"A plunge basin is a geological formation unique to a waterfall. As water flows over an escarpment, the action of the flow cuts through the rock and after a long period of time, forms what we call the gorge. The Falls originally was situated at a point miles upriver and has buzz-sawed its way back to this point. These rock walls all around us are the powerful visual evidence of the havoc a waterfall can wreak on the terrain.

"What people don't see is the damage inflicted at the base of the waterfall, where the full fury of the falling water is at its deadliest. The plunging water carves out a basin out of the solid rock riverbed; hence the name, plunge basin.

"Experts believe that if the height of the Falls is one-hundred and seventy feet, the depth of the plunge basin where the falls is presently, is at least that deep, and could be as much as two or three times as deep. That's the problem.

Nobody knows for sure what's down there. The current at the base is just too violent. With falling rock and debris from the river above, it's easy to understand why the Niagara plunge basin has remained a mystery to this day."

"Fascinating," Sara Wilson said, genuinely interested. "The more I seem to learn about Niagara Falls the more intriguing I find it to be.""

"What time is it?" I asked, eyeing the purplish darkness that now surrounded us.

I glanced at the clock on the wall. 9 PM. We'd just entered the red zone.

"Stick around Ms, Wilson," I muttered. "You ain't seen nothin' yet. My ancestors, the Iroquois, believed that a thunder god lived in those waters under the Falls. That's how the Falls got their name, but of course some say that's just superstition and myth."

" But not you. You believe in these myths?"

"Others can believe what they want. I've always thought that even a myth contained some element of the truth. As for superstitions…well as anyone can tell you, I'm a bit of a fanatic on the subject. You know the saying step on a crack break your mother's back. Well when we were kids one of my friends made it a point to step on every crack he came to. That night his mother fell off a ladder and broke her back. The other part of the story is that his little brother knocked her off the ladder when he rode under it with his tricycle which is also considered bad luck. I don't know which superstition claimed jurisdiction but ever since then I figured there must be something to it and I try not to invoke the wrath of such deities if I can help it."

"Perhaps if you developed a solid belief in one God, that faith would supersede all these idiosyncrasies."

"Perhaps. It's not like I don't believe in higher forces at work. I think with my mix of Irish and Indian and each having such rich traditions of folklore that having been exposed to so much its hard to settle on just one. I just seem to put stock in every one of them. Take the horoscope for instance. I mean how can you not pay heed to the alignment of the stars."

"But that's just someone interpretation of a particular circumstance. If your faith is strong you begin to realize that there are no coincidences-even the most minute detail is by intelligent design."

"I just find it hard to put so much faith in any one thing. Especially down here. When you see death so frequently in such a horrific display you start to realize how fragile life is-like a bit of butterfly and then it vanishes in the breeze. And you can't help but think that maybe the person would still be alive-maybe they could have escaped their fate if they had just done this little thing or that little thing. If maybe their life had taken a twist here or a turn there-at least your mind desperately wants to believe it because you don't want to see this kind of carnage anymore and you will grasp at anything that might provide the slightest avenue of escape and that's why I'm superstitious."

I realized that I had ended in a bit of a ramble but she would soon get a taste of what it was like to work down here. This river was a relentless teacher and its lessons taught me to believe in harsh realities. Sometimes I saw death every week, and if I was to choose one master of destiny – it would be the river.

Sara was not about to give up on me without a fight.

"But when your time comes that is not something that can be avoided and it is not this river that dictates it."

"I don't mean to be disrespectful but I think that what you say might apply to a normal river-not this river. The Niagara is not a normal river. Before this day is over even you will concede that there is some kind of phenomenon emanating from that plunge basin that indicates we are not being left alone to our own devices. Don't ask me to explain it because I can't but it's a perception I've had for many years now. You'll get your chance to make up your own mind about that, in a little while. Nevertheless to the Iroquois this stuff was very real, and many human sacrifices, usually young maidens, took place on these cliffs around us. This has always been regarded as hallowed ground to my people."

"You were saying that a third option existed for bodies coming from the Falls and you only gave us two, so far," Sara said.

She was getting very close to nailing a real exclusive, that is if, ultimately, she'd have the stomach for it.

"Yes," I continued. "The third designation for a body coming out of the plunge basin is that it never comes up. EVER!"

"You're kidding," she said.

"Nope. I'd say that it's my experience that one-in three bodies are never recovered. As I said, no one knows what's in that plunge basin, but it certainly is the key controlling factor. There's a reason why the Niagara Parks Commission built my little hut here. Over the years we found that if a body does come up, the current always brings it to this little bend in the river. Instead of chasing floaters all over the river; I just wait here. Of course the city wanted to keep the hut as conspicuous as possible so tourists wouldn't be wondering what we were doing down here. Not good for public image and that sort of thing. That's the part they don't want you to know"

"You could almost think of the Falls as one of those milk separators they used to have on farms. You pour in the milk and out comes cream, butter and cheese."

"I guess that's one way of looking at it."

"I hope you don't live down here in that hut.."

"Sometimes, it almost comes to that, but no I do have a real home. This can be a grisly business day in and day out and I'm lucky enough to have someone at home who understands that I have this thing in my blood about the river. It is almost like I don't have a choice. The trick is to remember not to let it take over.

"So you're married. I noticed you don't wear a ring."

"That's because of my arthritis. Got a touch of it in the

hands. Yep, been married almost thirty years and I have to give Susan all the credit for keeping me grounded and sane in this insane business."

"She sounds like quite a woman. Congratulations."

"You make it sound like I'm the only one getting something out of this. It's a two way street, you know. She gets a man who still loves her even after all these years. She gets a man who understands that a woman gets old too, no matter how many creams they put on, pills they take or sit-ups they do and accepts the fact that a caressing hand is going to run into a wrinkle or two. Besides as you get older you realize it's not as much outside as what's inside that really matters."

"And all she has to do is let you come down here to the river and play."

"That, and a round of golf now and then, not to mention letting me complain about my arthritis and these nasty winters."

"Sounds like a marriage made in heaven. I don't know if your wife realizes this but she married quite an enigma of a man. You would think that a a man in this job would have to be grounded by a strong belief system and yet from what you tell me you let your life be ruled by superstition. Your earliest and greatest fear seems to have been about Niagara Falls and yet your job is to come here practically every day and look it right in the face. And finally for someone as skilled and knowledgeable about the river and its articulations, it seems unfathomable that in all the time you've spent here you've only got one rescue to your credit and that was just the other day."

"I can see why you went into journalism. You do have a way with words or at least the way you frame them around a picture."

"But that's the key. I need the picture to build the story around and I have to admit I've never met anyone quite like you. You're quite an interesting snapshot."

I might have said the same about her.

Turns out we had a lot more in common than anyone could have imagined, as we would later discover.

"What you forgot to mention is this place. This place and this job. That's the real enigma, if you ask me. How many people have the privilege of having a job that lets them see the beauty of one of the greatest natural creations on the face of the planet, yet also tears through human beings like a paper shredder. I get to see both sides of that extreme on this job."

"I can see what you mean......any kids?"

"We had a daughter, a long time ago. She died in childbirth. We never had another. Susan couldn't stand to go through the heartbreak if it turned out the same way again. She would have been just about your age, had she lived."

"Sorry to hear that," Sara said.

"Sometimes I think about what might have been, but I learned long ago that you can't fight the plan of the gods. In a lot of ways the river is my child. The secret is not to let it become your lover and wife, like Charlie Knowales..."

"Hold it!" I gasped. I listened and looked out over the river, trying to see through the shroud of darkness.

I could barely make out the foaming pools of white, remnants of water violently agitated and still not in a state of calm.

Then I heard it. The telltale gurgling.

No other sound was quite like it and I could recognize its signature through a trumpet barrage on the walls of Jericho.

It was time to go to work.

In the old days, a river rat would get $30 for each recovery, now it was considerably more. I had to make a few preparations. First, the wintergreen under the nose, to combat the smell. I pulled on my rubber gloves and gathered a harness apparatus, which I placed on the rocks by the water. It was a harness used to lower animals safely into the holds of ships that I had adapted to allow bodies to be taken out of the river by a single man. I reached for my flashlight and my gaffing rod, a long aluminum pole with a hook at the end.

I was ready.

I turned to Ms. Wilson and said, "It looks like we are going to have another visitor, more precisely I am referring to my Three Day Dipper, in a minute or so, and you are welcome to stay. However, I must warn you that what you are about to see may be extremely unpleasant. If you'd like, I don't mind talking as I work."

I considered it blasphemous to do this to someone young enough to be my daughter, but after all this was her chosen profession and she would see plenty of life's dark side if she hadn't already. And she was entitled to the truth. Besides there are some things you just can't learn from books. Sometimes you have to learn about life in the classroom of the real world.

"You see," I continued, "depending on the water temperature and the length of time in the water, the bodies are in various stages of decay. Usually the internal organs tend to decompose first, along with any food in the stomach. The decaying action causes a type of fermentation to occur, which in turn produces gasses that build up internal pressure, resulting in the bloated appearance associated with many drowning victims."

Sara was scribbling away in her little notebook.

"The skin of a body can be so bloated as to completely hide a watch strapped around a wrist. Bulging of the eyes is also not uncommon. But contrary to popular belief, the eyes are not readily dissolved as most people tend to imagine. Actually the eye tissue is quite durable and stands up pretty well, if left alone. Of course, fish and insects that attack all tissue, do not discriminate. Often a bloated body will become discolored, and even turn black in some instances.

"One has to be very careful in the duty of extracting a water-logged body from the river. If grasped imprecisely or too harshly, an occurrence referred to as skin slip may result, where skin and flesh pull off the body in large sections. If the body is left to languish in the water for an extended period, eventually all tissue and even bone will disintegrate. Some people incorrectly assumed that skeletons would be prevalent when search expeditions reached the Titanic, due to the great depth and coldness of the water. But as photographs revealed, there was no trace of bodily remains.

"Although in some cases, bodies have been known to remain fairly intact, over a period of years, depending of course on location, type of water, and temperature. Here at Niagara, while the temperature and other aquatic organisms do take their toll, most of the damage is inflicted by the Falls. The Falls bestows it's own special treatment. Victims are crushed, ripped, and mutilated beyond recognition by the fall onto the deadly rocks below."

Sara Wilson had weathered all of my grotesque descriptions. So far, mere words had not caused her to flinch. How would she deal with a nightmare?

I turned and studied the water. After a moment I saw it. "Thar she blows!" I yelled, as though Moby Dick himself was breaking water. What I had seen would have been mistaken by anyone else as a log. The frothing water pushed the object right in our direction, as it always had in the past. I checked the time. 9:45. It was now 71 hours and 45 minutes from the time of entry. I got down to the water's edge and readied the gaffing hook. The object was almost within reach, still looking more like a log than a body. I took a deep breath of the wintergreen under my nose to prepare for its arrival. The skin had turned black as the night.

I felt my stomach drop to my feet. It always did and always would no matter how long I did this. I raised the hook and landed it in the chest region. It produced a sickly, mushy noise. One of the other local reporters, who I'd ignored entirely all evening, on instinct turned and retched. I had caught the gaff under a couple of ribs and started hauling the body in. The body was terribly torn, like discarded offal from a slaughterhouse. Both legs were gone, scythed off at the knee. Huge chunks of flesh were missing from other areas; all clothing gone. The master butcher had done its work well, once again.

"You want to give me a hand," I asked the other guy who hadn't yet yakked his cookies. "Try not to touch the body. That skin'll come off quicker than a dog sheds fleas. Float the harness under the body and we'll pick it up from each end. Here, you'll need this."

I offered the man the tube of wintergreen. The only thing that smelled worse than rotting corpse flesh was when my father had driven by a pig farm when I was a kid. Even after we had rolled up the windows, the smell permeated our clothes and the car upholstery for hours.

As we placed the harness, I saw the blackened face of the corpse. Not even the water had been able to erase an expression of utter agony. Once we'd dragged the corpse onto shore, there was nothing left to do but call the coroner's office to come and get it.

"Ms. Wilson, could I get that flashlight?" As she handed it to me, the light played over the face of the corpse.

I saw her eyes grow wide in disbelief at the corpse. She gasped and took an involuntary step back, but in the end she kept it together the way I figured she would. She had her exclusive, if she wanted it. She'd earned it.

The next question was inevitable.

"My God. Do they all look like that?"

"Every single one, ma'am. Without exception. Kind of kicks you right in the guts, doesn't it?"

There was something ghastly about the way the lips were pulled back taut exposing the teeth in such a forced, faux expression of a smile. That, in combination with the agony locked in the eyes tended to short-circuit normal sensory perception.

It looked as if their soul had been sucked from them. It was like looking at the face of pure evil. I believed that evil is always present among us-it just chooses the times and places that it wants to reveal itself. This was a glimpse of it disguised under the veil of mutilation.

I began to regret having exposed her to this. This woman had a gentle soul that wouldn't hurt a fly. I knew that police, firefighters, reporters and the like usually developed an immunity to such horrible sights after a period of time on the job but I saw her looking hard at the victim-perhaps in an attempt to fathom the suffering that this poor unfortunate must have experienced in his last moments. I knew that she was unafraid to confront life head-on, and would not look away even when it turned on its underbelly. Woman or not, this was a person that you wanted in your trench. There was no doubt that her mettle had been put to the test tonight, but I also felt that it wouldn't hurt to keep an eye open for her.

"That's enough for now, honey. It's not good to look too long. The show's over, anyway."

I pulled a sheet up over the face and nudged a rather dazed and silent Ms. Wilson in the direction of my hut.

That's the funny thing about it all. The more you wanted to look away the more you felt your eyes were riveted to the sight of it. If you stared too long you began to feel it change you.

After I made my call to the coroner, the reporters left. The dismissal bell had rung and school was out for the time being. It had been a long night, and Ms. Wilson had survived her first encounter with the Niagara "death smile".

It wasn't until later when I could reflect on that day that I began to realize the absurd irony of it-Ms. Wilson had spent her time trying to convince me of the existence of God and I had spent mine trying to convince her of the existence of evil.

For years I'd been trying to convince people that something unnatural was happening under the Falls.

No one believed it. Just another Niagara myth. Just superstitions.

It seemed as if no one was much interested in listening. No one that is, except Charles Knowales.

CHAPTER THREE
THE CIRCUS AND A SHOOTING STAR FROM THE EAST
COMES TO TOWN
Somewhere above Niagara Falls, Sunday, July 1st

"Look at that will ya! Look at that awful mess down there!" Luke Brown was speaking from high above the tsunami of Detroit steel and rubber that blocked roadways on both sides of the river. His mechanic Matthew Ford, was riding co-pilot in the Sikorsky S-64 helicopter and was a little on edge.

The S-64 Skycrane was a different kind of beast in more ways than one. First of all she was capable of carrying a ten ton payload. When she rode deadhead (deadhead being the term for no payload) she looked like a gutted fish. But that was the point of her design. The cargo was lifted into position where her eviscerated belly or fuselage would normally be. It gave her the appearance of a flying rail or beam while others often compared it to aviation's version of a dragonfly.

She still had a cockpit but it was highly modified. There were the standard pilots' seats facing forward, however the rear of the cockpit was glass as well. The crane or hoist operator sat here facing the payload area. In addition to cargo, a pod could be hoisted into position to accommodate passengers. It was very adaptable and had earned its wings quite admirably in the Vietnam conflict. This refugee had been acquired from army surplus by The Thrill Corporation and today she was being put to another kind of test.

"Yea, I would call that condition standstill," Ford remarked. "Somebody from another planet might be inclined to believe the world had just plumb run out of gasoline. There isn't a thing moving on those roads. It's actually kind of eerie."

The rotor blades tattooed the air with a strong steady rhythm, but nevertheless Ford was nervous.

"Stop gawking at the traffic, will ya? And watch where you're going. Are you sure you know what you are doing? I wish to God Phil Stinson had made this trip."

"You know Phil. He goes strictly by the book."

"Yea, well maybe we shouldn't be doing this either. It could be dangerous besides being illegal." As Ford finished his words, he once again checked the special cargo dangling from the crane.

"Relax, willya. Besides I didn't see anyone having to pry your hand open to put the money in it. If we just follow the plan we'll be fine."

"I wish I could be so sure. I'll tell ya one thing. It's been ten years since I had a cigarette but I sure feel like one right about now. If only Phil were here."

"Stop whining, will you. And he's got no complaints either. He had first right of refusal. I'll say one thing. Those Thrill folks sure got a knack for promotion. This is going to be one hell of an unveiling. Can you imagine the kind of publicity it will create by flying this load back up the river every day. People are going to think we're being invaded by aliens. That kind of advertising is priceless. You've got to tip your hat to that Knowales character, To tell you the truth he makes me a little uncomfortable but he seems like he knows what he's doing."

At this time their itinerary took them directly over the Falls and so far everything was secure.

"You know I never understood what all the fuss was about this place," said Brown.

"I mean from a distance the Falls looks no more than a low curved wall of water and yet people will drive from all over creation to come and take a look. I don't get it."

"I guess it's an understated kind of a thing, that you have to get right up to it to really appreciate its power," said Ford.

Below the helicopter, the waters of the Niagara River swirled and foamed, overlapping in spots, rip-tiding or forming little eddies in others, but always protective and careful never to reveal its secrets. What lay beneath its surface, in its dark recesses, in the icy cold and cavernous vaults of its plunge basin would remain hidden from the eyes of above.

For now.

It was a calm night up here, as if the whole world had stopped what it was doing to sit back and appreciate a sunset that was being painted stroke by stroke in soothing earthy tones.

By now Ford had the jitters. "We still don't have to do this you know. We haven't done anything wrong yet and there's still time to turn back."

"Are you kidding. I wouldn't miss this for the world. This is going to be one slam dunk of a stunt and we're going to have a front row seat. Talk about a christening. This is no time to get cold feet now. Anyway they wanted us to time it so that we get there right at dusk. It's just about time to make our cut in."

The helicopter with its most peculiar cargo in tow veered in from the path it was following down the river and headed to the east. Now it's journey over the city put them it in violation of FAA airspace restrictions.

"Time to light it up," yelled Brown.

Ford hit a switch to lower the mysterious cargo away from the bay and an array of fireworks began to ignite, lighting up the sky. As the whole exhibition continued to move in the direction of the tourist section of the city, contrails of sparks provided a tail to the apparition, giving it the appearance of a star or comet shooting across the night sky.

A misdirected flare from the fireworks display exploded directly in front of the cockpit temporarily blinding the pilot.

Suddenly the glass and steel of the Minolta Tower loomed directly in front of them. The mechanic yelled, "Look OOOUUUTTT....."

TOP FLOOR OF THE MINOLTA TOWER SIGN OF THE SNAKE, FIREWORKS AND ONE HELL OF A CLASS REUNION

Inside the conference room, the tension and electricity ran

as thick as bull's blood. I would have given anything to be back down in the quiet of the gorge. That was my world. This was a world created by madmen and fools. Yet I did have a commitment to fulfill as technical consultant and public relations representative to the Ultimate Thrill Corporation for which I was being well compensated. Hell, I'd have to pull a year's worth of bodies from the river to make as much.

I had to wonder if any amount of money was going to be worth this aggravation as I glanced down at the back of my left hand. CYFIC. I fingered the letters of scar tissue that had been etched there. The Can You Feel It Coming feeling I got sometimes even when I was away from the river felt stronger. For some reason. I could sense the presence of danger and whenever I did I looked to my CYFIC to remind myself to be careful.

I was just a rookie on the river when our crew made it's first rescue. A man had fallen into the river and was headed for certain death over the Falls when a whim of the current took him to one of the small islands at the brink. When we pulled him out I never forgot his words to me.

"It was the damnedest thing. I knew that I was in the current and it was dragging me toward the Falls but it felt more as though I was in a state of suspension and the Falls was COMING at me. A second seems like an eternity. Believe me, when you're in its grasp that thing is not static. Its got a personality that is relentless. It seems as if it can smell your blood in the water. I locks on you like the radar of a shark. It has a machine-like need to devour. You can feel it coming for you. You are its prey and it hunts you."

When the waves turn the minutes to hours.

Of course, everyone attributed such words to the trauma of the man's situation. Being just a first year man on the river maybe those words had more of an impact on me. I decided that the four-leaf clover in my pocket was not going to be enough so I vowed never to underestimate the deadliness of the Niagara and I had those letters hot-ironed onto my hand to remind me not to get complacent. I found it held up in many of life's situations.

Of course on the other hand just to balance things out was my snake tattoo. Why such a nefarious creature? The Indian culture regarded snakes as symbols of the river. There is no negative connotation to a snake unless it is depicted as fierce, for example with its mouth open and fangs poised to strike. Snakes were regarded with significance in many cultures such as those in ancient India Egypt and Asia. The image of the snake as being associated with evil or the devil is more of a Christian portrait not to mention that little piece of business in Ireland. But now it was time to get this puppy airborne, as they say.

"Ladies and gentleman,..please...please take your seats. This news conference is about to begin."

Sitting off to one side of the podium, Charles Knowales and Judd Blackadder sat as silent as zombies. I couldn't believe how much they had changed. We had grown up together and even though it had been quite a while since I had last seen them; in fact until recently, (I guess it went right back to that fateful day in Knowales' case), I thought I knew them. Now I wasn't so sure. I guess a lot of things had been set on course from that day's intersection. I realized I probably wouldn't be standing where I was if it wasn't for the events of that day.

And the change wasn't only on the outside but inside as well. These two had always been an odd pair, even back then they had been a study in contradictions. Knowales' good looks as a kid had evolved into an avalanche of white hair about his face and head. His long hair rolled back from his forehead in white waves of wool. His sideburns covered most of his cheeks in a passe style known as mutton chops. He looked like a prophet who had just stepped out of the pages of the Old Testament. His steely eyes could go for unnatural periods of time without blinking, a trait that made many uncomfortable in his presence. They were unusually large eyes-bulging eyes-sheep eyes-in fact with the hair and the eyes you'd swear you were in the presence of a human version of a sheep. Still he had the showmanship of a PT Barnum and the wiles of a snake oil salesman – a combination that had proven to be quite effective in the pursuit of his endeavors.

Charlie Knowales was the wizard behind the curtain for this venture. He had pulled all the levers, arranged the financial backing, coordinated the various aspects of the production, and in the final analysis, it was his baby. In word and deed he was Solomon, the Wizard of Oz and Faust all rolled into one. It was the Faustian part that was not in the mix when I had known him before. Back then he had seemed quite noble.

Now everything that he had become was wrapped around those eyes-those unrelenting piercing eyes that made you as uncomfortable as a screeching fingernail on a chalkboard. It was little wonder that he got his way on most affairs-people would do anything to avoid those eyes that seemed as if they would burn holes in you if you let them lay on you for very long. And they never seemed to blink! It was as if his eyes didn't require the moisture that normal people did or perhaps it was that he just didn't like not seeing what was going on around him for even a fraction of a second-for want of missing something. This Charlie Knowales appeared capable of training himself to be able to do just such a thing. Those sheepy eyes descended on you, surrounded you, devoured you. That was the man I had to deal with. That was the Charlie Knowales of now.

Then of course not to be forgotten, was the limp. Ever since the day that had happened Knowales had acquired two constant companions. The first was an ever present cane. This latest version which he held straight up in his hand next to his chair was not the same as was in his possession when we first met to discuss this Thrill adventure only some time ago. This particular instrument had a black wooden shaft quite narrow actually at the business end with a gold tip and capped at the other end by a gold plated snake's head. The snake was coiled to strike. It also had horns on the side of its head. A snake flaunted in such a disposition was a bad omen-had I seen this before I might not have signed on to this venture.

The second acquisition was the man sitting next to him. Speaking of snakes. Next to him sat Judd Blackadder. I found their seating positions to be a curious juxtaposition. The snake-head cane in Knowales' grip was between the two men and aligned at about the same level as their heads. I was astonished at the striking resemblance between the figure on the cane and Blackadder. Where Knowales had enough facial hair for a rock band, Blackadder had none. He was completely clean- shaven, bald pate and all. His nose was wide and flatter than most with eyes black and narrow. Freckles or some kind of skin spots lent the skin a condition that was further towards that of a reptile than a human. The lips were extraordinarily thin and in about two seconds I half expected a forked tongue to slither out and test the air. Nevertheless, Blackadder was chief architect, builder, and pilot of the passenger vehicle that would go over the Falls. He had once worked on the river as a river rat but had been expelled from this exclusive brotherhood after being found at fault over a rather ugly incident and although that was over fifteen years ago the tarnish on his reputation still lingered, as did my distrust of the man.

As both men sat erect in their seats I was reminded of a couple of wooden dummies animated by the black thoughts that had been cultivated by the tragic circumstances of a day that existed in the cobwebs of time's attic. Or was it the basement? Who pulled the strings of these puppets to make them act so cold, so driven, so ruthless? So changed.

I also saw Sara Wilson, and the other riders who would be on the maiden voyage. I couldn't see the face of a man in the rear, dressed in black trench coat, a black scarf around the lower third of his face, maneuvering skillfully among the shadows, but I could see that he knew how to find refuge in the shadows of a well-lighted room.

"Do you know how many people have died in that stretch of river over there," I said, pointing to the windows on the left side of the conference room, even though the curtains were drawn. Since I wasn't really waiting for an answer, I continued, "Well, I'll tell you that no one really knows, but I'd be willing to bet that if you took all the blood from every victim of Niagara and sent it over the Falls, the water would run red for a whole day. From the upper rapids to the Falls, through the plunge basin, through the lower rapids, and down to the whirlpool – it is a stretch considered to be the deadliest seven miles of river in the world. Let me illustrate by examples."

The house lights went down. As I spoke silent images of antique times and people long dead played on an overhead screen.

"This is Annie Taylor, the first person to go over Niagara. That was on October 1, 1901. She was lucky, and her wooden barrel went over the Falls at just the right spot, narrowly missing any rocks on the way down. She had the smoothest ride anyone could possibly imagine and yet her first words when she emerged were, "No one ever ought to try that again."

"She was right! Unfortunately, many did not pay heed to her words."

"Example number one. Everyone's journey begins here in the upper rapids. In 1951, Red Hill assembled a compilation of inner tubes and netting and set out through the upper rapids. There were almost a quarter of a million witnesses on the river bank, hearing of the venture mostly through word of mouth. His contraption called 'The Thing' disintegrated in the upper rapids. I can only imagine the sheer terror that must have seized him as he was delivered to the brink without any protection. He had to know that he was a dead man even before he went over the Falls. Red Hill dead at 36. That's the first obstacle; survive the upper rapids.

"Example number two. Next is the plunge over the Falls. In 1925, a man named Charles Stephens went over in a wooden barrel with an anvil in the bottom for ballast. He wanted to insure that he would land feet first. A stave of the barrel with

Stephens right arm torn from the socket were the only pieces ever recovered. Charles Stephens dead. That's the second objective; survive the trip over the Falls, a height of about 17 stories, with a possible crash landing into solid rock.

"Example number three. Then there is the plunge basin that must be negotiated. George Stathakis of Buffalo went over in 1930, holding his pet turtle. He used the biggest barrel yet, a one-ton wood and steel monster that contained sufficient oxygen to keep him alive for three hours. However, he was trapped underneath the foot of the cataract for twenty-two hours. Stathakis suffocated. The turtle survived.

Not only does one have to contend with the force of the water coming from above but there is so much air injected into the water that it actually becomes less dense. Objects can't resurface because there is nothing to push against in order to get leverage.

"Of more importance – no one knows exactly what's in that plunge basin or how it works. It is so dangerous it has never been surveyed. We surmise that its depth may be as great as three times the height of the Falls itself. Many people believe it is the key factor in a successful journey over the Niagara Horseshoe Falls. I would have to include myself in that group.

"Example number four. The next stop is the lower rapids, where the river actually convexes. That is to say that the middle of the river is higher than at each shore, if you can believe that. In 1975, a company attempted to conduct white-water raft trips through these rapids. The raft overturned and thirty-two people went into the river. Three died. The trips were discontinued.

"Example number five. Finally we arrive at the whirlpool. I assume everybody knows what a whirlpool is. If not, the best way that I can describe it is a tornado under water. Well, we've got one here at Niagara. Maude Willard tried to go through it or around it or something in 1901. Her barrel got sucked under and she also suffocated.

"And so, as you can see, danger and death lurk at every turn of this river. Everyone knows that the Falls is very beautiful, but don't be seduced. She lures you here with her thunder. She mesmerizes you with her water, tumbling effortlessly through space, glistening like diamonds in the sun. She entices you with her show of mist, like thick white smoke rising into the heavens. And then when you're hooked and you get a little careless, or maybe you get a little cocky and get a little too close, watch out! That's when she'll snuff you out like a candle and then laugh in your face. She can be the cruelest and deadliest of temptresses. Maybe that's why in all the history of this place, no one has yet to complete a successful navigation from the upper rapids to the whirlpool.

"That is about to change. It is our mission, the mission of The Ultimate Thrill Company to successfully complete such a journey through this hellish gauntlet of water. And not just once, but over and over again with passengers, much like the American space shuttle. It will be greater than any roller coaster ride or man made thrill because this is real. The river, the Falls, are real. The danger is real and we will conquer the fear and the danger, where so many have failed before. We intend to go down and look the beast right in the eye and walk away. It will be the ultimate thrill! As our advertising says, we'll sell you the whole seat but you're only gonna need the edge! And so without further ado, I 'd like to introduce you to the two men who have made this all possible, Charlie Knowales and Judd Blackadder."

The two men rose to their feet and were greeted by a blizzard of applause. In fact, the room almost exploded with noise. The display of appreciation took us all by surprise. My speech was intended to convey our intentions and create an atmosphere of enthusiasm for our project, but this exceeded our wildest expectations.

Charlie Knowales spoke into the mike, "And now you're all in for a real treat. I would like to introduce to you the craft that will take us over the Falls, in safety I might add; our own private ark if you will. So without further ado I give you the Hellion!"

The black curtains parted revealing expansive panes of glass that encircled the top floor of the Minolta tower, exposing the spectators to a blazing fireball coming right at them. It was the Skycrane with the Hellion hanging below it, ablaze in fireworks. It was a spectacular publicity stunt and the crowd applauded wildly.

But the Skycrane kept coming. And coming.

An errant flash of light exploded just outside the windows of the tower as well as the cockpit of the Skycrane, momentarily blinding those who were near. The Skycrane was close enough that it appeared it was about to crash its cargo into the conference room of the tower. And it was still coming. Someone screamed. The people near the windows tried to scramble away but there was nowhere to go within the crowded confines. A table overturned. Glasses crashed. Panic and helplessness awaited a disaster of monumental proportions. A disaster that seemed inevitable.

Inside the S-64. Matthew Ford pulled on the lever that controlled the hoist and the spaceship look-a-like Hellion just barely cleared the roof of the Minolta. It was a christening alright. A few inches one way or the other and this would have been the first boat to have been christened by crashing through the top floor of a tower. The crowd inside the tower was reeling around like it had been tazered enmasse. Then one person started clapping and was soon joined by others. They thought it was all part of the stunt.

That was the trouble. With Charles Knowales you never really knew.

There was that squirrel again gnawing at my gut-letting me know that the craziness was just beginning. As the ovation continued I took a second look around the room. There were probably two thousand people crammed into a room that was intended for half that amount. I imagined newspaper and television reporters from New York to Saskatoon. It was well known that stunts at the Falls had a history of drawing well, but this had all the earmarks of being the most spectacular media event of its kind in history. It was enough to make your tonsils sweat. However I was not going to let the fact that all these strangers had come together because of us -- Charlie, Judd, and me -- go to my head. Did they really care about us? Hell, they didn't even know us.

I've been on enough highways to see how the traffic slows down on my side of the road even though the accident is on the other side of the road. What is it that traffic guy in the helicopter calls them? Gawker blockers. You got that right, pal. That's the real reason for this crush of insanity. Plain and simple. Death. They came because there is a chance that someone might die. Give them a good show with a little death thrown in on the side and everyone goes home happy. Not only does it satisfy their morbid curiosity but it makes great copy as well. Let's face it, these people don't know Charlie Knowales from Adam and it wouldn't change their life one iota to have his guts splattered at the bottom of Niagara. Well anyway, I was rather hoping we could all put a nightcap on this dog and pony show and catch some much deserved z's.

Suddenly, there was a loud crash at the back of the room.

The applause petered out to pin drop silence. All eyes turned to a man dressed completely in black, still holding the handle of what was once a glass pitcher. Shards of glass and water littered the floor at his feet. The man was noticeably stooped over. A silk black scarf covered the lower third of the man's face, but not his bald head marked by curious protrusions – more like stumps – on the sides nor the black shark-still eyes that were focused directly to the front of the room where Charlie Knowales stood.

Those eyes shone pure hatred.

Despite his deformed posture the man was quickly across the room, noiselessly like a cat, before anyone could react. Knowales found himself face to face with the man, stunned and paralyzed. Only the snake-head cane separated the two.

"You remember me, don't you, Charlie?" the man hissed through the scarf.

Security guards headed toward him from various parts of the room. Judd Blackadder was the closest to Knowales and made a move to intercept the man in black.

"Maybe you remember when this happened." The man pulled the scarf down to reveal a disfigured mouth, taut lips exposing crooked teeth in a deformed rendition of a smile, a smile so garrish in nature that I felt as if I'd been stabbed through the heart with an icicle. There was a collective gasp from around the room.

Knowales, still trying to recover from the initial shock, stammered," Who...what the ....what's this?" But I could see the recognition in Blackadder's eyes, and his lips silently formed the name Rediens.

Kane Rediens from the old neighborhood! I remembered that they used to call him Lucky but that never made any sense to me because as I recall there wasn't one thing about him that was lucky. The three of them and the snake-head cane were all locked together in some kind of crazy waltz, as Rediens tried to get at Knowales through Blackadder.

Then security closed in. Before they could drag Rediens away he spat out something that made no sense, "I'll see you guys again soon. and we'll dance a real jig together..." followed by a hideous rush of sound through torn lips that was some kind of demonic imitation of a laugh. Knowales was visibly shaken, and the entire conference room buzzed with conjecture and theory. But I knew the truth.

I saw it as the beginning of things spinning out of control. They say that when someone finally conquers the river where so many lives have been lost, the tortured souls of the dead will finally be at peace. I wondered if there was any such solace for the tortured souls of the living?

Can You Feel It Coming?

CHAPTER FOUR
JINXED: THE BIG CAT CROSSES MY PATH

For me it had already begun. That's when the nightmares started. Again. I hadn't had a nightmare about Niagara Falls for years, but the previous night I'd dreamed that I was just a kid doing a little fishing in the calm waters of the river above the Falls. I was in my rowboat and I got a little too far out in the current. Next thing I knew I was struggling against the pull of water that wanted desperately to send me to only one place – where it sends everything else that falls into it's treacherous clutches. Over the Falls.

I rowed furiously on the oars until the left one broke. Now I was in real trouble. Still I paddled hard with the remaining intact oar. One side of the boat, then the other. I was fighting a losing battle. The noise and the mist that could only mean one thing, dominated all my senses, and made my skin crawl. Panic set in. I wasn't going to make it. Then I saw the little island, 50 yards from the brink. Gull Island, they called it. Not really an island, more like an outcropping of rock and a few sparse bushes. My last chance. I had to get out of the boat. I splashed into the river and flailed frantically for the island.

Just when I thought that all was lost, a last swing of current hurled me to the back end of the island. Before I was about to be swept past I caught one of the bushes that grew out of the rock. I hung on dearly. I was safe. The monster would not get me this night. Then a black cat with a head twice as big as the rest of its body, popped out of the bushes. It's teeth were crooked, but sharp. It smiled at me before it sunk it's incisors into the hand that was holding onto the bush. I screamed, but no sound came out. I let go of the bush and was swept over the Falls.

Everything always ends up at the Falls. Everything always ends up at the Falls. Everything alwaysendsupattheFalls.eve rythingalwaysendsupattheFallseverythingalwaysendsupatth eFalls.....then oblivion.

CHAPTER FIVE
THE TIGHTROPE AND A MAN SEES THE LIGHT

Consciously, what Thomas Barratt knew about tightropes could fit onto a post-it. Subconsciously he was no less than an expert on the art of walking a fine line because he had been doing it most of his life. He was a meticulous man to say the least, meticulous and austere yet in a somehow hollow way. Like a house made of straw-it looks formidable at first glance but upon closer inspection one recognizes that there is a lack of substance.

Barratt was a school-teacher-taught seventh grade at Quaker Road public school. The kids in his class hated him. It was like being taught by a robot. He always went by the strict rule of the book and never deviated-never showed any emotion-never showed that he was human. Except when he taught the lessons on the French Revolution-then he seemed especially angry as if the aristocracy had personally wronged him.

Even his demeanor was inflexible. He stood erect and he sat erect- always a model of perfect posture. His hair was cut short in a crew cut style and even the hairs seemed to stand at attention. The kids surmised that he must have applied some kind of grooming wax to get it to stand so erect. Even his mustache was trimmed short, never allowed to get too long and or droopy and it appeared that he treated that as well.

No, there was nothing droopy on the face of Thomas Barratt. The trouble was that all these strict features were applied to the face of a rat. His eyes were dark and beady and his nose short and thin and somehow his mustache even in its most rigid state looked more like whiskers than human hair. And to top it off he did have small claw like hands and a couple of prominent upper front teeth so that when he did smile which was almost never it was as if he just needed a piece of cheese to nibble on and the picture would be complete.. It was as if the discipline and regimen of a military man had been applied to the template of gnawing nocturnal rodent. That was just one of the dichotomies of the man and perhaps a microcosm of his whole life

He had gone to Catholic schools himself where there were all boys in his class. He never saw a classmate of the opposite sex until high school and by then he was so afraid of them he froze like a tin man in the rain. The Catholics taught you that everything was a sin- what you ate (of course they changed the rules on that one with the no more fish on Friday just to thoroughly confuse everyone not to mention a school kid trying to make some sense of it all.) what you drank, what you did and even what you were thinking. That one was a doozy. Ninety-five percent of the world would be condemned to hell if they were to be convicted on what they were thinking. And Charles Barratt knew that he had plenty of bad thoughts. On the outside though, he appeared as a young man who was faithfully complying with the dogma.

College only added to his confusion. The college he attended was run by an Augustinian sect of the Catholic church . When the priest who was his academic advisor and counselor wasn't running his hand up his leg as he did to all the freshmen- like he was chumming for a return reaction, the priest who lived at the end of his hall could be heard with women behind his door and the smell of pot seeping from the crack at the bottom. These incidents left their marks on an impressionable young lad who was trying to form his own ideas about God and religion and the world and where he fit into all of it.

Issues at home did not help clear the confusion. His father was of French descent and worked the tough life of a steel worker. He was also fond of pear whiskey and bought and drank it straight from the barrel. His motto was if you want to be a man you have to drink like a man. He was dead by forty years of age. The whole time his father had been alive he let Thomas know that he might as well have had a daughter. Thomas was never interested in sports , never did anything outdoors, never had any friends-just stayed in his room and read After his father died, not once did he ever go to visit his grave. Thomas lived in his boyhood home with his mother and after she died he lived there alone. His mother had a reserved plot by her husband in the cemetery but Thomas had her buried elsewhere so he would never have to go near his father again.

For years he lived in his yellow house, kept up his rigid rules and his rigid appearance and never missed a Sunday in church.

And it was all built on a house of rotten cards.

That was the tightrope that Thomas Barratt walked everyday of his life. Even his yard was meticulously maintained- from the immaculate weed-free flower beds to the religiously manicured lawn. From the outside, it appeared as if he was a model citizen of the community as well as a model neighbor. But no one ever got inside the little yellow clapboard cottage on Quaker Road nor the inner workings of his mind or they might have formed quite a different opinion of the rigid man who reminded them of a rodent.

It was as if Barratt had taken the ritual aspects of religion or the military (although he had never been in the service) and transposed that framework onto all aspects of his life.

On a school day he left the house at 7:13 am, started his engine and let it idle for exactly two minutes. At thirty five miles an hour, with one four way stop to negotiate it took him eleven minutes to reach the parking lot of Quaker Road School , where he parked in the last space closest to the fence that encircled the entire property. In two minutes he would be up the walk, then down the hall to the office to pickup the daily announcements and attendance sheets and up the back stairs to his second floor classroom. By the time he hung up his coat and opened the windows and got organized it would be 7:30 on the nose leaving him twenty minutes to go over the day's lessons before the first bell rang at 7:50. And the rest of the day followed in similar clockwork fashion. Always the same. Never any deviations. From year to year, only the faces changed.

Until one day Bridget Perry showed up in his classroom.

Bridget was a transfer from the New York City school system, had had sex two years ago at the age of eleven, had the fully developed body of a seductive woman and although she had a spectacular head of long dark hair it framed a rather plain face.

She dressed to the nines everyday in the tightest clothes she could squeeze into and wasn't afraid of anything. That included showing off her body and teachers. Never before had the students nor Mr. Barratt for that matter, been confronted with such a blatant and raw expression of sexual energy. It was as if it oozed from her every pore. She had a body that a stripper would kill for and even at thirteen she knew ways to dress and move that exploited every curve.

Despite the distraction, the class and Barratt tried to forge ahead with their studies, but it wasn't hard to know what was really on all of their minds. Never before had he called on students for answers, who had no clue, or were on the wrong page of the lesson. Some even had a book out for a totally different subject. Bridget flirted with anybody and everybody in the class and at recess she could usually be found in one of the remote corners of the school yard with a group of eighth grade boys around her. It was anybody's guess what was going on out there.

As for Barratt he could feel himself losing an internal battle within himself. On the outside he tried to keep up the same regimen of rigidity and inflexibility and the kids hated him as much as ever but inside he felt as if things were beginning to crumble-his usually sure-footed steps on the tightrope of his world were beginning to wobble. Seventh grade girls had never been a problem for him, but this girl was a new experience. She stirred sexual feelings in him that he never knew existed. During class he tried not to let her catch him looking at her, but at recess when he usually ate in the teacher's lunchroom – he began eating lunch at his desk and staring out the window.

He knew he was losing control when he brought in a set of binoculars and would watch as some eighth grader ran his hand up her t-shirt or down her pants before the yard duty came by. Another teacher who had come up to his room to drop off some work had caught him and forced him into an awkward explanation of bird watching, which even before he had finished, he knew was hardly believable. It was only a matter of time.

And there were other things. Although he had always had an appetite for pornography and over the years had assembled quite a collection behind the yellow clapboard walls of his Quaker Road cottage – his veracity and consumption had increased exponentially since the arrival of Ms. Perry. He was usually discreet and bought out of town-after all what would the school board think if they knew he was spending the precious dollars they paid him on such nefarious activities, but now he didn't care where he bought as long as he could find material that bore some resemblance to Bridget.

He knew that this carelessness would eventually lead to trouble but he couldn't help himself.

Two incidents pushed him past the point of no return. The first was the day that Bridget had on a short black skirt and had to write something on the board. In front of the whole class she dropped her chalk on the floor and then bent from the waist to retrieve it, exposing the fact that she had no underwear on. The class reaction to that experience could only be describe as a collective gasp of titillation and disbelief. Barratt should have written a referral to the principal about her attire being inappropriate or at the very least reprimanded her. He did neither and pretended that the whole thing never happened. For a man who always went strictly by the book, this represented a serious short circuit in the wiring.

The second incident occurred a couple of days later. It was after class and he was finishing up some work at his desk.

Bridget came in and closed the door of the classroom.

"Bridget, leave the door open. You know it's against school policy to be alone with a student in a closed classroom."

"I know but I need some extra help in private."

Before he could get up she was right next to his desk blocking his way with her scent intoxicating him into immobility.

"Quickly then, what is it you want," as he fought to resist the temptation.

She bent over the desk and revealed her firm supple breasts that were barely held in by a low cut top.

He couldn't stop his eyes from being sucked to the sight.

"Why Mr. Barratt I didn't know you cared", she teased in a voice that dripped with her own unique brand of sexual honey. It was seductive and free of inhibition and part of it made him want to throw his arms around her and fall in love with her and run away together and part of it made him want to kill her. Then she started to dance in front of him, writhing and running her hands over her body, all the while staring at him with her inviting brown eyes and smiling at him knowing that he wasn't going to lift a finger to stop her.

"Did you know that I was French? In French my name is pronounced Brigitte. Brigitte Anjanette. That's the French style. How do you like it Mr. Barratt?

That's when he knew that he would have to kill her. French style.

Barratt's house was going to be a problem because it was so small-only one story and a basement. The height of the basement was only nine feet high and he doubted if that was high enough to get the force he needed. Gravity required more time than nine feet would allow. He looked around the basement and spotted the laundry chute. That was the answer. It might still not be enough but it was going to get him into the second floor.

He started with the renovations that day-tearing out the laundry chute to make room for what was to take its place.

The chute itself had originated from an upstairs closet and that had to be cleared out but other than that it could be left intact and would hide the upper half of his device quite nicely. The bottom half would be incorporated into a bed. He bought the lumber and began assembling the frame work. Finally he was ready to install the main piece-a piece that he had custom made. He tested it from a height of sixteen feet on a watermelon and the results did not leave him satisfied it would do the job when the time came. There was no more height to be gained so he added more weight to the blade and reduced the resistance of the tracks by installing ball bearings. Everything was lubricated with a very fine machine oil. He tested it again and pronounced it fit for service.

The next day, as Bridget walked home along Quaker Road, he stopped to give her a lift, making sure nobody was watching and drove her to his yellow cottage. There he offered her a few drinks, got her to lie down on the bed in the basement and cut off her head with one stroke of his home-made guillotine. His last minute improvising had done the trick and the blade went right through the bone as clean as if it were the real thing. For the first time in his life Barratt felt liberated and wondered if that's how it was for the French peasants back in 1790.

That night the guillotine fell four more times removing all the limbs from Bridget Perry's torso. Barratt packed all the remains in plastic bags filled them with wet cement and dumped everything in Lake Nosbig, some distance from his house.

For the next month he continued to teach his class as everyone searched for the missing girl. One Saturday he was watching the news when pieces of her body were found washed ashore. Barratt knew the tightrope act was over. The police had ways of tracing it back to him. He packed a suitcase. He would need a place to hide out for a while.

He remembered hearing one of the science teachers at school talking about abandoned tunnels near the Falls. That night he found the entrance to one and followed it deep into the bowels of the earth. It ended in a kind of lagoon that must have been directly behind the Falls – judging by the rumbling and vibration that increased as he descended. And the lagoon, he surmised must have been fed by the water from the plunge basin below the Falls. It looked safe. As good a place as any to spend the night, maybe even longer if need be, he thought. He lit a candle, took out a snack and made himself comfortable.

That night he dreamed or at least he thought he dreamed that he was in the presence of something evil. It was an ancient, rotten evil. When he awoke after a rather fitful night of sleep, the tunnel smelled like salt. He went to the water and tasted it it and it too was salty. Now how could that be? he wondered. The lakes that fed into the river here were all fresh water. He hoped it was only a temporary situation, perhaps a salt deposit leaching into the water – because if he were to stay here for any length of time he had designs on drinking the water from the lagoon when his few bottles ran out.

He spent the day whittling a flute out of a piece of driftwood and that evening after he had put out his cooking fire he sat by the light of the candle-its flickerings throwing up macabre shadows on the tunnel walls. A melancholy tune spun sadly through the recesses of the lagoon as Barratt thought about his kids at Quaker Road School. As much as they hated him, he missed them. In about a month they would be getting out for summer recess.

That night he dreamed of the presence again only this time it was much more powerful. In the morning, the Lord's prayer was scrawled backwards on the tunnel wall with black charcoal from the fire and his writing hand was covered with it. He was running low on food and water and common sense told him that it was time to get out of here, but he couldn't leave. Something was holding him in place.

On the third night he vowed to stay awake and try to find out what was going on here. Huddled and shivering in a blanket, with only the warmth and light from the candle he waited like a frightened puppy for its master to come home. Around midnight he heard the water in the lagoon start to bubble and gurgle and the smell of salt and rotten eggs became over- powering. It rose from the depths of the plunge basin and drifted to within feet of where Barratt cringed in paralyzed disbelief and horror. He couldn't run, he couldn't move, he couldn't scream. He just stared until the sight of it nearly drove him out of his mind and until both retinas detached spontaneously. Now completely blind he could only feel what was happening to him.

It was as if he were in a vacuum and he was being turned inside out, although surprisingly there was no pain. Then he went completely limp. He sensed that the presence was gone as he flopped on the wet floor of the cavernous tunnel. He had some power to move but he felt like jelly. It finally dawned on him-this man who had always maintained correct posture when he stood or sat that his entire skeletal structure, backbone and all had been sucked right out of his body. He wasn't even sure how such a thing was possible because it was beyond his realm of comprehension.

On the other hand he had seen the "thing" and he knew that all things were possible.

He could move because of his muscles but without a framework for support he was reduced to flopping about like a fish. With the dexterity and agility of a slug he wriggled down to the edge of the water and lapped at the saltiness like a seal. He was sure to get salt water poisoning if he continued to drink but since he was already on the fast track to the depths of hell itself, did it really matter? All things considered that was probably the kindest thing that could have happened to him compared to the fate that lay in store for him. A fate he could not even imagine.

There by the water's edge he waited for the inevitable. Waiting was all he could do but it was the kind of waiting that twisted the mind.

The presence came back at dawn. Both entities knew how

it would end. When the candle went out this time it was never to be lit again. A final scream that could have curdled blood and stopped time in its tracks reverberated and then was dissipated by the winding tunnel walls. Sparse witness to the fact that Barratt's last black gasp in this world coincided with a rebirth in a whole new netherworld. Only in the vast recesses and silent vaults of the entity we know as time, was the event catalogued. It was the sixth hour of the sixth day of the sixth month when the hunter had claimed its prize.

CHAPTER SIX
JAG ROCK, DEMONS FROM THE PAST AND DESTINY SETS IT COURSE

The crowd was gone. At least for now. Even Judd Blackadder had gone home. The news conference had been a huge success. The chairs were now stacked in neat piles against the walls as two janitors geared up for the mammoth floor washing session that lay ahead of them. I grabbed a beer off one of the tables and went out on the observation deck of the Minolta Tower. Night had descended on the city below. Charlie Knowales had preceded me and was leaning on the railing.

Up here, on the top level 800 feet high, with a spring night air that was cool at level ground but stinging against our cheeks, it felt good to unwind. But I knew if I stayed out here too long it would play havoc with my arthritis. My hands and feet had been in the cold wetness of Niagara so many times before and now I was paying the price.

As I sipped the beer, I could see the Falls, brilliantly illuminated by artificial candlepower, 8 million strong. The beacons of light fanned out form their point of origin, behind Table Rock, and played on the falling waters in variations of colors--blue, red, white, pink and shades in between when the beams merged. Other rays of light tried to pierce the opaque curtain of mist but were reflected back in flashes of suspended color, almost as if the powerful searchlights were brushes, painting the picture of the Falls with sweeping motions. Kind of like a rainbow at night. That was the one thing about Niagara, if it was not possible to produce the real thing then the imitation would be manufactured. It was the illusion that was paramount.

Below, the Niagara Parkway, which winds its way beside the Falls and river and is intersected at Clifton Hill by Lundy's Lane, was a thick snake of white hot light, a result of the heavy volume of traffic that continued its assault on the city. The thick artery of light also coursed north up Lundy's Lane onto the Queen Elizabeth Highway, which leads into the interior of Canada. There were no vacancies in the Falls and people were heading further up north to find a place to stay.

"How many people can this place take anyway?" Knowales asked me.

"I don't know. It's hard to say. They say when Red Hill went over in 1951, the news was spread by word of mouth only a few hours before, and there was close to a quarter of a million people watching. I figure they'll line both sides of the river from Chippewa down to the Falls, then both sides of the gorge to the Rainbow Bridge. The bridge itself will no doubt be closed to traffic and turned into a viewing area, then all the towers. Hell, I'd say the potential exists for about fifteen million spectators."

This entire maiden voyage was planned around a whole week of festivities.. The plan was to make it a joint Canadian and American venture. Today was July 1st Canada Day, a celebration of Canadian independence, hence the introduction of the Hellion and the fireworks. On Wednesday July 4th, the American Independence Day, the Hellion would be given a test run over the American Falls in preparation for the inaugural run. Other days would be marked with publicity briefings, banquets and other honorariums that both countries were eager to participate in and promote. This was generating big tourist dollars on both sides of the river. The official launch day would be Monday July 9th, a day that held special significance for Charles Knowales. That was the day that Rediens had been referring to when he made his big scene earlier in the evening.

Maybe we oughta make the department of tourism cut us in for a share."

Even though he had tried to change the subject, I could tell that Charlie was still deeply affected by tonight's incident. And this was a man who was not easily shaken. Together we gazed at a Falls dressed in green.

"When was the last time you saw Rediens before tonight?' I asked.

"Not since *that* night when we were kids," Knowales replied.

"So what do you suppose he's up to after all these years. It's gotta be, what, about thirty-eight years?"

"I don't know. That's what has me worried.'

"I wouldn't let him get to you, Charlie. We both know that he's always had it in for you ever since we were kids in the Summerlane subdivision. But even you know that he's always been more hot wind than anything else. He's messing with our minds again He's like the black cat crossing our path. He can't hurt us if we don't give in to our superstitions. Hell, you knew that when you started this that it was gonna draw every psycho and his brother out of the woodwork."

My own words surprised even me-"don't give in to our superstitions". Who was I trying to kid. These days I was almost ruled by my quirks and even the sight of a gray kitten would have sent me scurrying in the opposite direction. Perhaps it was the years that had fallen between us that had encouraged such a display of metal on my part but anyone who really knew me –after they had done a double take on the origin of such an utterance would still be in shock or laughing uncontrollably.

Knowales to this point was not up to speed on my idiosyncracies and took no notice of my faux pas.

"I knew that going in. I just don't like the unknown. I like to know what's going on when it concerns me and my business. You know that I like to know everything I can about the Falls. That's one of the reasons that we brought you on. To insure the success of this venture. That, and some of that built in luck you Irish carry around to counteract the black cats of this world."

"I'm only half Irish and it seems my allotment of four leaf clovers ran out long ago."

"Nevertheless, nothing will be left to chance. We cannot,...

we WILL not fail. Failure is not even a consideration."

"Yes, you always liked control but as an old Indian saying goes, life happens."

"Still..." Knowales left the thought to drift away unsaid, his gaze drawn to the Falls now ablaze in pure white light.

"Charlie, you know that he always blamed you for what happened to him."

"I know, Ro, but I think it's gone way beyond that. I saw his eyes, Ro. Everyone else was looking at his mouth, but I saw the eyes. I saw the hate. I saw the evil."

It was unusual to see Knowales this rattled, especially in public. Rediens had really struck a nerve. I found it almost unthinkable to imagine that Knowales had an Achilles heel.

"There was something else. I couldn't quite put my finger on it but when we were in close quarters before security separated us....there was a smell. It came from Rediens and even though he was alive-it was the smell of death.

I had not mentioned the dream I had had the previous night and I did not think now was the time to bring it up. I'd never been one for putting much stock in the interpretation of dreams. On the other hand they did seem to be a window into the stream of consciousness of a higher order. In many instances it did seem as if a message were being whispered in your ear directly from the beyond. A message so immediate and pure it was as if at the time it was written in ink that was still wet. The trouble was in the morning when you woke up the ink had dried and faded like it was invisible and most of the time you couldn't remember what you had dreamt, good or bad.

Instead I tried to focus on the positive. "Well," I said. "The one good thing that's come out of all this is that security got a good look at Rediens so if he tries to come around again, they'll be on the lookout."

Something down deep and dark inside my gut told me that a return visit from Rediens was almost inevitable. He was one demon from our past that had not yet been exorcised.

"By the way," I said, changing the subject. "I want to commend you on your selection of Sara Wilson."

"Yes, I think she'll work out just fine."

I thought I detected a faint flicker of a smile dab its way onto Knowales' face. Also there was something about the way he said it that started to smolder within me. The lights on the Falls switched to yellow.

"By the way I was meaning to ask. What's with the cane anyway?"

"I thought you'd appreciate it. You know, a symbol of the river and all that."

"That's a little too malevolent to be taken for a symbol of life. A horned snake would be offensive. The Indian gods of the river would feel threatened, even provoked by that representation."

"Oh well, maybe it's better that way. Stir them up a little. Put them on their guard. Maybe it'll ward off evil spirits." I knew that this was an explanation that Knowales didn't really believe in but was using to brush me off. I decided not to press him on it.

I turned my gaze back toward the Falls, the star attraction in white, just as it was bathed in red light.

"Looks like blood," I said. "Blood gushing from some massive wound in the earth" The water fell, tumbled, and cascaded as if washing away the dirt of time with its own sacrificial blood. I thought of the day Charlie's younger brother, Ryan, died. I could remember every word said.

"If you're getting a cold, you better not give it to me," I warned.

"Ain't gotta cold. Just keep smelling something funny," Ryan said.

"You oughta try changing your socks," I said. Ryan had been sniffing all morning and it was getting on my nerves.

"Don't smell like that either. Smells like when my Dad took us up to visit Mamie's cottage on Cape Cod. Smells like salt." He sniffled. I put a hand on his forehead. "You must be coming down with something. There ain't no salt around here."

I couldn't make any sense of it but that was only the first of a lot of things that made no sense that day. I was only a kid then, but even today things that happened that day are still a mystery to me. We were all only kids, but I was 11, the same age as Charlie, who was the oldest of the two brothers. Knowales's father always told him that as the oldest he had to look out for his 9-year-old brother. This was the rule.

"Friends will come and go," he would say, "but you'll always be brothers for as long as you live." Corny as it sounds, he was right. Even after all these years, Charlie never found anyone that could replace the love and loyalty he shared with his brother.

Don't get me wrong. Watching over Ryan was not the easiest of responsibilities. He was always getting into some type of mischief or another. And then there was the mischief that Charlie was always getting into, that he had to keep Ryan out of. But Charlie never had to be forced to comply with his dad's rule. It was mostly a labor of love. Charlie loved Ryan, and they almost never fought.

One time I heard Ryan say that Charlie was the best brother that anybody ever had, but that was only after Charlie had repaired a part of the garage that Ryan had burnt, so that their father wouldn't find out that he had been playing with matches. I'm sure in this particular case his father would have waived his rule of big brother looking out for little brother but to Charlie, a rule was a rule.

Ryan was always copying him, following him, trying to be like him. That was his way of showing he loved Charlie. He looked up to Charlie. He trusted everything he said. Like the time Ryan fell off a swing and broke his ankle. Charlie had to carry him on his back for almost a mile, and Ryan didn't cry all the way home because Charlie told him it would be alright. And it had been.

"Sometimes," Charlie once said of Ryan, "I think his

admiration for me exceeded reasonable bounds, like the time at a pickup football game when he called the biggest kid on the field a sissy, or words to that effect, and that if the kid had any objection, I was volunteered to take it up with him.

Needless to say, with Ryan around, I got to be pretty good with my fists. Had to be just to survive. That's the way it was. Ryan got in trouble. I bailed him out. But I wouldn't have had it any other way. I envied my brother's fearless innocence. His spunk. That's why I knew I wouldn't be able to stop him from coming with us that day. I'd thought about leaving him at home, and naturally in retrospect I wish I'd had. But when I felt his forehead, he had no fever. He was just sniffing all morning because he smelled something funny."

We took knapsacks of food and cooking utensils, a tent, sleeping bags, an axe, and a couple of pellet guns. The five of us, Charlie, Ryan, Judd Blackadder, me, and a bizarre-looking kid, Kane Rediens, looked like an army detail about to go on patrol. Rediens was a new kid who had recently moved into the neighborhood with his family. We didn't know a lot about them outside of the fact that there was Indian blood in their background-a fact Rediens felt compelled to confide in me (which I always regarded as a way to gain favor with us) but we could certainly sense the overzealous initial attempts by Rediens to impress our little group.

The day immediately got off to a bad start. We'd been filing our way down Quaker Road. Whether it was intentional or accidental, one of the guns went off, firing a pellet into the side of a passing car. Most of the time the motorist might have thought the plunk of the pellet striking the door was just an errant rock and not paid any attention to it. Not this car. The brake lights flashed and the car skidded to a halt about 100 yards away from us. Gorilla Monsoon and King Kong got out. One look at the scowls on their faces and I knew these two meant serious business.

Tension hung in the air as both camps planned strategy. I didn't particularly like the odds but I knew we had to keep our heads. To panic would prove fatal. Besides, if you disregarded their size and the steam coming from their ears, these two didn't look like the were going to be invited on "Jeopardy" anytime soon.

"Listen you guys, these two are pretty big and if they grab us, there's no doubt we're dead meat, but that doesn't mean they can run that fast. We know we can run, we know the area, and we've got a head start, so head for the cornfield and don't let up."

I had to hurry the last few words as the two men from the car bolted for us. This was high drama. As high as it gets in the young lives of eleven-year-olds. We hopped an old wire fence surrounding a cornfield and tore down the rows towards the woods at the far end. For us it was a race for life. Not that the two King Kongs would actually kill us, but for sure, a severe beating was in store. One mistake, a fall or a trip, and that boy would incur all of the wrath for the dent in the car.

We liked to think of ourselves as a fairly loyal close-knit group, but on occasions such as these loyalty went out the window, and it was every boy for himself. The survival instinct in its rawest form. Except when it came to Ryan. Charlie purposely let him get ahead, even though he was a faster runner, that way if Ryan fell, he could help him, or if things got worse and it looked like Ryan might get caught, Charlie could give himself up, allowing Ryan time to get away.

We reached the woods with no appreciable gain from the two men who were still thrashing and flailing about in the leaves of the cornstalks. We, being much shorter, had been able to run under most of the leaves without much interference. Now, we were on our turf. The woods. We knew all the paths and trails in the woods, where they led to, even where they faded out. On these we could travel faster and quieter, as they guided us to our destination. Eventually King and Kong reached the woods also. I could hear the crunching and crashing of sticks in the distance behind us. We took full advantage of our trail prowess and quickly widened the gap between our pursuers. The crashing noises soon faded off further in the distance and I knew the game was over. We were safe. We stopped for a rest.

Charlie, breathing and perspiring heavily, gasped, " Jeez (inhaling) that (exhaling) was close. Who the hell fired that shot, anyways?"

Reluctantly, Rediens spoke up. Like I said, he was an ugly kid with thick wads of hair for eyebrows and a widow's peak that was creeping down his forehead as if it were trying to touch his nose. He seemed to have bowls instead of eye sockets. Although it hadn't quite manifested itself yet Rediens was in possession of a gene on the long arm of chromosome 17. It was this gene that had been mistaken for the condition known as elephant man disease. The cause of that disease was later identified as the proteus syndrome. What Rediens had was neurofibromatosis, a condition marked by skin discolorations, growths on the eyes that would eventually result in blindness, scoliosis-a severe curvature of the spine and excessive bone growths that could show up anywhere on the body. While the neurofibromatosis was not in evidence yet the excessive hair growth and the peculiar angles of his face were conjuring up images of a pubescent Neaderthal. Subhuman. Jungle-istic. By the end of his teens, thick hair would grow to cover most of his body.

"I was just swinging the gun by my side," he said, "and just as I squeezed off the shot that damn car went by."

This didn't wash with Charlie.

"Jeez," he said. "Watch it next time willya? You almost got us damn near killed, you shithead." He was not deliberately picking on the kid. God knows as ugly as Rediens was he was gonna have enough trouble in life without anyone adding to it-he was just one of those characters whether by luck or overzealousness or whatever the reason that would show up every time with fork in hand when they were passing out free soup. Of course, Charlie would have said the same thing to one of the others if they had been the perpetrator. I could tell he didn't like having Ryan put in jeopardy because of someone else's error.

After about a half hour catching our breath and mockingly putting our ears to the ground (as Indians do to listen for footfalls) and even to the trees, we headed back.

Pecker's Pond was our destination that day. It was located about a mile behind the Summerlane subdivision in a section of wooded area just off Quaker Road. Although I didn't know it at the time, the pond fed into Chippewa Creek, which was a tributary of the Niagara River. What I'm trying to say is the same water that ran in the stream and pond would eventually go over Niagara Falls. Measuring about half the length of a football field, it served as the reservoir for the Peckinpaw farm during the dry season.

Ever since old man Peckinpaw had stopped farming his fields, the pond had lain dormant, overrun by weeds and frogs. Dormant that is, until the kids from the Summerlane founded it as a natural playground. Pecker's Pond was the ideal spot for dawdling on the way to and from school. In fact, you could tell quite a lot from who dawdled there and when. The kids who hated school dawdled in the morning, and the kids who hated to go home dawdled in the afternoon. Sadly to say, some kids were in both groups.

Very rarely, did we ever pass by it, without at least stopping to skip a few stones on it's glassy surface or scare up a few frogs. It was our way of saying hello to an old friend each day, a friend that had afforded us countless hours of pleasure.

On Saturdays, it was usually the site of a full-scale, all day invasion. A whole gang of Summerlane kids could be seen marching across the fields and through the woods to the pond. The pond was easily accessible by way of Quaker Road, as was the case during the school week, but the woods was the more adventurous route. It afforded a more back-to-the-land-Huckleberry-Finn feeling. Perhaps that was its greatest attraction, that it allowed us to become pioneers, discovering new, untainted lands every Saturday morning.

The waters of Pecker's Pond were also witness to a lot of growing up on its shores. It was a good place to talk about your problems, or the problems of growing up, in general, or to just shoot the breeze. Girls and sex soon became the dominant topics, as we reached that particular stage in our lives. And more then one of us experienced the pleasure of his first orgasm, masturbating into the waters of the pond. One time, a girl from the block, Rebecca Elliot, went skinny-dipping in the pond to the wide-eyed stares of the boys on shore. We also smoked our first butts on its banks, often until we were so dizzy that we fell into the water.

The one drawback to the pond was its waterfalls, well, not really the falls so much, but Jag Rock at its base. The pond was deep enough to permit diving off its 20 foot cliff, if you were careful enough to avoid Jag Rock. So named for its jagged edges, most of the toy boats and other objects that were sent over the falls ended up in pieces on Jag Rock. But every once in awhile, especially in the spring or early summer, after a heavy rainfall, the current was sufficiently swift enough to propel an object past the peril of Jag Rock.

Finally, there was the Ark. You couldn't talk about Pecker's Pond without mentioning its crowning jewel. The Ark was a raft built out of various scraps and odds and ends. Judd Blackadder was the principal designer and builder of this water contraption, a vocation that seemed to have followed him 38 years later.

The raft was an incredible device, at least in our eyes. The task of building the raft had fallen to Blackadder, who else but Blackadder, the mad scientist-inventor of the group. Blackadder had access to all kinds of nautical equipment because his father was employed by the St. Lawrence Seaway Authority, which controlled, among other things, the Welland Canal, which was built as a by-pass to the Niagara River. Blackadder's father would take us to see the lakers go through the locks at Port Colborne, and once we got to ride up in a train bridge that spanned the canal.

Blackadder had scrounged a couple of steel drums from his father's garage and had bolted some wooden planks onto them. The craft was then fitted with oars for power, and a moveable board at the rear served as a rudder for steering, although the craft never went fast enough for this to be really tested.

It was even equipped with a trap door allowing us boys, garbed in underwater masks and fins, to submerge into the depths of the pond. Huckleberry Finn never had it so good. And this raft changed configurations faster then a chameleon changes colors. One day it was a submarine, Captain Nemo-style, carrying its warriors to do battle with the giant octopus; another day it was Long John's pirate ship off to Treasure Island; and another day it was a landing craft on the shores of Normandy during the invasion of D-Day. The raft's only limitations were the imaginations of its young sailors.

We had gained the pond by late afternoon, without further incident, and began setting up camp. We alternated our duties with dips in the cool pond. When firewood had been collected, we broke open our supplies, and it appeared that franks and beans would be the menu du jour.

While we were sitting around the banks of the pond waiting for the fire to build, an event occurred, that had it not been overridden by the tragic circumstances of later in the evening, this would have been the centerpiece of our memories when we recalled the day. At first, I thought that the noise I heard was another annoying ploy by Rediens to grab attention.

"Shut up," I implored.

"That wasn't me."

We stopped all activity and all of us listened again. Above the crackling of our fire, off in the distance, it sounded as if a baby was crying. However the sound was coming closer and as it did it became more distinctive. It was an animal. Bleating. And it was coming from the stream that fed into the pond.

Five sets of eyes swiveled as though on the same axle toward the waterfalls. To our combined astonishment what looked like a bale of cotton with legs flailing swooped down the swollen stream and was propelled over the falls. It was a lamb from the Peckinpaw farm that had apparently ventured too close to the swift waters of the stream and had been swept away.

The ball of wool easily cleared the danger of Jag rock but landed with a splash and an awkward thud on the edge of the free floating Ark. The bleating and the thrashing ended abruptly. I was still in my shorts so I dove into the pond and reached the animal before it disappeared under the waters. The poor lamb was suffused with a limpness that conveyed a severe departure of its life forces. Its face stared back at me with eyes bulging as if any second they would pop. The lamb had broken its neck in the fall. Had it not still had air in its lungs it would have plummeted to the pond's recesses with the speed of a sack of silver dollars. As it could only have weighed a brick's worth this side or that of thirty pounds anyway and was still quite buoyant, it was no more difficult getting to shore than a bundle of three or four heavy duty sweaters. It lay motionless on the bank with its unblinking bulging eyes long enough for even the unbelievers among us to finally pronounce it dead.

"Put away those dogs boys," announced Rediens, "We're going to have a real meal tonight."

He went over to his knapsack and extracted a pretty good replica of a hunting knife.

"What are you going to do with that?" someone asked.

"I'm going to skin it and we're going to eat lamb chops. We're going to have to make a spit over that fire."

While Rediens was already in action, stripping down to his shorts, the rest of us were skeptical if not downright stunned by this declaration.

"Do you think he knows how to do that?" someone asked.

"Well, he does live on a farm of sorts, I guess," someone answered. "Maybe he does."

I interjected what I knew into the conversation,"He told me his mother was part Indian."

The whole idea seemed to make more sense to us the more we thought about it. After all we had not killed the animal nor had we trespassed on Peckinpaw's farm to get it. It was just going to be eaten by other animals or worse yet, rot in the sun. So why not. Besides we were all kind of intrigued by the prospect of preparing and cooking our own fresh game just like the pioneers must have done for hundreds of years . Of course Rediens would be doing all of the preparing. There was not a one among the rest of us who even had a clue.

We watched with fascination as he picked a tree on the far side of the pond and hung the animal by its rear legs from a branch. A small length of rope helped him do this.

Then he drew the blade across the throat of the animal several times, probably owing to the sharpness of the instrument. On the third pass the blood began to flow. It ran down one side of the sheep's black nose and soaked into the ground. After a few minutes of waiting, Rediens slit the sheep down the belly. There was more blood and some slippery slimy objects that we guessed were the stomach and intestines. Rediens continued to hack away at the lamb and at one point peeled back the woolen hide and laid it on the ground. By now he was so completely covered in blood that only his eyes glistened white in the gathering darkness. Next with great difficulty he removed the head and the lower legs so that all that remained of the animal was a solid parcel of flesh. In the process of this transformation the lamb had gone from an entirely white creature to a slab of red while Rediens had gone from a white boy to the incarnation of the dark avenging angel, Lucifer himself. This refugee from Dante's inferno cut the meat down and handed it to us.

"Here's supper. Run a stick through it and keep turning it so it roasts. The other stuff has to be buried or we're going to be attacked by bugs and any other thing that smells it. I'm going swimming." With that he dove into the water.

It was my job to bury the offal. Even as I covered over the head with dirt I could still see the bulging eyes of that thing staring back at me and in the growing blackness, it gave me the creeps. I finished the task as quickly as I could and hurried back to the campfire. After his dip in the pond it appeared that Rediens had returned to our world, at least on the outside.

We all had to admit that in spite of our reservations in the beginning our entree was smelling quite appetizing. The honor of carving up the beast again defaulted to Rediens. One thing was a given he certainly seemed to know his way around a knife. I came from Indian stock as well and I found myself being repulsed by such activity.

I'm not sure beans was the appropriate companion to leg of lamb but even so, the fresh air had rendered us to the brink of starvation and we ate like hogs at a trough. The whole endeavor had proven rather fruitful except for the image I still carried in my mind of unflinching bulging eyes.

Although the tent was up, we were planning to sleep under the open sky, in our sleeping bags. As dusk laid its dim blanket on the pond and the recesses of the woods, we gathered around the knapsack of Judd Blackadder.

"I lifted these awhile ago off my big brother, but I was saving them for a special occasion, and I guess this is it." He opened his hand to expose three neatly rolled joints. "Columbian, man oh man."

Immediately, Charlie flashed "the look" over to Ryan, and Ryan understood. Charlie usually included Ryan in everything, but not when it came to pot. Most of the other boys had experimented with grass, but Rediens had not tried it as of yet. It took a lot of coaxing on the part of Judd Blackadder, but he finally gave in. Blame it on the day we'd just had. What's one more crazy thing gonna matter? He coughed roughly every time the joint passed to him and he took a drag. It was a lot harsher than cigarette smoke.

"No, no. Like this," instructed Blackadder.

"Hold the smoke deep in your lungs for as long as you

can."

Rediens followed suit on the next couple of hits, which he washed down with a beer, one of several Blackadder had confiscated from his father's supply.

"Hey, you guys, save the empties, will youse?" Blackadder said. "I have to replace them sose my old man won't know I was in his booze."

We laughed at this, ridiculously giddy. Rediens did not see anything funny. In fact, he felt nothing except a little heady from the smoke.

"That stuff don't work. I don't feel anything."

"Give it a little time," we told him.

"It usually takes a little longer to hit the first time."

In a few minutes, Rediens began to feel a tingling sensation in his fingers and toes. Then an overwhelming rush of well-being seemed to wash over him. His face looked hot and flushed. He began to laugh at the silliest things, or nothing at all. He noticed that his shoelace was untied, and in attempting to retie it, he discovered that he had forgotten how. By then, we were howling in fits of laughter.

"Look, look. He's shit-faced."

Rediens began to feel at his face for a foreign substance. This action sent the rest of us off on yet another laughing convulsion. Rediens was being made a fool of. We were having a real blast at his expense. Normally, this would have bothered him, but somehow he didn't seem to mind. Or so the rest of us thought.

Someone came up with the idea of paying a visit to the graveyard, so, without giving any thought, we staggered drunkenly out to the road and towards the cemetery, half a mile away. By the time we reached the cemetery our laughter had dissolved into a heightened sense of awareness and even some downright serious contemplation about God and the impossible nature of infinity.

The cemetery was an ancient relic of a place no longer used or visited except by weeds. Many of the gravestones had crumbled from age and neglect. Long ago, it was rumored to have been an ancient Indian burial ground. Hedging the borders of the burial ground was a row of weeping willows. Willows are the creepiest sort of trees, I thought. Their hanging vine-like branches often resemble long thin fingers dangling about, fingering the ground. But just let someone come within reach of their grasp and they would rigidly come to life, wrapping themselves around, and then crushing the life out of the victim. No, I thought to myself, I would not go anywhere near the willows.

In the rear center of the graveyard loomed a massive vault of concrete.

"What's that?" said Ryan

"Hopkins Tomb." answered Rediens.

"Oh, yeah, what do you know about it?" Ryan asked.

"Something I heard."

"I bet it's probably another one of his bullshit stories. Where does he get this crap from anyways? Probably living in that haunted farmhouse he calls home."

To say that Ryan never liked Rediens would be stating the obvious. He had never trusted him, even though Rediens had never hurt Ryan to my recollection. Just a kid's intuition, I guess. Or were they the like poles on a magnet? For some reason, although I could never put a finger on it and had never expressed it to anyone but myself, I felt the same way about Judd Blackadder. But then kids have lots of gut feelings that they can't explain.

In truth I think Rediens was jealous of Ryan and Charlie because of their close brotherhood, and I think maybe Ryan sensed this. Besides, Ryan did have a point. Rediens was always coming up with these strange stories. At first we thought he was just lying to gain some attention. Trouble was most of the stories usually turned out to be plausible, as well as scary.

Rediens had a particular affinity for the macabre. And the house he lived in didn't subtract from his general aura of eeriness. It was an old farmhouse, set back from the road. Trees planted in the front yard had been allowed to grow wild, obscuring any view of the house from the main road. All the other houses in the Summerlane were basic clap-board capes, a popular construction choice after WW II. Each sat proudly on equally divided half acre tracts of land. Rediens' house stood alone in both age and irregularity and may have been one gene away from being haunted.

That aside, nobody really knew much about the people who lived inside the house. Rediens never talked about his parents or where they came from. Most of the other fathers in the subdivision worked for one or another of the two steel mills in Welland. Nobody knew for sure, but it was said Rediens' father worked for the Parks Commission that maintained property connected with Niagara Falls.

"And how come you always dress in black colors?" pressed Ryan.

"It's because I don't have a big brother to dress me," taunted Rediens.

It was time for me to step in, "Let's hear what he has to say, Ryan."

"Legend has it (a standard Rediens line) that old man Hopkins was a rich bugger and that his wife poisoned him to death one night. Then she had this massive tomb built with some of his fortune she had inherited. Probably to make sure he stayed inside. But I heard Hopkins or his ghost gets revenge on anybody who invades his privacy. One time a fraternity from Fonthill High School tied a guy to one of the gravestones in front of the tomb as part of the guy's initiation. They left him there all night, and when they came back to get him in the morning, the guy was dead from a heart attack. There were no marks on him at all. His heart just gave out. Oh yeah, and one more thing. His face was frozen into a incredible smile, a smile of intense fear, a smile of death."

This last part about the smile had not been included in the story that had been related to Rediens, but he had just recently seen the movie "Dr. Sardonicus" on television about a man who had a death-smile frozen onto his face, and he thought it added a nice touch to this particular tale.

How ironic would this turn out to be, in retrospect.

"Anyway," Rediens continued, "the theory is that old man Hopkins came out of his tomb and scared the kid to death. They say that if you want to get him to come out of his tomb you have to wait until dark, and then knock three times on the door of his tomb."

Silence.

A breeze rustled through the weeping willows, causing the vine-like fingers to stir. It was as if the fingers of the tree-hand were beckoning us to come a bit closer within reach of their grasp.

"No way," I said, talking to the trees.

"What did you say?" said one of the boys.

"Nothin'," I replied.

The strawberry moon hung full in the sky, almost surrealistically, just above the arch portal of the tomb, and the gigantic concrete house itself cast its shadows to our feet and beyond. Ryan walked up to the steel door of the tomb and pounded on it with a clenched fist. The dull echoing thuds reverberated inside of the chamber. The rest of us assumed our best pugilistic stances, fists raised forward in preparation. Blackadder had taken a little karate and flashed palms open.

Silence.

A distant plane droned far overhead. Then faded.

Silence.

"Come on Hopkins, you mother. We're ready for you!" shrieked Ryan, shattering the night.

More silence.

Then a grating sound of steel against concrete emanated, and it appeared in the dark shadows or in the stoned imaginations of the boys, as if the large steel door of the tomb was beginning to swing open. Every man for himself again as we all turned on our heels and fled out of the graveyard, knocking over a few headstones in the process. The Three Stooges could not have staged a more haphazard exit.

Only when we were safely back at camp did Rediens reveal that the scraping noise was just his knife rubbing up against a nearby tombstone. He was laughing too hard to mention that it had been intentional. Old Rediens was giving us a little payback for making fun of him earlier. He had always taken great delight in messing with our minds.

I always maintained that what would happen next was our punishment for desecrating a sacred burial ground. I didn't believe in ghosts, but still the dead deserved some respect. Rediens never put much stock in that.

"Lets go shoot Jag Rock!"

The idea was Charlie's.

It was not a particularly bright idea in the first place, but considering the darkness and the condition of our group, it was that much more foolish. It was Knowales's determination, after studying the waterfalls in the moonlight, that it could be done. It was true, the current did seem to be extra forceful tonight, after a heavy rainfall the previous morning.

"C'mon, boys. Just look at that current, will ya? It'll never be any stronger until next spring. It's now or never if we're ever gonna do it."

"I'm game," Ryan said. He seemed to be determined to answer any challenge when he was around Kane Rediens.

The first task was to get the Ark into the stream above the falls. It took all of the boys in the party and a couple of ropes to portage the raft up the steep path on the side of the waterfall. Charlie manned the steering apparatus in the rear, with Blackadder. Ryan , Kane Rediens, and I rode up front. When all had boarded and were settled in place, I gave the order to cast off. There were two ropes, the one in the front for mooring the craft and the one in the rear with anchor attached. The ropes were dragged in and coiled into two piles on each side of the raft.

The Ark started sluggishly at first, then began to pick up

momentum.

"Get down as low as possible," instructed Blackadder. "We can't afford any wind drag."

The excitement and anticipation of the moment ignited the adrenalin in Charlie's veins like gasoline on water. He lived for doing things like this. Laying flat as he could, Ryan couldn't help but glance back at his brother, silhouetted against the night sky. Ryan saw the excitement in his face and felt the courage that Charlie exuded. The courage and self-confidence of his brother had carried young Ryan through many a situation that, if alone, he would have given up on. Ryan admired his brother Charlie. He wanted to be just like him. He did not remember a single day, when he did not feel proud to be the brother of Charlie Knowales.

"Charlie, I smell that funny salt smell again. Only this time it's a lot stronger."

"I don't know where you're getting this from, Ryan. There's no salt around here." "Anybody else smell anything?"

We shook our heads, no.

"I think you better have Mom check that out when you get home."

"Okay guys, brace yourselves, we're getting close. And remember what Judd said, hang on tight and stay low."

In the excitement and my efforts to lie as flat as possible, I never saw the hand that intentionally knocked the anchor rope into the water. We were moving at a surprisingly brisk clip, now. Even I, who had doubts about the whole operation in the beginning, was now almost convinced that we were going to make it. Knowales steered the craft expertly.

"It's showtime!" he called out as the Ark neared the brink. Despite the nearly insurmountable logistic of the operation, we probably would have cleared Jag Rock, but right at the crucial moment before going over, the trailing anchor rope caught on a rock. The raft skewed sideways. Precious momentum was interrupted. The current upended the craft, dumping us, then the Ark, over the edge of the falls.

Ryan's last words were, "Charlie, Charlie," he called as he took the brunt of Jag Rock, with a sickening thud. He died instantly, neck broken, head almost completely severed from his torso.

I was thrown clear. Kane Rediens was smashed face first into a flat section of Jag Rock. When I swam over to him, his mouth was a gurgling mess of blood, teeth, skin, and bone and there wasn't much I could do but I attended to him the best I could. I would later go on to make a career out of doing just that. For the most part, Blackadder had escaped unscathed as well. Not so Charlie Knowales. The tumbling raft had crushed his hip condemning him to limping his way through the rest of his life with the aid of a cane. But that night it didn't stop him from reaching his brother.

Charlie thrashed about in the black water until he reached the floating form beside Jag Rock. He cradled his brother in his arms, watching the last of Ryan's lifeblood ooze into the cold waters of Pecker's Pond. A neck chain with a cross Ryan always wore had settled into the hideous neck wound, glistening in the blood. Then his eyes rolled back into their sockets until only white showed. Blackadder pulled the Knowales brothers to shore and Charlie and Judd had been inseparable ever since.

Ryan's dying words, "Charlie, Charlie, Charlie seemed to echo over us, even from that night as we looked down at the bloody Falls from the tower. I looked up as Charlie spoke.

"It's funny though, because from that day on, I knew what had to be done for my brother. I knew the minute I laid my eyes on this place that somehow my destiny was tied to this creation of God. It was all connected Jag Rock, the Falls, God, Ryan's death and my fear. I made a vow to Ryan that day that I'd beat this thing one day, once and for all. I guess you could say it was also the day that I broke from God. A God who I never understood because he had taken the life of the one person who I had loved the most in this world.

"Then the nightmares started.'

All I could think of was *Join the club, pal.*

"I had nightmares about this place for years. It's like everything gets sucked to the Falls. Everything always ends at the Falls. In my dreams, if I was on water, say in a boat somewhere, no matter where, it could have been a pond in Alaska, it always led to the Falls in Niagara. And no matter what I did to prevent it, I always got swept over. If I was in a boat, and the boat was tied up, the rope would somehow break. If I was swimming in the water, no matter how hard I tried to swim upstream, it was like my arms would get heavy, and I would still get sucked over. One time in a dream, my arms just fell off and floated away, leaving me defenseless against the current. At other times, I would dream about climbing those wooden stairs beside the Falls (once part of The Cave of the Winds) and I would slip on water-slicked steps. I was forever slipping on those steps. Even so, when I went to grab onto the railing, the wind and mist would buffet me endlessly, trying to make my hands lose their grip. I would resist, yet in the end, the railing would break, and I would go over again.

"They say that you never actually die in your dreams. That's a crock, because I've died a thousand deaths at this place and felt the pain of each one as if it actually happened."

My hands were throbbing, and I'd decided I'd had enough childhood reminiscence for one evening.

"You know Ro, even after all these years, I miss him like nobody's business."

Charlie said goodnight and went home. Maybe it was the drink. Maybe it was all the remembering. But in the few hours of sleep that came grudgingly, despite his weary condition, Charlie Knowales tossed and turned fitfully. Niagara had not entered his dreams for years, but that night he dreamed that he was swimming in the waters above the Falls. He suddenly felt himself getting colder and colder. He looked down at his skin and it was getting whiter and whiter. His neck tingled with electricity so he put his hands to his throat. To his horror, blood was surging out of gashes in his neck. He tried to plug the gashes with his hands but to no avail. He began to lose control of his neck muscles; his head bobbed and dangled wildly. Then he ducked under the water and the river sucked the blood out of his entire body through the wounds in his neck. Leaving his skin transparent white, like empty sausage casing, and turning the whole falls red.

A beautiful red. A brilliant red. A blood red. A premonition? A portent of things to come? This dream was only the beginning. His mind began to turn over and over and over. Everything always ends up at the falls. Everything always endsupatthe FallsEverythingalwaysendsupattheFallsEverythingalwaysen dsupattheFallsEverythingalwaysendsupattheFalls.........then oblivion.

CHAPTER SEVEN
THE CEMETERY AND A DEADLY OBSSESSION

There is no rhyme or reason to the Niagara Escarpment. It's edge meanders throughout the region, winding its way from Niagara-on-the-Lake to Stoney Creek. It was carved up by receding glaciers millions of years ago – its role varying from one vicinity to another. At the Queenston end of the escarpment, the water that flowed over its edge instigated the birth of the present day Niagara Falls. Near Welland its ledge is the waterfalls at Pecker's Pond and Jag Rock. Towards Grimsby it forms Balls Falls, a popular swimming area. At Effingham, its steep descent is traversed by a paved road.

The summer after Ryan died, Simon Schultz tried to run the Effingham hill on his bicycle without applying the brakes even once on the way down. To do so one ran the risk of being the latest brand of chickenshit for the day or longer until the next challenge. He didn't make it. He lost control on the last third of the hill when he was going the fastest and slid the remainder of the way to the bottom on his face. I've never been run over by a lawn mower but I can only imagine that's how it felt. It looked even worse. When skin meets tar and stone even at a low rate of friction most two-year-olds know the outcome. It would take 350 stitches and more before he once again had a face that he could take out in public without pieces of it coming off in his hand. It would take another six months of recovery before he could go out and not set dogs barking and babies crying.

In Fonthill, at Lookout Point Country Club, the escarpment affords one of the best views in the Niagara Peninsula. A clear day to the north will lend a view 90 miles to the CN tower in Toronto. To the southeast, the Skylon Tower in Niagara Falls and sometimes the taller buildings and the factory smoke of Buffalo NY are visible. The clubhouse of Lookout Point is also the point of convergence of three of the best damn golf holes in the world, the first, the tenth, and the eighteenth. The first and the tenth have their tees in front of the clubhouse on the top of the escarpment with greens far in the distance below.

I caddied at Lookout when I was 12 in order to earn free golf privileges every Monday when I was just learning how to play. To tee it up on number one was a dream come true ever since I first laid eyes on it. I remember as I lined up the ball preparing to launch it into the sun peeking out from the horizon, I felt like I was master of all I surveyed.

It's hard to hit a bad shot on number one or number ten. Even a ball that is flubbed is guaranteed to roll almost halfway to the hole. A good strike often produces a spectacular result. Since then I've been a member for many a blissful summer and while I've played on plenty of other courses nothing can compare to the take-your-breath-away thrill I get every time I tee it up on Lookout's number one.

The eighteenth hole is just as sensational, except in the opposite direction. The tee box sits on the lush valley floor, and the green is scooped out of the escarpment three quarters of the way to the top, right in front of the clubhouse. It takes nothing less than ball strikes right on the screws to overcome gravity and the terrain of the eighteenth. Other holes, while not as dramatic, provide similar challenges so that one taste of the Lookout Point golfing experience often proves addictive.

The only drawback for me was that the Canadian winter cropped the golfing season preciously short, especially for a man with arthritis and susceptible to the earliest chills out of the north.

"I swear one of these days," I would say to my wife "we're gonna chuck all this and head south where the only snow is in a cone."

Susan would just laugh, secure in the knowledge that we weren't going anywhere.

"As much as you hate the cold and the snow," she'd say, "you know that you'll never leave the river, not to mention your golf. You'd never be satisfied at another course."

"One day, you'll see," I kept repeating this like a mantra

usually after the first frost hit.

But in the end, she was right as "one day " never seemed to arrive.

Finally at Queenston, the Niagara Falls cemetery lies in the protective shadow of the Niagara Escarpment. I suppose General Brock, who saved Canada from an American invasion in 1812, is the most famous person buried there, but not the one I had in mind when I invited Sara to meet me there.

Brock's Monument towers above the collection of tombs, stone markers and plain white crosses. It was cool and quiet as I waited in the shade of one of the trees that sheltered the grounds. Sara arrived by cab not long after I had.

"There was something that I wanted you to see. Something that I thought you might be interested in," I said. "Maybe it will give you a little more perspective on what is going on around here."

"I think I got a pretty good dose of perspective the other day down in the gorge. I'll tell you one thing, after that day I will never look at Niagara Falls in the same way again."

"I'm sorry about that. That was a little extreme. But on the other hand it is the reality, and I didn't think you wanted anything less than the truth. This place is not what it seems. The more you delve beneath the facade erected for the tourists the more you'll realize that this is not a place for the squeamish. Just like the river and the Falls themselves, life here at Niagara is teeming with treacherous undercurrents. One must be careful where one treads."

"And will today's lesson be another warning to the unwary? I must say Mr. Patric, first the gorge, then a cemetery. Your choice of venues as schoolhouses is certainly not for the squeamish."

"I suppose I could have done without the cemetery, but if you see it first hand you might appreciate what I'm about to tell you a little better. Besides, there are worse places to be than a cemetery if peace and quiet is what you seek."

"Fine, Mr. Patric, I'm sure it will have it's desired effect.

Well, if the teacher is ready, the student is set for her lesson."

She did have a way of looking at you that made even a rogue like me feel guilty for not having done the right thing.

"No more games, I promise. But before you get all dressed up for this dog and pony show that the Thrill people are putting on I think that there are a few things you ought to know about the folks you are dealing with.

"Why Mr. Patric, Now if I'm not mistaken you are being paid by the Thrill Corporation and I would have thought your loyalties would lie with them."

"They're paying me all right. For what I know about the river. My loyalties aren't included in the bargain. Those can't be bought-they have to be earned. I figure with what you put up with the other night you earned the right to know a few things, so I'm giving you the special customer tour. Now if you'll come over here."

I noticed that she was about to step on the corner of one of the grave sites.

"Hold it! You don't want to do that. It's bad luck to step on a grave with weeds growing on it. That means an evil soul is buried there."

"Will this stuff never end with you?" Sara was exasperated. "Fine I will go around. I wouldn't want to be said that I was the one that jinxed your life."

We stood in front of a grave marker that listed a C .J. Carpentier as the assumed occupant with 1987 as the interment date.

"There's nothing in it but a foot."

"You're kidding ? How come?"

"That's all they found of him after he went over the Falls. You see your pilot Judd Blackadder has quite a checkered past. Not only was he there the night Charlie's brother died but he was in the center of quite a controversy on the river and unfortunately this man paid the ultimate price."

"That's a story I'd like to hear."

"Back in those days Blackadder worked a stint on the river

as a river rat. Pretty good with a boat too. He and this man Carpentier were assigned to patrol the upper river above the Falls. One day they spotted a forty foot Searay that must have slipped its moorings on Chippewa Creek and was being taken by the current towards the Falls. By the time the two of them came upon her she had already drifted past the intake apparatus and was entering the swifter current near the point of no return, but they still had some time in order to salvage her."

"Was there anybody on board?"

"There didn't appear to be, but that's something C J. didn't want to take for granted and it would ultimately cost him his life. The runaway boat was tossing and bouncing too much to get close enough to board her so after a couple of attempts they snagged her with a grappling hook. Had they not been in such rough current they might have even been able to tow the errant boat back in but now it was all they could do just to keep her in place.

Carpentier, knew that time was running out, and wanted to double check that no one was aboard so he went hand over hand across the rope that wedded the two boats. It was an unwritten code among the rivermen that the helmsman, Blackadder would not leave without him. Carpentier, having gone below and discovered the lower cabin empty, was about to return, when it must have hit upon him that maybe he could still save the Searay if he opened all the seacocks. If she took in enough water she might ground. The water poured in as he unscrewed the seacocks and somehow he slipped and got his foot wedged between a ladder and the gunwale. He began calling to Blackadder that he needed help. By now Blackadder in the other boat could feel the strain on the tether line because of the added water that was pouring into the Searay. He radioed for a helicopter and then cut the line and headed his boat to the safety of the upper river. Stinson and I took the call and we had our helicopter over the spot in four minutes. The trouble was that even with the seacocks open the Searay went over the Falls in three and a half minutes.

They did find pieces of the boat, especially the piece with Carpentier's foot torn from his body. Blackadder later claimed that he had no choice but to cut loose because the additional weight of the water that was coming into the other boat was dragging him backwards as well. But all he had to do was to hang on for another minute and that would have given us time to get there. Even if he had held until the rope broke which was almost a certainty it would have bought Carpentier more time. Many in the service felt that Blackadder had abandoned a comrade without exhausting all possible options. Others thought it was an out and out act of betrayal that went to the very essence of the fraternity of the men who risked their lives on the river , and although such allegations were difficult to prove and even harder to prosecute, Blackadder was given his discharge from the river service. As for me, and this goes back to when we were kids, I never trusted him as far as I could throw him."

"Wonderful. How reassuring to know that that is the man who holds my life in his hands as we go over the Falls."

"I just thought you should know what you are getting into with these characters."

Now we stood in front of a tombstone with *KNOWALES* etched at the top in bold letters and below that in lowercase ryan, with the inscription, "We will never forget you."

"Charlie Knowales's younger brother," I stated. Then I told her everything that happened that night at Jag Rock.

"What's important to remember here is the final date."

Sara read the date off the headstone, "July, 9th ,1964."

I guided her to another section of the rambling grounds and another headstone, this one for *JAMES HONEYCUTT*.

Again, Sara read the date of death, "July,9th,1964. What's the connection?"

"In a lot of ways, none. And in fact what may be most relevant to this matter is what is not here. Honeycutt was a 40-year-old adult. Ryan was only 9-years-old. The two had never met and never knew of the other's existence, and both died in different places. I alone of all the people in the world may be the sole link between the two. I was there at Jag Rock on the day that Ryan Knowales died and my father was working the river the same day when James Honeycutt died at Niagara Falls. My father pulled his body out of the river three days later and then told me the story of what happened. What follows is an account of a miracle."

July 9th, 1964 was hotter than most days, hot enough to blister paint. At that time, Niagara Falls, New York had been transformed into a massive trailer camp during the construction of the Robert Moses power plant. Eleven thousand men from all over the country pooled their collective skills to build the plant, the reservoir, and the conduits that would feed water into the mighty turbines. Many of these workers were accustomed to the roving lifestyle that led them across the country in pursuit of well-paying work.

Frank Woodward was no exception when he arrived at the Sunny Acres Mobile home park with his carpenter tools and his wife, his 17-year-old daughter Deanne, and his seven-year-old son Roger, who would now be entering his third school in a third community in the last three years. Employed by Balf, Sarin and Winkleman, Woodward's park was not far from the river or the Lynch Trailer Park in Wheatfield where Frank's foreman, James Honeycutt lived.

On that hot Saturday afternoon, Honeycutt offered to take the Woodwards for a boat cruise out on the Niagara, an offer that Frank and his wife passed on. Although the two Woodward children could barely swim, they were allowed to accept the invitation on the condition that they never be without their life jackets. Strictly adhering to their father's warning they suited up and eagerly piled into Honeycutt's 12-foot aluminum craft, with its seven and a half horsepower Evinrude outboard motor.

The trio departed from their Grand Island dock, and while the Woodward children were river neophytes, Honeycutt was highly experienced as both boatman and swimmer. He'd had six years experience as a lifeguard in North Carolina and had traveled extensively throughout the upper Niagara south of Grand Island.

For some unknown reason, this day Honeycutt headed the boat under the Grand Island bridge, north where he hadn't been before. The waters here were new to him and more turbulent, and some speculate that he may have been trying to give the children a little excitement. They would end up with more than they bargained for.

The heat was sweltering even out on the river, and Roger almost took off his life jacket but remembered his promise to his father. It would prove to be a fateful decision.

Honeycutt allowed Roger a turn at steering the boat, seemingly unaware of the dangerous direction they were heading. Ahead in the distance the mist of Niagara rose like a mystical, whitish tower into the sky. The newly arrived Woodwards would not have understood the connection between their leisurely ride on the river in their father's friend's boat and that murderous marking that was the crest of Niagara.

Surely it wouldn't have occurred to a seven-year-old caught up in the ecstasy of piloting a real boat for the very first time.

When they struck the rock, everything changed in an instant. With the propeller sheared off and no drag on the motor, the Evinrude went into a high-pitched convulsion. Honeycutt hauled the engine out of the water to assess the damage. The situation couldn't have been more critical. They had no power. Seizing the oars Honeycutt began to row furiously for the American shore. The children couldn't help but notice his frantic intensity.

"What's the matter?" Deanne asked.

Honeycutt didn't have time to answer.

They were caught in the Canadian current and being sucked through the rapids by Goat Island. The dramatic swells struck fear in the helpless boaters.

"I don't want to go swimming. I don't want to die!" sobbed Roger.

"Don't be scared. I'll hold you," cried Honeycutt.

It was evident that they would not be in the boat much longer. They survived one mammoth wave but a second one hurled them into the raging river. Deanne was trapped for a few moments underneath the overturned boat but managed to struggle free. Honeycutt, despite his most valiant efforts to hang onto Roger, was torn loose in a violent explosion of water. Sheer panic and terror engulfed the three as they pinballed off the rocks in the channel.

In his last moments, Roger could see people running horrified up and down the fenced Goat Island shoreline and wondering why they wouldn't help him. It was all so surreal. The look on their faces was enough to tell him that he was going to die. Seconds from death, a calm came over Roger.

Slow motion. Out of body. At peace. It seemed as if there was a presence that comforted him. As his life passed before his eyes, he wondered what would become of his pet dog Fritz, named for his idol, Fritz Von Erich, a local wrestler who lived in the same trailer park. He wondered what his parents would do with his toys and his clothes and his tiny bedroom. How sad they will be when they learn of his death and how much sadder when they recall that he followed up on his lifejacket promise to his father right to the end.

Then he was catapulted over the Horseshoe Falls.

After the boat had capsized, Deanne had hung onto its side then lost her grip and struck out for Goat Island. Weak swimmer that she was, her chances were slim. John Hayes, a black bus driver from Union, New Jersey was taking in the view of the Falls that afternoon from Terrapin Point, when he spotted black objects in the water above the brink.

"Oh my God!' was all he could gasp as he watched the overturned boat slide over the Falls followed by two human figures.

Someone screamed "There's still a girl in the water. Someone help. For God's sake, someone please help her."

Hayes dropped his camera and ran to the railing, spotting the red life jacket of the girl a few feet from shore as she was about to be swept to her death. He climbed the railing and reached out, but she was beyond his grasp. Hayes ran along an 18-inch ledge just above the water, then, hooking one leg over the railing and arching his body as far as he could, he screamed to the girl to kick her legs.

"Kick harder!" he commanded. "You're fighting for your life!"

Deanne was about to give up, then, in a last ditch effort, she splashed furiously for shore and made a lunge for Hayes' outstretched hand, barely catching his thumb. They were both only fifteen feet from the edge of the cataract, and for a moment it seemed as if Hayes would lose his balance and both would tumble to their deaths. But somehow he managed to right himself. He was able to hold Deanne, but it was impossible to haul her to safety. His foot hooked around the railing was the only thing that kept them both from going over. He called for help. The crowd of onlookers, stunned by the spectacle before their eyes, had grown roots.

A short distance away, John Quottrochi, a sheet metal worker from Pennsgrove Pennsylvania, and a veteran of five European campaigns in WWII, sprang into action. He handed his young son to his wife, dropped his camera, and squeezed underneath the railing, bumping his head in the process. He leaned from the railing, grabbed Deanne's free arm, and together the two men hauled her in to safety.

Narrowly escaping death herself, her first concern was for her brother.

"My brother! What's happened to my brother?"

"Pray for him," Quattrochi told her.

Tears streaming from her face as she knelt in silent prayer.

In the mist of the drenched maelstrom below, Captain

Clifford Keech had just lit his pipe and was preparing to bring the Maid of the Mist about, having run her in to about two hundred feet from the Falls, as close as she could go without being swamped. He had made this run for about twenty three consecutive years, but the sight of the young boy floating in the orange life jacket was a first . Roger saw the Maid of the Mist turn away and began shouting and waving, thinking she was leaving, but Keech was just angling his boat to keep the propeller away from the boy.

From the starboard bow, first mate Murray Hartling and deckhands Jack Hopkins and my father tossed life rings to the bobbing figure. On the third attempt a ring landed within two feet of the boy, who grabbed it and slipped inside, finally being pulled to the safety of the boat's deck.

"Save my sister. She's still in there." He cried.

From Terrapin point, John Quattrochi had witnessed the rescue of Roger and informed Deanne that her prayers had been answered. Except for some bruises, Roger was unhurt.

Three days later my father pulled out the battered and ravaged body of Honeycutt. He looked as if he had fallen off a mountain, there was no other way to describe it.

To this day, Roger Woodward remains the only person to have gone over Niagara Falls with no protection and lived to tell about it.* He alone, even if it was purely by accident, had found the sweet spot, the chink in the armor of that engine of devastation.

"That was an amazing tale but I still don't quite see the significance of it." Sara said.

"The initial significance is that the Thrill Expedition has charted Woodwards' route and plans to follow his path over the Falls, but in our case it will be by design."

More importantly the significance of this day was never lost on Charlie Knowales. You see he could never quite understand how on the same day, within hours of each other, God could take the life of his brother at one small insignificant waterfall and spare the life of another at one of the mightiest waterfalls.

In fact, Knowales comes to the grave every year to honor his brother's memory. And that's why the Thrill expedition will conduct its maiden voyage on July 9th, to commemorate Ryan Knowales. It's where we met up again almost one year ago on July 9th when he brought me on board the Thrill project. I can remember distinctly his very words.

"Ro, we have to do this for Ryan, so the world won't forget that he lived, that he was here on this earth. We have to do this for ourselves so that people will know that we were here and we left our mark. And I promised myself that I would do it for him."

Charlie pointed to a grave next to his brother Ryan. John Knowales, Charlie's father had died some years ago.

"Didn't you ever wonder how I came up with the name Hellion for our craft? It's because of him and all the men like him. It's a story that you, Ro, will recognize because you lived it with your father."

"I'm not quite sure what you're getting at,' I said.

"Look, my father had to quit school in the fifth grade and go work in the tobacco fields to help the family through the depression. While that would have been a blessing for some, for him it was a curse because he was no dummy and he loved to learn about new things. But he was the oldest and he never shirked the responsibility of taking care of his family and allowing his younger brother to stay in school and get an education. Then when the war came he answered his country's call. To his way of thinking the air force was the branch to be in. The life span was shorter than the other branches but as long as you survived, conditions were pretty decent back at the barracks. And if you didn't make it the end would probably pretty quick. No time for lingering in a hospital bed. But the trick was to try to survive,

He was a tailgunner in the B-17 bombers and at the height of the war the average life-span for a tail-gunner was 30 days. The German fighters focused on the gunners first and if they could knock them out, the rest of the plane would be easy prey. My father somehow survived the war and by shooting down three planes, took care of his crew in the process. Hell, they should have given him a medal just for surviving."

"I would have never known that about your father. I was around plenty when we were young and he never mentioned a word."

"Are you kidding? He never mentioned any of this to me. I got the story in bits and pieces from my mother and my grandparents who had talked to some of his buddies from the war. You couldn't get word one out of him about the war. He never talked about it. I can only imagine the horror of the things he saw as an eighteen year old. Ever notice it's the cooks and the book-keepers, the ones that were 10 miles away from a shot fired in their direction that have no problem blathering on about some exaggerated role they may have imagined they had in the war. All of a sudden their soup ladels turn into tommy guns and they're leading assaults across the Rhine."

"But it was the guys on the frontline who saw the real war and the indiscriminate destruction that went with it. It was so overwhelming and their chances of survival so slim that the only way to get through it was to pretend that you were already dead. It was the only thing that made sense. It was the only thing that your mind could accept as rationalization for any of this utter inhumanity. It was expected that you would be killed. To not be killed was anti-climactic. These guys in the thick of things would be as surprised as anything to come through it alive. And now that they had, they sure as hell weren't going to relive it by talking about it if they could help it.

I'm sure a lot of them couldn't if they wanted to. To put yourself in that state of mind has to be life changing. My grandparents always told me that my father was never the same after the war. Before he was rambunctious and headstrong, after softspoken and reflective."

"Those are not necessarily bad qualities to have," I said.

"No, but the point is, he seemed to have his spirit, his zest for life, sucked from him. There was a spark that was missing. Anyway the smart thing to do would have been to take advantage of the G.I. Bill and catch up on the education that he placed such a high value on, but maybe he was looking for that spark. And then again maybe it was just a little comfort that he seeked.

"Anyway he met my mother got married and next thing you know he had a family to support. Without an education, the only game in town was the blast furnaces of the steel mills and once again he did what he had to to take care of the ones who depended on him. He had to stand by and watch as others not half as smart as him went on to become lawyers and businessmen, while he went to a job that he detested and despised. While he never said a word, you knew that it was killing him inside."

"One time he told me this story about the cooling rack. The cooling rack was this monstrous steel conveyor belt that took the red hot pipe after it came out of the furnaces. The pipe was so hot at the point of entering the cooling rack that you could bend it like a noodle. Then it stiffened up on its journey over the cooling rack. At the end of the cooling rack was another conveyor belt that transported the straight pipe into the next department.

It was my father's job to remove any of the crooked pipe from the cooling rack while it continued moving. He was supplied with asbestos gloves and a metal hook. It was hot and Dangerous up on the rack because sometimes the metal pipe was really disfigured and as it tumbled it could come at you in a way you would not expect. It was not unusual to get whacked with a near red hot pipe.

Some guys took to wearing long sleeved shirts to protect their arms but the extreme heat forced most to wear tee shirts. You could always tell that a guy had rack duty from the burns on his arms. The most important thing was to get rid of the bent and twisted pipe so that the straight stuff could be sent through without stopping the production line.

My father had rack duty when an unusually twisted and tangled mass of steel came onto the rack. He started to separate and extricate the twisted pieces from the straight ones. He followed the jumble continuing to remove the bad pieces as it neared the end of the rack and the next conveyor. Bending down to pick up one piece another steel pretzel caught him on the side of the face and knocked him onto the next conveyor. That operator seeing what happened to my father shut down his conveyor thus shutting down the whole line. The foreman on the line was in a lather. They were more concerned that the line had been shut down than worried that a man had been hurt. And that, my father said, was life in the steel mills."

"The first thing he would do when he got home on Friday at the end of a long work week was to take a hot shower and wash all the crud and sweat away. But for him it was more than that, it was like a baptism back into the human race, for at least a couple of days anyway. Then he'd head to the library, just like clockwork, and check out six or seven books for the week. That man loved to read. He may have not received a formal education , but he possessed a wealth of knowledge and it was all self taught due to his voracious reading appetite."

"Yea, your father was a smart man. We all knew that even as kids," I interjected.

"I apologize if I sound like I'm making a speech here but it's the way it was. My father, your father, all the fathers in the Summerlane, they all made up that blue collar environment. Someone who didn't grow up there might think I'm talking about Jimmy Stewart in It's a Wonderful Life but it wasn't like that. No one ever gave my parents anything, and if there wasn't enough money for something then we did without. But we always had a roof over our heads and food on the table and my father never missed a single hockey game of mine or my brothers'."

"When Ryan died, my father never said much but he was

absolutely devastated. Then at 62 years of age the steel mill gives him yard duty in the winter. That kind of cold can age a young man 5 years in one winter. It's what killed him. He worked all his life and then when it was his time to retire he dies at 65."

"So when it was all said and done what did it get him. The world hardly knew he was here. All of his life he took care of the ones around him and did he get any thanks from society. Hell no."

"Society and its rules stripped him of his opportunities, then asked him to be a man way before he should've had to be, sending him into the nightmare of war and then killed him off in virtual anonymity. It took guts and courage to live that life. You want to talk about sacrifice and no greater love hath a man. Some men die in battle and it's over in a second. He sacrificed his life and it took 65 years, so that those around him would have better lives. And the irony of the whole thing was he never went to church a day in his life and yet outside of a priest you would be hard-pressed to find another man who lived a more Christian life. There wasn't an ounce of glitz or flash about the man but he was rock solid-a foundation you could depend on. And isn't that the kind of man Jesus wanted to build his church on – Peter the rock. I wanted to say all this at his funeral but I choked up. So I named the craft the Hellion after one of his favorite books. I think it was written by Joseph Conrad but it was about being free from the constraints and bonds of society, not caring what others think and living life to the fullest. In honor of my father and all the fathers of the Summerlane I christened her the Hellion. And on her we're going to raise havoc with Niagara and the world."

"And that's the speech that Charlie Knowales used to recruit me for this expedition. After that performance how could I refuse. I guzzled that story like it was cheap beer because I wanted to believe in it. Sometimes I think the man could sell humps to a camel."

"Don't you think his preoccupation with his brother, and

now his father, while in some ways is noble, is a little strange. I mean most people honor someone's memory by celebrating their birth. The only death remembrances with that kind of fixation that I can think of are JFK and Jesus Christ," Sara said.

"Well, normally that's the end of the story, but here comes the interesting part and the part of the lesson that carries the message to be wary. You see the way that Charlie Knowales saw it, especially through eyes clouded with grief, is that Roger Woodward stole the life that should have been his brother Ryan's. He was obsessed with Woodward's life after the rescue. The reporters were calling it The Miracle At Niagara."

"Charlie cut out every article he could find on Woodward in the years that followed. He knew that his family had moved to Florida and that Roger attended the University of Mississippi where he studied music and education. He followed with great interest his enlistment in the Navy, his career as medical equipment salesman in New Orleans, to his promotion to sales manager of a business machine firm in Orlando, where he got married and raised a family."

"I heard rumors that Charlie looked up his address at that time, went down to Orlando, and stood across the street and just stared at the house for hours."

"Creepy. You can get arrested these days for that kind of stalking."

"It's what I've been trying to tell you. Don't take these men and what they are capable of doing, lightly. I've known them since before forever and even I'm not sure what I'm dealing with here. They've changed and not for the better. The one thing that I do know, is that being fixated on one thing for 38 years has to do something to the mind."

"In other words CYFIC."

"Exactly. Then there was that trouble in 1990. In 1990, Charlie caught wind that Roger Woodward was coming to Niagara Falls to revisit where his life had been miraculously spared, and he made sure he was there. Right there at Table Rock amid all the spectators and the reporters there was a scuffle. Charlie was yelling, 'I won't let you forget him,' before they hauled him off to spend a couple of days in jail. Some say it was harmless enough, just a man distraught over the death of his brother. But others swear he was trying to push Woodward over the railing that day, using his cane as if it were a hockey stick in a cross-checking motion, although it would never be proven."

As a river rat, it was my duty to be entrusted with the safety of the public, the protector, if you will, so in keeping with that tradition I never let on to Sara how scared I really was.

But my God how deep the undercurrents they did run here at Niagara.

CHAPTER EIGHT
UNDERBELLIES,FISHEYES, PANIC ON THE TOWER AND
IN THE PLUNGE BASIN (ABOVE AND BELOW)
Wednesday July 4th

"Where the hell was Judd?"

"I told him 9 o' clock sharp. He was never late." I guess I was going to have to handle this alone. I would have preferred to have the builder of the craft here as I did this, but it didn't look like that was going to happen.

"I trust you folks slept well last night," I said, trying to sound chipper in spite of the night I'd had. God only knows the night I'd had. Night sweats and a headache that would kill a small pig. Today was trial run day for the Hellion. She would be given her baptism of fire. We had planned to send her unmanned over the American Falls where the rocks were the most treacherous. We wanted to see how she could withstand the stress under the worst possible conditions that she was likely to encounter. I was showing the three would-be passengers around the complex; a huge hangar like building, part of which ran out onto the Niagara River and housed the Hellion.

Three people would accompany us on our historic first run over the Falls. Each rider had paid a $30,000 fee. "We'll sell you the whole seat but you'll only need the edge." Each rider had been interviewed extensively by Charlie Knowales. Paul Martin was a wealthy business man from the world of finance and had been involved with the financial structure that had gotten this project off the ground. Mark Young was a test pilot associated with the Canadian Spar Corporation, a company that specialized in the design and fabrication of space age material, well known for it's development of the mechanical arm that was used on the American space shuttle. Finally, there was Sara Wilson, reporter for the Washington Post. She would cover the events first hand for the journalistic world.

Our tour had ended up at the Hellion's dry-dock. Even now, technicians swarmed over her in final preparations for the test run. In thirty minutes she would be in the water, but there was still no sign of Judd Blackadder.

Miss Wilson stood next to me on the platform. All morning I had been aware of a funny smell that had teased my nostrils. It wasn't strong enough to come right out and identify itself, but then when I wasn't paying it any mind it would sneak up on me again. As I stood here trying to accommodate my guests and wondering impatiently where Judd was, that smell came back again. Teasing. Subtle. And then I realized what it was.

Sara Wilson was wearing perfume.

My God! How long had it been since I had smelled a woman's perfume during working hours. There weren't many women down on the river. Most of my co-workers were men that I had worked with for many years. We shared a unique bond that only came from time spent in a factory of danger. In a way I thought that it was good that some of the things that we saw down in the river were spared from gentler eyes, as Miss Wilson could recently attest . Before, us, the black Hellion hung suspended.

"She's a real beaut, ain't she?"

"Just look at those lines," I whistled.

While the thought probably wouldn't have crossed Sara's mind because that's just the way she was I could have just as easily been referring to her instead of the Hellion. Still I wondered if deep in my unconscious that connection wasn't being made and I had to purposely remind myself that it was utter foolishness for me to have any thoughts along those lines.

First of all, I was married and she was young enough to be my daughter, which also meant that I was old enough to be her father. I know what year it is but in the circles I was raised in that still meant something to me. Often when I thought back on that day I wondered if it was just the intoxication of a pretty woman's perfume or if there was something more to it.

Sarah rapped on the side of the Hellion's outer casting like you would kick a tire on a used car.

"Not just any old kind of plastic, I take it? Some kind of polymer looks like."

"You're right," I replied. But that was all I could say with any confidence. Judd should have been here to explain it. I took a stab anyway but I was strictly winging it on what I had been told. "Yea, its a special fiberglass and polymer laminate developed by Spar. Let's see, how can I explain it? If you've heard of the Fiero that Pontiac makes, you know that you can kick the hell out of the body and not make a dent. It doesn't crack like the fiberglass in a Corvette. It gives and then comes back into it's original shape. It's what's known as material memory. The off shoot is the stuff they're putting in mattresses now. Tempurpedic was the pioneer in that field if I'm not mistaken. The polymer blend is what gives it this characteristic. So in effect, the whole outer shell acts like a giant shock absorber. Giving under pressure then springing back. You wouldn't suspect it because it's hard to the touch. And durable. Almost impossible to scratch. But..."

"But it's not indestructible," Sara finished for me. I must have looked a little stunned.

"Don't look so surprised, Mr Patric. I know I'm the only woman on this trip and you fellas are the experts on this sort of thing, but I only ask that you go about your technical matters as you normally would. Don't try making things simplistic just for my benefit. If I don't understand something I'll ask, but let me be the judge of that. When I'm assigned to cover a story I don't go along just for the ride, no pun intended. I like to know what makes things tick. I'm not above nuts and bolts."

"I know, I was just..." I sputtered feebly. I had to hand it to her. She was tough and smart, and if she was going to cover it she wanted to be a part of it.

"Sorry. I'll try not to let the fact that you're a woman get in the way again," I said, even as I took another whiff. Fat chance of that happening. Her perfume smelled too good.

"Anyway," I continued. "The Hellion is not indestructible. The outer layer is three inches thick over a steel mesh infrastructure, with a row of clear panels designed for underwater viewing and which, incidentally, gives the craft its spaceship like appearance, but it has its limits. Everything has its limits. In this case that limit is 20 tons of pressure. To put it in perspective, that's ten times what the Falls can dish out. Of course once we are submerged, interior cabin pressure will counteract some of the exterior water pressure. Nevertheless, you can never have enough testing, and that's the reason for our trial run today. By the way there are no moving parts on the outside like propellers to get damaged. Jet propulsion is the way we get around that. There should never be an engine failure due to any external force and that is probably the most critical element in determining the safety of this expedition, aside from the protective outer shell. Any further information is contained on this sheet of specifications," which I handed out.

Height: 5 feet. Diameter 15 feet. Weight 1 ton empty. Water displacement, loaded: 1500 gallons. Stress capability: 20 tons. Horsepower: 100 from 2 jet propelled engines. Air supply 48 hours without engine power. Indefinite with engine power. System support: Double redundancy in all systems, triple in some.

"What is that?" Sara asked, pointing to a shiny stainless steel plate about four feet square suspended on the belly of the Hellion. Had the Hellion not been out of the water in drydock, the shiny device would not have been visible. As I stared at the device, I realized that the one thing I feared would happen when I reluctantly agreed to conduct this tour in Judd's absence, had happened. I had no idea what that device was.

Even though I had a pretty general knowledge of most of the equipment on board, no amount of staring at this particular piece produced an answer. I looked like an idiot. I cursed Blackadder's name under my breath, but at the same time I was damned curious to know what it was myself. What exactly was that thing, anyway? I opened my mouth to say something idiotic, and that's when Judd Blackadder finally showed up.

"Hey where the..." Before I could even finish, Judd brushed by us like soup through a goose and disappeared into a side office in the complex. A second passed then he re-emerged with a pair of binoculars. He brushed by us again, giving no more notice of our presence then a wall-eye salmon would of Thanksgiving. Out on the dock, he focused the binoculars upward and pointed." Look!"

I took his binocs and said, "Just what exactly am I supposed to be looking at?"

"Look over at the Skylon. Up at the top." I focused the powerful lenses on a tower about 3/4 of a mile down river. Standing on the roof of the observation deck was a man. I could see the wind blowing his coat and long black hair as he tried to maintain his balance. Through the narrow view of the lenses, I followed the shaft of the tower down to ground level where a collection of people and police cars had gathered, providing me with all the information I would need to complete the picture. A bad feeling from deep down started its ascent.

"Any idea why he's doing it?

"I dunno. The Indians around here used to sacrifice themselves to the Falls all the time. But that went out of style back in the 17th century."

"Think it's got anything to do with us?"

"Who can say. You know this place. It attracts the crazies like flies on meat."

"What's he waiting for then? Maybe we should postpone our run." In the excitement I hadn't heard Charlie Knowales come in. He'd overheard my last words. I took the binocs from my eyes and glanced at him. He gave me a withering look, and just for a second I got a glimpse of his obsession and

its underlying madness. The moment passed. It was then that
I realized that these guys were not about to let anything, even
a life, come before their mission.

"Out of the question." Knowales's tone was sterile of
emotion. "Besides he could be up there all day."

"Then again maybe he's waiting for just the right moment,"
I surmised.

The roar of a Sikorsky helicopter engine starting up
signaled that it was the moment for us to get underway.

"C'mon," shouted Blackadder,"it's time to get aboard!"

Outside the skies had been lightened considerably by a
sun nudging its apex over the horizon. Everything was still
drenched in a grayness, and numerous shadows were being
cast westward. The three men and one women were ushered
aboard the gigantic Sikorsky. As I climbed aboard I kept
thinking about the man on the tower and I didn't like the
queasy feeling I was getting. There was something familiar
about the man's face. I was burning out brain cells trying to
place it and at my age I didn't have many to spare.

The powerful helicopter was a refugee from the Vietnam
war, but it had been completely refurbished. The Thrill
venture had purchased her from the U.S. Navy at a bargain
basement price. Aside from her price she was coveted for her
three powerful turbine engines and her spacious payload. She
had ample room in the payload pod to accommodate all of
the tracking equipment and electronic gadgetry that had been
loaded into her with space left over for a few passengers. Her
engines were strong enough to hoist the Hellion right out of
the river if such a rescue or recovery mission was asked of her.
(Some helicopters of this class had been employed as flying
mine sweepers during the Vietnam War because of their lifting
power.) Of course, after a successful navigation of the Falls,
the Hellion would have to be transported back upriver to its
complex and for this main duty the S-64 would be deployed.

Blackadder was already on board, situated behind a
paneled array of flashing lights and dials. A specially-fitted

plexiglass cargo door airlocked shut and the cumbersome vehicle slowly left the earth. About six hundred feet up we leveled off. The expansive electric door of the dock complex slithered open allowing the Hellion its freedom. Blackadder flipped a switch and the Hellion began easing out of her sheltered berth into the impelling river current. The test run was underway.

"She's responding to remote. I am switching on video cameras now. Have you got her on screen yet?" Blackadder barked to the tracking crewman aboard the helicopter.

"She's just coming up now."

"This is air control to ground control; have you got the Hellion on your screen yet?"

"This is ground control. Affirmative," came the transmission from Table Rock.

"Okay," said Blackadder. "Am now pressurizing the air chamber and retracting the out rigging." He flicked another switch.

Knowales and the others peered through the cargo door and watched as an outrigger apparatus lowered to the craft's water level. This test run was aimed at the American Falls, a narrower and rockier landing than the Canadian Falls. That was okay, at least, for the purpose of this trial. We intentionally wanted to land on rocks to test the craft's strength and to see how she fared. And the American Falls passage guaranteed this end. Nothing would be left to chance on the day of the historic run. Every angle was being covered.

Before the current got any stronger, Blackadder brought the second jet engine on line and steered the Hellion toward the American shore of the river, just skirting the tip of Grand Island by a snitch and a snicker. The craft bucked in the savage current as she gradually made her way to the American side of her approach to the American Falls. The helicopter followed.

"She's having a rough time out there going cross-current but the out-rigging is keeping her stabilized," yelled Blackadder back to the passengers in the cargo bay, above the din of the helicopters rotors. We watched the Hellion's progress as she arduously fought the current. It would be a few minutes before she reached her appointed destination. While we were waiting, I handed Sara Wilson the binoculars.

"Let's see how its going at the Skylon." I shouted.

Our path had taken us down river to a point where we were now no more then 500 yards from the tower. As we hovered there with the Falls on our right and the tower on our left, the tiny speck of a man was visible on the Skylon even without field glasses.

Sara zeroed in on the tower and reported back to us, "He's still up there, but now he's on the outside of the top deck." I wondered if we would be able to pick up anything on the police scanner. I fumbled for the right frequency and sure enough...

"This is it. Listen."

"Joe, are you having any luck talking him down?" crackled a *voice over the scanner.*

"Not at the moment, Lieutenant. From what I can gather he's not one of the standard loonies. He's not saying anything, not a word so far on why he's doing this. He's just standing there, smoking a cigarette."

"Well, you tell that joker that he's already broken the law."

"I'm not sure that would have any affect on this guy."

"Well, is there any way you guys can get close to him, get a hold of him somehow?"

"Well, at the moment he's on the other side of the screen barrier up here, and he's hanging on, but he says if we get any closer, he's going to take a big dive for sure. If you ask me he's going anyway. He's got that look in his eyes."

"Exactly what look is that, Joe?"

"I don't know it's hard to explain. It's a look that he means business, I guess. The only way I can describe it is to compare it to the look a killer has in his eyes. You know, that dead, cold-blooded, fish-eyed look that most of them walk around with. Like he's been hypnotized into a trance. This guy has those same cold fisheyes. I

definitely think he's going over. And if you ask me he's just getting into position."

"You know there's no point in us setting up a net down here. Not from that height. It would be useless. If this guy's going to be stopped at all, you guys are going to have to do it from up there."

"Yeah, I know, Lieutenant. Don's talking to him now. We'll do the best we can."

I felt the knot of dread tighten in my stomach. What I had suspected all along was apparently coming true. We did have something to do with Fish-eyes being on the tower. Exactly what, I'm not sure, but it sure looked to me like he was waiting for the Hellion to go over the Falls. I was betting on the two making the plunge at the same time. Even Sara Wilson could sense something coming.

"There's no reason for this." Her voice had an edge to it as she continued to train the glasses in on the tower.

"Keep a watch and let me know if anything happens, " I said.

When the Hellion had arrived at the desired point in the river, Blackadder turned her toward the American Falls.

"There's still a chance she'll drift over towards the Horseshoe, so I want to keep the engines on for a while longer," Blackadder informed us.

"You guys all set?"

"Ground control set."

"Okay, here we go."

The combined force of the river current and the engine thrust began propelling the circular ship at an increasing rate of speed. We watched in eager anticipation as she lurched off rocks and rode the threatening swells of white water. She was now about a half mile from the brink of the American cataract. There was no chance of diverting her course now. The American current had her in it's grips, and it was not about to let go. Blackadder shut down the two jet engines and let the flow of the river take her the rest of the way.

The craft careened down the river now, slowly revolving

in a counter-clockwise motion with no engines to provide direction. The craft was now about two hundred yards from the brink. The skies had almost broken into full morning daylight. Off in the distance and across the river, the two Canadian observation towers loomed like two huge spikes driven into the earth. Blackadder flicked another switch.

"Outrigging retracting." This was to protect it from incurring damage as the craft went over the Falls. To all of us high above in the helicopter, it seemed funny to watch the water-bound craft perform all these functions when no one was aboard to control it. Chalk another one up for modern science.

Blackadder pointed down and yelled, "The draft of the Falls here is much shallower than the Canadian Falls, which is about three times deeper, ten feet over the American Falls, thirty feet over the Canadian, but since the Hellion only rides about three feet into the waterline with passengers, there should be no problem."

Although the American Falls was narrower and shallower it was swifter, and with the outrigging now retracted, the river hurtled the craft along like a small, toy top.

"I don't believe it. That's impossible! Whose got the binoculars? Take a look at the Hellion. I swear I saw something moving inside the craft!"bellowed Blackadder.

All eyes went to the vehicle bobbing in the rapids. Sara had the benefit of lens enhancement, "You're right. There is something in the cockpit. I can't quite make it out." She thumbed the fine adjustment to bring it into focus.

"It doesn't matter who or what it is-there isn't a force on this planet that can prevent that craft from going over the Falls now," commented Knowales.

"You're not going to believe this. It looks like....like an animal. Is it possible-a sheep?

"Are you sure? Let me see those glasses. She's right. That's what it is. I don't know how it got onboard but it looks like we have a guinea pig for our test run," I confirmed as I handed back the glasses.

"Let's hope it enjoys the free ride on us because this is what it looks like, when something is swept over the Falls. Here she goes!"

Blackadder's running commentary had added just the right touch to an already exciting scene as it unfolded below, and all four of us strained for the best view of the climax. A rack of fireworks exploded on the American side of the river saluting the arrival of the Hellion.

The Hellion crested at the height of the American Falls, tottered in the air for a moment as if reluctant to go, then dove vertically into the rocky base. A few diehard photographers, newsman, and sightseers had set up a vigil at the Table Rock area hoping to capture the trial run. As the approaching helicopter blades grew louder, they figured their wait had paid off. They kept looking upriver from the Canadian Falls for a sign of the Hellion, fully expecting it to do its breaching over the Horseshoe.

The craft never appeared in the Horseshoe current, and it was to their complete surprise to look over and see the Hellion spilling over the brink of the American Falls. No one had a chance to reposition their cameras as the Hellion collided head on with a flat section of rock at the base of the Falls, stopping her downward progress cold with a force that would have shattered almost anything else. She hung suspended for a moment, then rolled over completely, one time, glanced off a pylon of rock , and then began to slide down yet another flat section of rock.

She slithered with a splash into the depths of the river just as a log might barrel into the water from its flume. Most of her downward progress had been arrested by the rocks, so when she finally hit the river, she only plunged to a depth of about twenty feet. Once she disappeared from view of the helicopter, Blackadder raised his crew members,

"Have you got her on the screen? What's up?"

"This is ground control. Yeah, I got her on the monitor.

She's only about fifty feet down and she'll probably rise on her own. Boy, she really took a crack on the nose, didn't she?!"

"Well, that's what we wanted to see. If she can survive that she'll withstand anything this place can dish out."

I had fully expected to hear from Sara by now about the man on the tower.

"Anything from Fish-eyes?" I asked anxiously.

"Nope he hasn't budged. Mr. Patric, I believe you have the instincts of a good reporter." Apparently she had suspected a timed jump from Fish-eyes, as well.

"Looks like we were both wrong," I said, breathing easier than I had since the test run began. There wasn't much left to do now but wait for the Hellion. However, the craft seemed to be taking an inordinately long time to surface from fifty feet. The mist near the Falls had thickened quite considerably since the inception of the test run and it was with increased difficulty that we now tried to follow the events in the plunge basin. Also quite prevalent. The smell of sea salt.

"What's happening on radar," Blackadder yelled tersely.

"She's sinking deeper. She's at 100 feet now."

At this point several things seemed to happen simultaneously, like rapid concussions.

Sara shrieked, "Oh, my God!"

Those words caused an anvil to crest and lodge in my throat.

The police scanner crackled alive with, "He's going! Watch out below!"

I yanked the binoculars from Sara.

The man clung to the outside of the barrier despite the high winds whipping at him. He went into a crouch and pushed off backwards. The wind velocity caught his body for a second, then blew him outward like an unfurling flag. He dropped like an anvil. People on the ground started screaming.

The searchlights followed the plunging black shadow right down to the pavement, where it exploded, in a mass of tissue, his body reduced to pulp. Initially, Fisheyes landed feet first. But when the unprotected human body slams into immovable concrete at a speed of over 100 mph, it really does not matter in which position it lands. As the victim's feet made contact with the pavement, a few of the toes began to pop off and a cloud of red mist enveloped the ankles. The blast of pain had already flashed to Fisheyes' brain, obliterating his consciousness. Next the ankles snapped.

Even before the ankles had a chance to buckle under the pressure, the fibulas of both legs unhinged at the knees and were telescoped into the thigh tissue alongside the femurs. At this point if the action could have been freeze framed, it would have appeared that Fisheyes was kneeling on the ground, when in fact his legs had disappeared from the knees down. The body was being chopped and compressed, section by section, as if it were being devoured by the ground. By the time the shattered femurs were propelled into the stomach organs, fisheyes was dead. Jagged bone protruded through the rib cage. What was left of the upper torso began to topple backwards with enough momentum left to dash the skull against the pavement like an eggshell. What seemed like eternity was only a second and reduced the human form to half its normal body mass. In the end, the remains of the head were twisted completely around facing towards the back of the torso. For anybody familiar with such intricacies, it was a scene that conjured up the mutilations associated with a little known ritual referred to as a black mass.

What I had witnessed had left me stunned with a taste of gun metal in my mouth.

Sara Wilson had turned her head into my shoulder, a reflex action without a doubt, but it was a natural reaction to circumstances so horrific. I wanted to protect her from the nightmare I'd just seen. She had already shown that she could be tough when she needed to be but she was also not afraid to show her vulnerable side. It was this compassionate side, this humanness in an occupation that could be cold and cruel that made the people who knew her fall in love with her.

The Hellion was still in the plunge basin and Judd was fighting with the controls, totally consumed by the same obsession that I'd caught a glimpse of in Knowales. Blackadder frantically worked the engine switch oblivious to everything else around him. Suddenly the engines caught life, and the Hellion started her ascent to the surface. Blackadder looked ashen, completely drained by the Hellion's ordeal. The baptism of fire had turned into more like a baptism of blood.

Later when we examined the craft we found the sheep inside the cockpit. The animal was dead but there was not a mark on it with the exception of eyeballs that seemed to be bulging out of their sockets. I know this sounds crazy because animals usually don't register emotions the way humans do but I'd swear on a stack of bibles that that creature had an expression of terror on its facial features.

I don't know how he did it but I'd say this was the work of our friend Rediens. If I didn't know better I'd say he was trying to send us a message. Everything he touches turns into death," said a shaken Knowales. This was the second time in three days that Rediens had found a way to get to him. Neither would it be the last.

Lost in my own emotion of the day, I had completely forgotten about the stainless steel device on the Hellion's underbelly.

CHAPTER NINE
WALKING ON WATER, A MAN GOES INSANE AND I
STILL DON'T SAVE ANYONE
Maid of the Mist Dock, Thursday July 5th

"We will not be responsible for this!"

"I want it on the record that the Thrill Corporation does not in any way sanction this undertaking," I said, with as much restraint as I could muster.

"Relax, Mr. Patric," Sara said. "We realize that. This operation is being underwritten by my newspaper, and it will assume full responsibility."

"That's fine, and I respect your initiative, but no matter who is responsible, this is not a good idea." I was firm in that belief.

I watched as a tall lanky figure, his leanness accentuated by the skin-tight rubber suit that he had somehow applied to himself, cleared the air from his respirator. Two steel tanks back slung, fins on his feet, and a face mask completed the man's costume.

"Mr. Patric, aren't you the least bit curious after what happened yesterday?"

"I'm always curious when it comes to my river. The day I stop being curious is the day six feet of worms will have the apartment above me, but there are other ways to do this without sending a man down there. It's too dangerous. By the way, could we just make it Ro? You're making me feel old with that Mr. stuff."

"Okay, Ro. We thought of that. We looked into getting a remote controlled apparatus, but we can't get it here in time. Besides, why hasn't that been done before now? We're in a new millennium for heaven's sake and there's still no survey of that plunge basin on record."

"It's been tried," I said defensively.

"And?"

"They had problems." I knew at this point that Sara had

the opening that she needed and she would exploit it to her advantage. It was true though. Mechanical underwater robots had been attempted in 1992 and 1997. Both times equipment failures had sabotaged the missions. Then for one reason or another, it kept getting shuffled to the back of the deck.

"Would those problems be the same as the problems with the Hellion, yesterday, Mr. Patric? I mean Ro."

I could feel the oxygen being sucked out of my fire.

"Look Sara, far be it for me to pretend to be any kind of expert on the matter, but I do know that with all this sensitive high tech equipment around, malfunctions are a part of the territory. And because of the remote system, you also have the potential for communication breakdowns."

"That's why I want to try a diver!"

"A diver could never get anywhere near the base of that falls. It's too violent, I tell you."

"Laz, assures me that he can." Sara stepped aside unveiling a jet-ski-like machine tethered to the dock. "On this."

It looked like a torpedo with handlebars.

"This is a water rocket. It's equipped with sonar, a camera, all the latest technology. This will take me where I want to go." Diver Laz offered.

I found the diving credentials of Laz Harrison to be impeccable. He had four years as a Navy diver. Still, I was worried even after he had promised to exercise the utmost care. I knew how capable Niagara was of turning the most diligent safety record into so much shredded wheat, just like the slicers in the cereal factory on Portage road.

"Hey for two grand an hour, I'll go down and piss on Davy Jone's locker, if that's what you want."

I did not share in such enthusiasm. Harrison readied his equipment. Since Sara knew that I could not stop the dive from taking place she tried to massage my defeat.

"What really got me thinking yesterday," she said, "is the way Fisheyes waited on that tower. He didn't jump when the Hellion went over the Falls. No, he waited until it got into the plunge basin. Don't you see? It's like you said. The plunge basin is the key, not the Falls."

"I won't deny that there have been some strange occurrences emanating from the basin. You saw evidence of that first-hand on the face of the victim I fished out of the river that night."

"It goes a lot deeper than that. I've been doing some investigating and I've turned up a few nuggets of information that should be of great interest to you. Now I don't want you to get defensive but this first item will not exactly enhance your reputation."

"That's okay. Let me have right between the eyes. It won't be the first time this river has humbled me," I said.

"Okay, well I interviewed that woman Marie that you were credited with talking off the ledge at Goat Island. By the way I read a transcript of your words to her and I personally thought they were brilliant."

"I appreciate the attempt to soften the blow Miss Wilson, but please let's just have it."

"Don't say I didn't warn you. Technically your record of not saving anybody on the river is still intact. According to her, the mist had more to do with getting her off that railing than anything that you said to her that day."

"The mist? What do you mean the mist?"

"Seems she saw something in the mist that day. She couldn't exactly describe it but she could feel its presence. Scared the hell out of her even in her condition and she got out of there as quick as she could."

"I do remember the mist being particularly thick that day but I didn't see anything and I was right next to her."

"Well apparently she did. Said it smelled too. Like an ancient evil ocean. What else can I tell you?"

My emotions ran from disappointment to puzzlement. I had smelled the salt air on other occasions as well.

"There's more. On the day of the test run, most of the photographers were caught out of position but even so their pictures would have been of the Hellion going over the Falls. This was taken from a Japanese tourist from the Skylon tower just before Fish-eyes jumped off."

Sara extracted a photograph out of her pants pocket. She continued as she handed it to me.

"That's one thing about the Japanese. They'll film anything that moves. If the wind were to blow over a pile of dogshit they'll have it captured on film. And nowadays they've got cameras in their phones, in their wallets and everywhere else."

"I don't see anything but a bunch of grayness." I replied.

"Look closer in this area." She attempted to point out an image with her finger nail. "I know it's not perfectly clear but you can detect an image. It's kind of snake-like. It's got a very sinister appearance."

"That may be true, but it's not conclusive of anything. In fact it's a rather subjective interpretation. Many people thought they saw evil images in the pictures of the smoke coming from the terrorist attacks on the twin towers in New York on 9-11. Others couldn't see what they were talking about."

"Exactly, and that's the real kicker here. These two pictures were taken on either side of Fish-eyes." She handed me two more photos.

"The image in the first one is not present in these two," I concluded.

That's right but they were all taken within the same time frame. And I've checked other photographs from the same time. Nothing. Only this one shows anything because it was taken almost right over his shoulder only he was on the outside of the tower. This was the exact perspective that Fish-eyes would have had on the Skylon."

"And?"

"And as a reporter I wouldn't be doing my job if I didn't follow up on every angle." I think it may have something to do with him being up on that tower in the first place. And it gets worse. If I didn't know any better I would say that this "thing' in the mist chooses when and to whom it reveals itself."

"You've got to be kidding?' I exclaimed.

"I know it sounds crazy. But you were standing right near that woman Marie and you couldn't see anything and neither could anybody else. But she swears she did. She had every intention of jumping that day and it's the reason she didn't follow through."

"So now you're thinking that there might actually be something down there in the plunge basin?"

"I don't know, but you have to admit the connection between Fisheyes jumping when he did and the Hellion losing power seems too strong to just be a coincidence. I just want to see if we can get some kind of a reading on things down there, is all."

"All right, I'll go along. Anything to prove to you that there's no Loch Ness monster down there."

"If I come across any monsters, it'll cost you extra," quipped Harrison.

Let's get on with it," Sara said. "You're not getting paid to crack jokes."

"See, you in about an hour," Laz said.

It would be the last intelligible thing he would say on this day, as he disappeared into the cold, icy waters of Niagara's belly.

Clouds of gray mist and fog lifted off the river and lingered above the gorge walls like a shroud. I looked long and hard at the mist and I'll be damned if I could connect the dots between any bestial images. I guessed it was like looking at the stars at night. You can see the constellations if you know what you are looking for. Still I was not willing to rule it out either. There may be something to it. All the recent coincidences were too difficult to deny.

The early hour of the day had not afforded the spring sun a chance to burn off this condensation. Less than a half a mile away, as the sound of falling water droned ominously in our ears, we were just two lone figures on the dock enveloped in the gray solitude of morning on the river.

Sara paced the dock either out of nerves or to keep warm against the water's chill; I did not know which. I stared into the roiling foam so prevalent at this juncture of the river, my eyes drawn to a dead carp that drifted by as more evidence of the brutality of Niagara. She granted nothing free passage. Birds, animals, fish, humans, all were treated equally. And the appetite of the " beast" was veracious. No amount of blood or destruction seemed to sate her thirst No amount of death could slake her lust. Like a mill of death, her waterwheel churning and grinding. Always churning and grinding. No matter what else you did at Niagara it was always about the Falls, ticking away in the background. If you lived at Niagara you couldn't escape it any more than you could your breath or your heartbeat.

I watched as the battered fish caught in an eddy. In other times, this place would have been a perfect hunting ground for a bear or a fox. Now the carcass just swirled about with a few cigarette butts. One of the butts went to it's mouth so, for an instant, it looked like the fish was smoking. It would have been laughable if it hadn't made me think of the previous day's sad turn of events. The police had not yet identified the suicide jumper in the black trench coat. His fingerprints were not on file so it would take some time. I had a feeling that Sara was right about the man jumping when the craft was in the plunge basin. But to what end?

Even the police seemed convinced he was not a publicity seeker, but more inclined to have a purpose in mind. But what did he accomplish, other than his own death? An hour after he jumped, the pavement had been sprayed, disinfected, and sanitized like nothing had ever happened there. I watched as the carp turned over and sank from view, interred forever in a watery tomb.

After only twenty five minutes, the silence was broken by the whine of the aqua jet. Harrison had pierced the surface, about 100 yards away from the dock.

"Hell, that didn't take long," I said. "It probably just goes to prove that's there's nothing down there to concern us."

I watched as the aqua jet skimmed across the water in the general direction of the dock with the diver in tow. At a glance, everything appeared okay. But as the diver got nearer, Sara noticed that Harrison only held onto the jet with one hand. The other hand dragged limply in the water beside the diver's body.

"I hope nothing's gone wrong," Sara said. My eyes remained riveted on the approaching diver.

"What could have gone wrong?" I asked, keeping the answer - "Plenty" - to myself. Can You Feel It Coming?

The diver got nearer.

"Ro, look. He's not driving the jet, it's dragging him!"

She was right. The body of the diver seemed lifeless behind the ski jet, and it appeared as if the hand that was holding on was actually entangled in the apparatus. The diver's head was face down in the water.

"Something's happened! He's gonna come right by the dock. Quick! Hand me that netting."

Sara grabbed a length of old netting piled with some other equipment on the dock. As the diver neared, I tossed the netting over the jet ski and entangled it. But then a strange thing happened. When the jet ski snagged, the momentum continued to carry the body of the diver forward. It appeared as if he were walking on the water. Then devoid of impetus he started to sink. Sara noticing that I was caught up in the netting, dove in and floated him to the dock. The engine of the jet ski whined like a sick mule, until I could de-tangle myself and reach the switch to kill it. The two of us struggled to get the lifeless form onto the dock, the pain of my arthritic hands dulled by adrenaline.

Sara checked his pulse. "He's still alive!"

Harrison's diving mask was clouded with condensation, so neither Sara nor I could see his face. I leaned over the diver and slipped the mask off. Then, as a matter of reflex, I jerked back.

"Holy smokes! Look at this."

The diver's features were frozen wide-eyed in an expression of intense fear.

"Better call an ambulance," Sara muttered.

"Is he gonna be all right, doctor?" I asked in the hushed atmosphere of the waiting room at the Niagara General Hospital. After two hours of operating on the diver, sweat stained the doctor's hospital fatigue.

"Well, he's not going to die if that's what you mean."

"Thank, God for that. We were worried stiff. We kind of feel responsible because Mr. Harrison was working for us when this happened. Can you give us any information at all, on what happened?"

"Well, all I can tell you is that your diver suffered a serious lack of oxygen. We had to operate to relieve the pressure on his brain. A few more minutes under the water and he would have been gone. As it is he has suffered some permanent damage."

"Would it be possible for us to talk to him, doc? We'd like to find out exactly what happened down there. It's very important!"

"That's impossible. He's under sedation."

"We understand. Well, maybe in a day or so we can...."

"That's impossible." He seemed very tired. "Maybe I haven't made it clear to you, but you will never be able to talk to that man in there."

"But doctor, you said he was going to live."

"That man will be nothing more than a vegetable for the rest of his life. I'm sorry."

It was as if he'd hit me with a baseball bat. And so another thread was knitted into the fabric that was Niagara. A shroud donned as comfortably as a widow at a perpetual funeral.

CHAPTER TEN
A SHADOW IN THE WOODS ENROUTE TO THE
SUMMERLANE SUBDIVISION
Friday July 6th

To be sure, the autopsy on the adventure in the plunge basin produced a grim tally. One man in the hospital with a prognosis of permanent incapacitation, no pictures on the aqua jet's camera, and no recordings of any value on the onboard instrumentation. Worse yet, no one was any closer to the truth. Before that, we had a loss of power on the Hellion, and Fisheyes taking a header off the Skylon. Sara decided it was time to shift to a new venue to look for clues.

"Now why would anyone want to do that?" Sara asked. "Clear all of this land except for the strip of woods around the house and driveway."

It was quite obvious it was by design.

"Whoever did it certainly did a good job. From the main road, you can't even tell that there is a house out here."

I had been coerced to come along, but I was hoping that we were not compounding one mistake with another.

"I can't believe I let you talk me into coming out here, especially after what happened at the Maid of the Mist dock." Secretly though, I had to admit I was curious about coming back to the old neighborhood where we had all grown up.

"I'm involved in this now," she said. "What kind of a reporter would I be if I didn't run down every angle. Besides you get a free trip back home."

As she drove, I stuck my hand out the window and played with the passing air.

"Some things are better off left alone," I responded. I should have took the advice of the song that was playing on the radio. It was an especially well timed tome from Eddie Money who was chanting about the foolishness of thinking one could go back home after a period of time away and expect that everything would be the same as when one left.

Its hook line was singed into my train of thought- "I wanna go back but I can't go back I know..." That was certainly a theme that would have resonance with me this day.

As we passed by the woods and fields on our way to the Rediens farmhouse, we crossed paths with Pecker's Pond, and I thought of everything that happened those thirty-eight years ago. Shrubbery and weedy undergrowth had conspired to choke off all access to the pond's banks. Only a trickle of water now cascaded over the waterfall area. As I remembered it , it was always a robust flow, but then a youthful memory is always a great enhancer. Everything seemed a lot smaller than I remembered it. Of course one had to take into account that I was also larger now. Maybe that was it.

The one thing that didn't seem to have changed over time was Jag Rock. There it was, still protruding defiantly out of the waters of the pond, menacing and deadly as ever, like a black jagged iceberg. In fact, having been witness to the events that occurred here, and the impact that it had on my life as well as others, the physical presence of the rock seemed to have increased in stature, rather than diminished. It stood as a monument to young lives shattered. Everyone who came out of those waters that day had their lives set on destiny's path. Knowales became a cripple, lost a brother and his belief in God. Blackadder became the builder of the Hellion forever tethered to Knowales like a stalker. Rediens became disfigured spiraling into tailspin of hate and revenge. And even though I never really rescued anybody there it's where I got my inspiration to choose the career that I did.

The overgrown condition of the pond told me that it wasn't seeing a lot of visitors these days.

"Kids are more interested in computers and video games nowadays," I thought. "They don't get out and play like we used to in the old days. Hell, give us a simple rubber ball and that could keep ten or fifteen of us occupied for hours. Today everything has to be sophisticated and played by the rules. Maybe it's just as well. Too many people have their lives tied up in the tragic past of this place as it is..." My thoughts were interrupted when I saw movement and yelled, "Did you see that?" A startled Sara swerved the car onto the shoulder and then righted it.

"What?" she exclaimed somewhat annoyed.

"There was something moving over by the woods, next to the pond. I couldn't make it out exactly; it was a dark figure. It was moving fast. It was down on all fours like a cat, heading in the same direction as us."

"Ro, I don't see anything. You sure it wasn't a cloud shadow or something?"

"I swear it was heading for the farmhouse. It's gone now whatever it was."

The raw movement of the thing had projected an air of the sinister that I could not have begun to describe to Sara. For the rest of our sojourn I swore to keep my eyes open.

"Tell me about Kane Rediens and Knowales. They had some kind of rivalry, I gather," she probed.

"Not much to tell. They just didn't mix, right from the word go. You see, in those days, Charlie Knowales was a golden boy of sorts. He could do no wrong. Smart as a whip in school with hardly any degree of studying. Athletic, a good looking kid even then. He appeared to have a very promising future. He was so good at hockey that he seemed a can't miss for the NHL. Of all of us, he was the one who seemed destined to succeed at whatever he chose, and naturally a lot of others gravitated toward him.

"While, he was very popular, there were others who were very jealous. Kane Rediens was the best example of that jealousy. Believe it or not, early on, Rediens had his own following, even though he was relatively new to the neighborhood, but it was mostly composed of kids who didn't feel they were good enough to hang around with Knowales. Kind of like the dregs of our little microcasm. Knowales and Rediens were like leaders of opposing gangs. Anyway, they got into an argument, I think it was over a girl, and they got into a fight. Charlie should have won easily being much more athletic, but there was a crazy fierceness in Rediens. He fought like he was possessed, and even though Knowales bloodied him up pretty good, Charlie developed a whole new respect for Rediens. Some say, it was fear. Whatever he saw in Rediens that day, from then on Charlie tried to keep Kane at arm's length.

"However, Rediens was not the type of kid to forget such things and remained ever vigilant for a chance to get even. Meanwhile the jealousy only increased as Rediens, who was not all that good-looking to begin with, began growing body hair like crazy at an extremely early age. Of course, then came the thing at Jag Rock. By his late teens I had heard that he had developed a type of rare affliction that really did a number on him physically. The kids started calling him Lucky but not for the reasons you'd normally think. It was more in the vein of "Boy are we lucky we're not like him." It was kind of a reverse play on the word. Personally I'd never heard of anybody having such a run of bad luck as him."

"Charlie was never the same after his brother Ryan died. He just couldn't seem to recover from it. I don't know if he was consumed by guilt or what, but he is caught in a time warp of the past. Some people are like that. All of us like to go back in our past and pull up old memories. Memories are what make us the people we are today. For some, the old memories are the best times of their lives, like the quarterback in high school who ends up working in a steel mill the rest of his life.

"Then there are the others that have a traumatic experience and can't seem to transcend it. It paralyzes their future. Rediens and Knowales's lives intersected that day at the pond and neither one has recovered. Knowales, especially, could have been a success at a lot of things, but it was like he just lost interest, never even played hockey again. After high school he just drifted from job to job. He never dated much although he had the looks."

"Eventually he did get married, but that ended a few

years ago the same time he began working on this project. He doesn't have time for anything including marriage. He will let nothing come between him and this obsession he has for going over the Falls. It's like he's trying to make up for all the lost time in his life in this one last ditch effort. He's knocking on 50, and it's his last chance to make his mark on the world. Of course, everything he accomplishes will be dedicated to his brother Ryan."

"I know a lot less about Rediens. Naturally, you've seen what the rafting accident did to his face. I can only imagine what going through life like that would be like. Although most people don't know this, he too had a couple of younger brothers. I think one, Mark I believe was his name, got taken away when he was quite young. Nobody knew them all that well. The family was always considered to be strange and reclusive. Word had it that because they were part Indian they didn't mix well in white man's society. Anyway they just faded from view. Castoffs from society.

"Word was that Kane worked as a night watchman for a time. That sounded like a perfect fit for him, alone in the solitude of the night. He always liked black. He seemed to live in the shadow of the underbelly of society. You can be sure of one thing though, he never stopped hating Charlie Knowales and he never will. And now you've talked me into coming back into that world. Don't you know that some things are better left undisturbed?"

"You're talking to a reporter. What you just said is sacrilegious."

"This could turn out to be a wild goose chase. You don't even know if he still lives here."

One look at this place though, and I felt sure Kane was here all right. Hell, talk about strange, this place was it. Cubed.

A narrow driveway filtered up from Quaker Road for about 100 yards leading to an old wooden two story-frame house. The driveway was not paved but was one of those dirt lanes, two strips centered by a corridor of grass. The wheel ruts had remained grass-free, but certainly not from traffic passing through. Maybe they had been oiled.

But that was not the strange part. The strange part was that the forest on either side of the drive extended all the way back to and encircled the house. Everything else beyond this configuration was all open field in every direction.

Up close, the house's ramshackle condition was even more apparent. Boards that no longer held even a trace of paint hung loose; windows on the main floor were boarded up, making the place look condemned. If Rediens was still here, he was surely no handyman. Either that or he just didn't care. Then again who was going to see the place way out here?

We knocked on the door. No answer. We checked all the doors and windows on the ground floor. Everything was secure.

"We're going to get in trouble for this," I said.

"We're just trying to find out if someone lives here. If anything happens I'll take full responsibility."

"When have I heard that before?"

We removed the boards off one of the rear windows and punched a hole in the glass. The tinkle of the broken glass seemed to be the only sound in this particular part of the world. The air inside the house was quite musty, making it difficult to breathe. I cautioned Sara to watch her step until I found a light switch, not sure it would even come on. But, to our shock, they did.

There was dust everywhere. It was hard to believe that someone could actually live here, but someone had to be paying the electric bill.

"I guess Rediens doesn't believe in maid service," I tried to joke.

"What maid in her right mind would come out here?" said Sara.

I was for getting out, but the arrival of light had also revealed something more disturbing. In the center of the room was a bed, covered in dust. In the center of the mattress, was an S-shaped trench.

"Something had to be laying on that mattress for years to have caused that kind of indentation."

"How about a body in the fetal position," intoned Sara.

"Yea, that would do it....But how..."

"Just a case I reported on. Guy wasn't found for a long time. Made a mark just like that."

"I'm sure something like that would be of great interest to the police. C'mon, let's get out of here."

Sara had stopped in the doorway of another adjoining room, "Hold on. Take a gander at this!"

I was stunned at what I saw. Pictures of Charlie Knowales, Judd Blackadder, and even a couple of myself were pinned to the walls along with cutout newspaper articles of the Thrill Corporation's project from it's inception. Somebody was taking a great deal of interest in our endeavors, and it didn't take a lot of imagination to guess who that someone was.

While there was not one picture of Kane Rediens, among the other pictures was a photo of a young man, I knew I had seen somewhere before.

"Funny," I muttered to myself, "I don't recognize this person as being associated with the Thrill project."

And then it hit me. I recognized the face. " We have to get out of here, and I mean now!"

I pushed Sara towards the door, "Ro, what's..."

"Sara, trust me when I tell that we maybe in grave danger and we have to leave immediately. For once in your life, no questions, please!"

I slammed the door behind us, and we jumped in the car.

"Lock your doors!"

As I scanned the woods around the house and the drive, my heart pounded in my ears. We pulled out onto the main road and made our escape. It wasn't until we were over a mile away that I finally felt safe enough to take a breath and another two miles before my hands stopped shaking.

"I think we need to head for the police station."

"Not until you tell me what this is all about."

"Fine, if I had any doubts that Kane Rediens still lived in that house they were dispelled today."

"How can you be so sure?"

"I remembered where I saw the face of the man in that picture before. It was in my binoculars. On the tower. Two days ago. The man in the picture is Fisheyes. Fisheyes is Kane Rediens younger brother! Don't you see. The guy that jumped off the tower. He sacrificed his own brother. He'll stop at nothing in his quest for vengeance. The whole time we were there I had a very uncomfortable feeling of being watched. I remembered rumors as a kid that there were hidden tunnels behind the Rediens place."

It's strange how you can feel eyes upon you and not be able to see the thing that is doing the looking or have the specific knowledge that something is indeed training its faculties on you. It's as if the power of vision disturbs the air like the ripples of a stone cast into a pond. The waves are transmitted so that the receiver feels them as an almost imperceptible pressure but nonetheless, a palpable percussion that was not there before. Two conditions must exist for this to happen-the observer must be intent on its subject-a casual observance will not suffice and the object of the observation must be receptive to the possibility that a scrutiny may be a distinct reality.

Computers are sensitive to such prying eyes by detecting from the millions of eyes out in the vastness of cyberspace, the ones that are aimed at its master. This device is called spyware. I always likened this feeling to the time my father took me camping overnight in the remote woods of Algonquin Park, in the northern reaches of the Canadian province of Ontario. I was ten years old and it was the summer before the chaos at Jag Rock I had never experienced such isolation before that. No television or radio or friends. It was just him and I-or so I thought. I soon learned differently. That nature is a component all to itself. Like a third person that has to be considered and communed with. That it is always

around us even in the city if we just take the time recognize
its existence.

Even though it was still daylight we saw plenty of signs
of animal life all around us as we set up camp. A hawk kept
a circling winged vigil above us. Beavers playfully splashed
about in a nearby stream. Squirrels performed precarious
acrobatics on limbs that were so thin they didn't look like
they could support the weight of leaves. Even a curious fox
peered at us from behind a distant tree -a rarest of occurrences
because this is an animal that treasures its stealth and for it to
have been spotted by us indicated a serious breech of its most
sacred covenant. Later my father took me down to the stream
to show me the tracks of deer and a moose.

But it wasn't until night that the woods really came to life.
Or death depending if you were the stalker or the stalkee.
Every now and then a shriek or screech that was cut off in
mid-expression told us that something was having supper
and something else was supplying the meal. Sitting by the
crackling light of the campfire I could feel the weight of every
animal eye in that forest watching us and yet I couldn't see a
one in the darkness of the night. But I knew as sure as I could
see the moon and the stars that they were out there.

I imagine it is an experience similar to that of stage actor
when the house lights go down. He can't see the audience
but he knows that they just didn't get up and walk out either.
They're there. Our stage that night was the campfire and our
audience was the denizens of the woods. I suspect we hardly
made a twitch that night that wasn't recorded in the register
of every animal out there.

Sara broke the spell of my thought, "In a way I would
have like to have interviewed him. Too bad he wasn't there
for a little face time."

"He was there all right, as sure as I'm talking to you now.
You'll have to trust my Indian blood on this."

The thought of the cat-like shadow in the woods sent the
breath of a Canadian January down the knuckle by knuckle

length of my spine.

BOOK II

Shine Shine on
The darkness was hiding me
When you call to me
When you call out my name
When you show me how to shine
Taking me higher and higher and higher
Shine Shine on
By Farrenheit

CHAPTER ELEVEN
THE PILGRIMAGE AND A RIDE TO HELL

Night had fallen like a black curtain. Kane Rediens waited until the car was gone before coming out of his beloved shadows. He had lived among them for most of his life but this time he knew the jig was up. He knew that he could probably live in the tunnels behind the barn for a period of time if he had to. The tunnels were well hidden and would be hard to discover even by the police, who would come soon. They would find out things, then put the pieces together. It was better this way. Besides, with his brother Bela gone, and mother years before that, he was all alone now and he knew it had to come to an end some time.

Some people are born into this world under a curse-some are destined to toil their lives away under a bad sign-and others are doomed to not be in this world for very long. Kane Rediens wore all three of those albatrosses around his neck. Nevertheless he was not about to go gently into that good night. He had decided that he would create as much a ruckus as he could on the way out and that was how people in these parts would remember his name-and to hell with them if they didn't like it.

He knew that he would miss roaming the fields of the farm at night. He loved the cool breeze from the woods near the pond. On the warmer nights he went naked. Rubbed himself black with charcoal from the fireplace and he would be gone, running free and wild into the night. He loved to run on all fours like a shaggy bear. The scoliosis had deformed his spine to such a degree over the last few years so that it was a posture that was quite accommodating actually. He could not achieve top bear speed, but he was quick, his hands developing the necessary calluses from frontal usage. He loved being low to the ground. Sometimes he could come upon a cricket or even a frog and catch them clean right in his bare teeth. He loved the feeling as they squiggled down his throat, still half alive.

Other times he would sit by the pond and think of the life he never had.

"Never even got out of the gate, really, did I?" he would say.

In his wallet he carried a crumpled time worn picture of himself as a diaper-clad three year old romping on Lake Erie's Nickle Beach with his father. It showed him to have a magnanimous smile even for a three year old. To look at it you could almost feel the joy and happiness emanating from the crinkled celluloid. It might have been the only time in his life when he felt the pure joy of being alive. After that the reality of life starts to take hold and the process of corroding the soul begins. To say that he ever had a family, would have been really stretching the truth. In reality they were just a bunch of strangers living at the same address.

It was shortly after the picture at the beach, that things went bad. After his brother Bela was born, his father was committed to a mental institution where he died a few years later. They say he was hopelessly insane at the time.

"Mother raised us alone after that but we pretty much stayed to ourselves, only going out when we had to. Mother herself began showing signs of a mental affliction. Dementia, was what they called it," he would say.

After that he and his brother were pretty much on their own , so even when they came home from school one day to find her body hanging from the rafters in the barn, it was no big change in lifestyle.

Of course there was no need to report her death and the social security checks kept coming to the house. It was one way that Indians could get retribution for the white man's persecution. They still slept with her on the big bed in the downstairs bedroom, mother in the middle and one boy on each side, just as they had always done.

While life at home was normal, at least to Kane, it was school where he was beginning to have problems. He locked horns with Charlie Knowales. Where others usually yielded in the face of his bizarre assaults, Knowales stood his ground and actually got the better of him. Rediens was not used to this kind of resistance. His usual tactic of bullying had not worked with Knowales as it had with so many others. But something about Rediens made Knowales tentative about his victory, and even Rediens could sense that wariness. It allowed him to stay in the game when he should have been eliminated.

So the two remained rivals of a sort, crossing paths every now and then. As Rediens began growing hair all over his body due to some rare affliction, his appearance became more like that of a gargoyle with each passing day. His grotesque nature was the real reason people tended to avoid him but somehow Rediens believed that Knowales was responsible. Rediens knew that he could thank Charlie Knowales for his decline. Knowales had put the first chink in his armor and also offered a safe haven for others to defect to. Rediens was left to wander through the social terrain of his teen years as a virtual castoff.

Even though Kane was uglier than ever, he just didn't command the same respect as in the pre-Charlie Knowales era. This soon escalated to a point where the other kids were merciless in their teasing, slowly tearing down any last bastion of self-esteem and destroying his spirit from within. The internal scars would never disappear. They started calling him Lucky, a nickname he loathed. The rafting accident and the horrible disfigurement to his mouth just moved the scars from his soul to a place where it was available for public consumption.

Then in his early twenties the neurofibromatosis began to manifest itself. And that really was the end for Kane. The first signs were dark blotches on the skin. When his hair growth began to escalate Rediens resorted to shaving to keep it under control. Now it was a choice between the hair or the blotches. Rediens stopped shaving. There was nothing he could do about the growths behind the optic nerves that tended to give the eyes a bulging disposition. But he did try to do something about the bone growths on both sides of his head. Bela often helped him and together they would saw them off with a hack saw. It made a bloody mess but it didn't hurt as much as one would have imagined. Apparently there weren't many nerve cell in the bone growths. For a while Rediens hair would cover the stubs of the growths but of course they would continue to grow. The lowest jobs, no friends, no relationships, hiding in the shadows. It was a life that was only distinguished by the depth of its failure. But in one respect it was a new beginning. His hatred of Charlie Knowales reached levels that even Kane would not have thought possible. It centered upon Knowales and built itself layer upon agonizing layer for 38 years. Every frustration, every rejection, every failure added another layer. Finally the scoliosis set in and Rediens stopped going out in public. There was no more point in cutting off the bone growths now. They grew like horns out of each side of his head.

But enough reminiscing about the good old days, he thought. The cops were coming and he had some preparations to make. It was better this way, and besides it was not like he didn't have some place to go or something to do. He did. There was a pilgrimage to be made and it had long been in coming. So there was no point in delaying the matter; might as well get right to it.

The first order of business were the turtles. The turtles were his brother Bela's pets, the last thing given to either one of them by their mother before she died. When they arrived in a small water-filled cup each turtle was no more than an inch long, and they had been in the family ever since. Now each bore a shell about a foot in length as they swam with various gold fish in the huge water tank in the living room. Bela had never missed feeding them and would watch them for hours on end.

Kane was going to miss Bela, and even though he was a little slow, Bela always did what Kane told him to do right to the very end. Too bad thought Kane, but it couldn't be helped.

He wished he hadn't let Bela wear his black trench coat. He was gonna miss that coat, but Bela was a good soldier.

"What the heck," he thought, "Bela deserved to go out in style. "

In general, since Kane rarely left the farm these last few years, Bela was Kane's link to the outside world. Because Kane wanted him to, Bela had run the errands, cashed the checks, paid the bills, cut his horns and jumped off the Skylon Tower.

Kane plunged the sledgehammer into the glass and stepped back. In what seemed slow motion, the glass tank imploded inward for a second, then blew outward in a shower of glass shards, colored pebbles, and water. A wave of water washed over the floor and died at his feet.

Somewhere inside Kane, a primal trigger was pulled. His brain was spinning, swirling, smoldering. Two orange goldfish and the two turtles flopped on the floor, high and dry. One fish lay still but the other continued to wiggle around. With the heel of his boot, he ground the head flat with as much emotion as he would have had if he were grinding out a cigarette. The body of the fish remained intact but the head was just a pasty mush. Again the headiness struck. Waves of it. Swirling dizziness.

With sudden swiftness he rendered a sledgehammer blow to the back of one of the crawling turtles. The shell shattered like pumpkin rind; blood and a greenish fluid spurted out the turtle's mouth. He picked the second turtle from the floor, and it ducked into its shell. Rediens waited until eventually the turtle head came peering out, perplexed. That's when Rediens caught it by the neck in his deformed jagged-toothed wreckage of a mouth and bit down as hard as he could. At first the flesh was tough, rubbery, but then he could feel the gush of liquid spurt into his throat.

The head was the same size as a frog or a field mouse and he swallowed it whole discarding the headless carcass.

"Thought you could hide in the darkness of your world,

did you. Well no one knows the darkness like I do. Been living in the darkness all of my life. In my world, I am the master of the darkness."

He was out of his mind, and he wanted this to be his legacy.

As the fog in his head grew thicker, he grew calmer.

The second order of business was mother. He headed out into the barn.

Mother's skeletal carcass hung from the rafters where the boys had placed it after many years in the house. Underneath was a barrel of sulphuric acid, once used around the farm to clean metal. Rediens undid the rope and lowered the skeleton into the barrel. The bones were still foaming when he returned to the house.

Back inside the house, Rediens put on black slacks and a black turtleneck. He would have liked the trench coat also but Bela had placed final dibs on that garment, so the turtleneck would have to suffice. It was just as well. He needed to travel light.

He hesitated a moment. He'd gotten an idea. He went into the bathroom and applied some of his mothers makeup. He painted on a garish red smile with lipstick, some white skin color, and black mascara on the eyes. The end result was a freakish clown characterization of himself.

"I'll be the clown that this world always wanted me to be. Now they can all have a good laugh at Lucky."

Stuffing a crisp new hundred dollar bill in his front pocket, then tucking a manilla envelope addressed and ready for mailing under his shirt, he hit the cool night air.

Night around the house was black as cancer because of the trees, but once he got out into the field the fullness of the flower moon greeted him. He wrapped his damaged mouth around a howl that was as haunting and beautiful as any wolf would have offered up. Then he ran like a wolf on all fours for two miles through moonlit fields until he reached the 406 extension where he hailed a cab.

The cabbie almost didn't stop because of his outlandish appearance, but Bart Fraser had had a pretty good night for himself because of all the visitors in town. One more fare would eclipse his all-time one night earnings.

"What, the hell are you all made up for buddy, eh?"

Rediens had forgotten about his appearance. "Oh yeah. Yeah...uh..I. Uh. I just came from a costume party. Gotta get back home now."

"I gotta tell you, that's pretty good makeup, especially around the mouth. Very interesting."

Out of habit, Rediens pulled the collar on the turtleneck as high as it would go.

"And I love the effect with the horns. Don't tell me. Let me guess. You're a clown, a grizzly bear and a devil all rolled into one. Right?"

"Yea, I always been regarded as kind of...unique. One of a kind, you might say."

"Where are you headed, buddy?" the cabbie asked through the rolled down passenger side window. He was not about to allow this weirdo into his vehicle until he checked him out first. Besides the crazy make-up job, Fraser was suspicious of Rediens' ability to produce his fare.

"Can you take me to Niagara Falls?'

"Niagara Falls! Are you nuts pal? That's twenty miles away and you don't look like you could pay to get down the street. Besides it's late and this would have been my last fare and then I was headed home."

It was after two in the morning. A full moon leered from the blackened sky.

"Listen, I know its late, but I can pay and it's important that I get back."

Rediens fumbled in his front pants pocket and produced the c-note. Fraser's look of doubt ebbed away.

"Listen, I'll give you the whole hundred if you take me there and if you do me one favor. Just drive me. No talking any bullshit. Just drive."

"Okay, buddy. It's your dime, and I haven't seen the day yet when I turned down an extra fifty bucks."

He leaned over the front seat and unlocked the back door to admit his fare. Rediens slipped him the hundred and climbed in.

"Sorry I gave you a bit of a hard time, but in this business you can never be too cautious, especially with all the nuts running around because of that Falls thing."

Fraser was a scroungy, wily individual of about 40, thin frame, greasy black hair face like a ferret. He would have looked equally in place riding on the back ledge of a garbage truck, which happened to be his daytime occupation. He started running the hack for some extra cash, trying to get ahead of the game, always out hustling. Despite his efforts, however, he was the kind of guy who always managed to remain one paycheck removed from the street.

"Where abouts you headed in the Falls?"

"Just take me to the Falls themselves. I'll walk home from there."

"Okay, you got it. I suppose you're here for that Falls ride too, like everybody else is."

"Yeah, ..I'm waiting for the ride." An ugly evil smile formed on Rediens' lips.

After this exchange, the driver kept to his word and maintained his silence. He was not to be denied the company of a radio however.

In the darkness, Rediens drifted off into insanity. One minute he would appear to be okay, sitting calmly erect. In the next moment, he would be rolling his head back on his shoulders, his eyes wide open, staring, but not seeing. It was kind of comical because once in a while, a low moan would escape from Kane's lips and the driver would peer in his rear-view mirror for a look-see. It just so happened that this would coincide with one of Kane's more coherent moments and the cabbie would be greeted with Kane staring back at him, normal except for the grotesque and sinister smile coursing his lips. The cabbie would put his eyes back on the road, and Rediens would spazz out again. This game of backseat chess continued on for the greater part of the forty-five minute ride.

At one point in the ride, the cab had to wait for a red light. Kane was in total oblivion in the backseat. His body was convulsing under great tension. His feet were still on the floor of the cab but his back was arched right off the back seat. His head was twisted so that it appeared almost upside down in the rear window, where it lolled and jerked about on his neck. His eyes bubbled wildly in their sockets. He was really losing it when the Mustang pulled up behind the cab, its headlight illuminating the rear window like the stage in a high school gym.

Janet Wilton and Myra Holder were returning from a party and both were a little tipsy. Janet knew that she was probably over the legal limit of blood alcohol to be driving but as long as she took it slow, she figured that they would be all right. And as long as they didn't get pulled over by the police. The two teenagers kept up a running conversation in order to stay alert in their homeward navigations. As they pulled up behind the cab, both immediately noticed the hideous spectacle in the rear window of the cab.

"Do you see what I think I see?" Janet gasped.

"Yeah. I sure do," said Myra.

"Then if you can see it too, that means it's not just in my imagination," Janet said.

The playing of the bright lights, the ghastly makeup, and Rediens' cadaverous facial contortions combined to produce a grisly apparition.

"What the hell's he doing anyway?"

"Freaking out is what he's doing!"

"Jeez, look at that! That guy's really gone! Look at him! Look at his eyes."

"Must be freaked out on drugs, maybe acid."

"C'mon, let's get the hell outa here!"

"Next time I have too much to drink I'm calling my parents to come and get me."

The light had changed and the girls squealed past the cab, staring into it as they passed. Fraser, taking note of the alarmed looks from the passing car, once again shot a glance into his rear view mirror, and once again he was met by Redien's staring face, with it's hint of a deathlike smile.

The timing was uncanny.

The yellow cab sped on under the moonlit sky into the myriad of lights that was Niagara Falls. Now they were on the Niagara Parkway only a few minutes from the Falls.

Rediens was locked deep in the throes of a trance.

His time was coming and he knew it.

Nearer and nearer.

The cab braked to a halt in front of the roaring beast itself. It seemed to welcome him as he knew that it would. This was not the first time Rediens had been here. Many times he had gazed into the falling water crystals spinning their hold over him. He had heard the callings before and had sensed the presence of something greater. He knew without a doubt that there was something down there. He had seen the image in the mist and had made a pact with it. He knew he would someday make a pilgrimage back. This was how it was intended to be. It was only a question of time. And now it seemed as if it expected him.

Kane sprang into action. He opened the car door, taking the manila envelope from the seat and depositing it in a nearby curbside mailbox . He shook hands with the driver through the open window and while still grasping the cabbie's hand, he leaned in as if he wanted to whisper something in his ear. It was like reaching into the yellow shell of a gigantic metal turtle.

"Hey mister, thanks for the lift." Then he sank his teeth into the cabbie's ear and came away with the majority of the organ. Blood spurted down his chin and chest and down the driver's door of the yellow cab. Fraser shrieked with the pain and almost passed out. Rediens spit the remnant of the ear in Fraser's lap and bolted in the direction of the Falls. Fraser tried weakly to summon him back but Kane was gone. He would have been wasting his breath on the wind.

Kane was a man on a mission, not to be deterred. He raced on all fours by startled passers-by on the sidewalk and arrived breathless at the iron railing at the brink of the Falls. He paused for a moment to catch his breath, a breath that filled his lungs with salt air.

The Falls roared in utter delight!

The nearest bystander was at least one hundred yards away. As he stood transfixed in the darkness of the precipice, a familiar feeling of seductiveness came over him, just as it had before when he came here.

This particular vantage point was unique. First of all, it was about the closest you could come to the Falls without actually going over, and secondly because it offered a singular perspective. The water could be seen rushing over the pinnacle point just ten feet below your feet, then everything just fell away to a misty distant point far below. It was as if the two planes, that of the beginning of the waterfall and it's end, were juxtaposed in an illusion of a few inches apart. Common sense tells you that the fall was vastly greater than just a few inches.

Rediens was usually a man of the shadows but it seemed that most of his previous visits here had been in the daylight He could remember gazing into the cresting torrent until it mesmerized and induced him in some way to join their flow. It was a powerfully seductive invitation.

"C"mon boy. Ride me," it's seething watery voice beckoned. I'll take you on a ride like you've never had before. Ride me ...Ride me."

He never knew what had kept him from going over those other times. Yet he never forgot the calling. Once it connects, even if you resist it at first, you never forget the calling. And if you're lucky like Kane Rediens you will come back to it.

So there would be no stopping Kane tonight.

Tonight was his night to ride, and the Falls knew it too.

Could sense it.

And wanted him.

Ride me. Ride me. Ride me.

"I Kane Rediens summon thee from the recesses of the dark, Amen evil from us deliver but temptation into not us lead..."

Ride me. Ride me.

"And us against trespass who those forgive we as trespasses our us forgive and..."

Ride me. RIDE ME!

"BREAD DAILY OUR DAY THIS US GIVE..."

RIDE ME. RIDE ME.

"I'LL RIDE YOU, YOU MOTHER" he screamed.

And he did on this night of the full moon of the rose, right to the end of its raging abysmal depths.

The moon hung full and the big black cat Lucky, with one last mournful wail, blood dripping from his teeth and the horns of a devil glistening in the starlight, jumped into the void of darkness, into the gates of hell.

What Kane could not have achieved in a thousand lifetimes of struggling, he had now acquired with one bold death stroke.

Freedom. It was his time to shine. He truly was master of the darkness.

But Kane didn't die.

Not exactly.

CHAPTER TWELVE
REVELATIONS
Saturday, July 7th

The car shot down the dirt road kicking up dust into
billowing clouds behind it. It had been almost an hour now
since the tires had last touched blacktop.

"Are you going to tell me where the hell we're going?"
Sara was peeved having lost patience back on the blacktop.

"You'll see. We're just about there. You're not the only one
who can play out their hunches, you know."

I aimed the vehicle through a gate in a fence that was badly
in need of repair, braking in front of a row of six long buildings.
They looked like Army barracks with their rounded roofs of
corrugated tin reaching down to meet weather-battered walls
of wooden shingle. Many of the wooden shingles had fallen
off, exposing bare patches of black tar paper. In a weeded field
behind the buildings, cannibalized remains of old automobiles
lay strewn about like lizards, rusting in the afternoon sun.

A number of people were gathered in front of a huge
fireplace. An open compound wrapped around it. A large
black pot hung suspended above the fire that burned in the
brick structure. A few of the men dozed in the sun on the steps
of the dilapidated buildings. Some empty bottles of liquor
littered the ground nearby. From the worn, ill-fitting clothes
to the hungry faces of the people near the fire, the place reeked
of poverty.

"It looks like we caught them at supper time," I observed.

"This is an Indian reservation. What are we doing on an
Indian reservation?"

"Just someone I have to see."

"Wow, I heard stories that these reservations were not
faring too well, but seeing it in person is really depressing."

We approached the group by the fire, mostly woman and
young children,

"Excuse me for interrupting your meal, but I'm looking

for Tom Rees. I was told I could find him here."

Judging from the reaction I got, which was no reaction at all, I wondered if perhaps another language was needed, maybe even sign language. An aroma drifted from the pot but I couldn't decide if it smelled good or not. Finally an old woman pointed to the door of the fifth building.

"Thank you ma'am," I said

We approached the door.

"Boy they're not much for words are they?" Sara said. "And I wouldn't want to guess what they're cooking in that pot."

I knocked on the wooden door.

"C'mon in," said a voice from the inside. "It's not locked."

Tom Rees sat at a desk in a small room that was lined from wall to wall, ceiling to floor with shelves of books. Various pieces of artwork depicting scenes from Iroquois folklore hung from some of the shelves. He was a white-haired man of about 65, but the glint of his smile and the twinkle in his eye made him appear much younger and certainly a lot friendlier than the group we had encountered outside.

As we shook hands I happened to notice out of the corner of my eye a very worn, black book to one side of Rees' desk. I've always marveled at what a wonderful place the corner of one's eye is. It is a place where so much information clandestinely flows, innocent of the observation of others close by. And yet time and time again the knowledge gained in this furtive and fleeting manner proves to be just as true and reliable as that gained in circumstances allowing for head-on scrutiny.

In this case, as I said, the book in my eye-corner's scope had a black cover, not very thick as it was wrinkled and dog-eared from handling and probably age. It did not have a conventional binding but the pages were held together by nine wire rings giving it more the appearance of a binder or a manuscript. There was no title or any other words on the cover, the only marking of any kind being that of a white twisting symbol.

While Rees had no knowledge of my observation there was no indication that he would have taken offense to it, after all it's not like the book was hidden.

"Don't worry about them; they're a little reticent around strangers but once they get used to you they'll be fine. How can I help you?"

"I've been told that you are an expert on Iroquois history and legend. I'm seeking some information."

"Yes, I can help you but first it is time to eat," invited Rees.

I could tell that Sara was not enthused at this prospect.

"If you don't mind, I just ate a short while ago. You'd be surprised how much a couple of Big Macs can fill you up."

Rees sensed her unease and laughed.

"C'mon it won't be as bad as you think."

I whispered to Sara on the way to the compound that it would be considered an insult to these people if we refused their offer of hospitality. It wasn't in Sara's character to offend such simple and humble people.

We were treated to a surprisingly delicious meal of fish stew, and fresh loaves of bread prepared Indian style on an open fire.. The pot didn't look overly huge but it held enough to feed all the people in the encampment and there was still plenty left over. I didn't think it was possible, but the group did open up to us as Rees predicted, with a warmth and friendliness that made us feel welcome in their home, in spite of its squalor. In fact, once you got past their initial aloofness the kindness that these poor people extended was really quite overwhelming. Many of the woman and children tended to gravitate to Sara sensing immediately that this was not a stranger who held herself above them but a down to earth person who sympathized with their plight and tried to identify with their situation. Soon they were proudly exhibiting some of their arts and crafts for us to admire. While some of the other children were playing Sara spotted a forlorn little boy standing near the door of one of the barracks.

"Why does he not join in," she asked.

"That's little James," a woman replied. "His mother died last winter. He's blind and now his dog is sick."

Sara went over to the boy who cowered as he sensed the presence of a stranger. She scooped him up in her arms and the softness of her voice was like salve on a wound, putting the boy at ease. He led her to his dog and it was obvious that the boy relied on the dog to get around as well as for companionship now that his mother was gone. The dog just lay listless in a corner of the room, but its breathing was labored. Sara felt its nose and her hand came away warm.

"He went out one afternoon and he came back sick," the boy said.

Sara had seen this before with her aunt's dog.

"I think your dog has heat stroke. He probably saw a rabbit out in the woods and chased him a little too hard in the afternoon sun."

"Will he be okay?" the boy asked worriedly.

"I think so", soothed Sara. "But first I'm going to need a couple of wet towels."

She wrapped the dog up in the wet towels with the skill and gentleness of a nurse. I watched all this with amazement. And here I was the one that was trained in first aid.

"Now let's let him rest for a while. In the meantime you can keep me company."

We went back outside and the boy sat in her lap while she stroked his black hair. The two of us were also surprised at how articulate and educated Rees and some of the others were.

"Yeah, most of us have had schooling and some have even gone to university," said Rees.

"Why do you stay in these appalling conditions? Why not go out and make a better life for yourselves?" asked Sara.

"If only it were that simple. It's not a lack of education that holds us back. It's more a sense of alienation than anything else. Many of us have gone out and tried to make a new life for ourselves. Some have been successful. But the others, they just keep drifting back They feel they just don't fit in anywhere.

Indians have always been tied to the land. It's in our heritage. It's in our blood. The white man who pushed us onto reservations could never understand that mindset.

In an Indian's eyes one can never own land. The land was given to us as a gift from the gods and we are stewards who take care of it for them. The land is sacred-places are sacred. In that respect Indian is reverent man and the white man is Prometheus man who razes everything he touches. He rapes the land and then cries about global warming. Maybe it was the Indians who had it right in the beginning-who treated the land with reverence and respect.

Think about it-the white man pushes us onto useless tracts of land and our whole way of life changes. If that is not bad enough-as in the case of the Sioux in the Black Hills of South Dakota-once gold was discovered the greed of the white man forced them from their sacred lands. To be dispossessed in such a manner is devastating to an Indian. We can't seem to deal with living in cities and the complications of living in modern civilized society. Unemployment, alcoholism, suicide rates are all much higher on the reservation, no question about it. But that doesn't mean we are not proud. Sometimes too proud to a fault. Our goal is to create our own social indoctrination center that will preserve our heritage in our own way but teach us the skills that will allow us to successfully integrate into the world outside this reservation. If you give a man a fish you feed him for a day; if you teach him how to fish you feed him for life."

Night had fallen and darkness bathed the compound. The three of us sat alone, our silhouettes illuminated by the warm light of the fire. The other members of the tribe were assembling to partake in a ritual dance. The boy had fallen asleep in her arms. A pipe with an herb-like tobacco was passed around.

Sara's face never looked more beautiful than here in the soft fire glow under a starlit sky. I realized that she hadn't changed since I first met her, but since then we had gone through some things together and I had gained insight into her character. She was such a gentle presence. She didn't nag or pressure or preach but she had a way with a simple look of the eye or touch of the hand that was enough to inspire others around her to do what was right.

I sensed that no matter what she wrote as a newspaper woman her greatest legacy would be that she recruited the best intentions from the souls she encountered. It was as if she was on an unsolicited mission to inspire the rest of us to be better by setting the example. I found myself trying to resist treating her like a woman and being protective and not being able to help myself. At this point every man that worked on the river was hopelessly in love with her.

I recalled the day we met, I had just come from a situation in which a mother was grieving over a daughter that had thrown her life away on drugs. Then in complete contrast on the same day, this girl comes into my life, so vibrant and alive, loaded with enough spunk and energy to take on the world three times over. It's a crazy place, this world that we live in.

The intelligence, spirit, and kindness that she had displayed conspired to create an inner beauty that transformed plain features. Of course she was headstrong and independent, but still we shared a bond together. I knew that if I had had a daughter I would have been proud if she had turned out like Sara.

However it was time to get down to cases. I never let on to Sara my purpose for coming out here. Something Charlie Knowales had said to me after the press conference continued to chew at me, but I knew that Tom Rees could provide me with the information that I needed.

"How did the elders of the tribe select a candidate for sacrifice, in the time when that was practiced?" I said, getting to the point.

Sara looked at me like I was nuts. Rees smiled at the question, watching the dancers who were limbering up. A low slow drumbeat had begun to mark time.

"Take Kira, over there for example," Rees said, indicating a young woman with a smiling face on the far side of the fire. She held the hand of a child to either side of her as they prepared to dance.

"Had she lived in those times, she would have been considered for selection, although her life then would have been far different than what it is today. First of all she would not have had to live by the white man's rules. A white man's reckoning would have been of little concern to her although even then there were early signs of influence. There would have been a few things, mostly from the white trappers, who sometimes came by and traded for furs.

"There would be the red woolen blanket her brother Inoue had traded for. It would prove to be not as heavy as the bearskin, but on the really cold nights neither would it be as warm. On most other nights it would be serviceable. Kira would be able to wrap herself in it, for it seemed to breathe better than an animal skin, and thus she would not sweat as much. She would like the color. The fabric would be courser against the skin than the deer hide scraped smooth by many hours with a knife or stone, but that was because the cheaper grades of wool out of the English factories were the ones that made it to the frontier. Although an Indian maiden would have no knowledge of that.

"Then there would be the black cast iron kettle that would be far superior to the clay pots her tribe would have used before. It would not have come cheap, requiring many furs, and while it would be shared by many families in the tribe, it would have been worth it. Wahay, which means like a rock, was how the Iroquois referred to steel. It was more precious to them than gold. The Iroquois had never seen anything like it and had no concept of how to produce it. The hard steel of the white man could withstand many fires and still not crack and it held the heat much longer than clay. Although it was very heavy, the Iroquois did not move around very much. Later, hatchets and knives and eventually guns would be prized items of trade.

"At some point Kira might have seen some men of white skin with writing sticks, but that would pretty much be the extent of the white man's influence on her. She would not get to see the diseases the white man would bring later that would ravage her village, or hear the lies that would be told about the Iroquois in white man's wars over land that was stolen from the Indians in the first place. Finally, after the Indians had served their purpose, the white man would turn against them in the end.

"Kira, which means fawn in the woods, would not have been around to have seen any of these things come to pass. She would have only been familiar with the simple Iroquois life. Everyone worked hard but that was because it took hard work just to live. That would have only made her appreciate the simple pleasures of her world. She would come to love, as all Indians did, the beauty of the land, the coolness of the woods or a pristine stream on a hot summer day, the warmth of a blazing fire on an icy dark winter evening.

"She would love the every day bustle of the Iroquois village and the camaraderie of people, all with the common purpose of trying to survive by helping each other. Men and horses going off to the hunt, the women cooking, babies crying, children playing games in the fields or the woods, dogs chasing around the stick and mud dwellings, barking and fighting each other for scraps.

"Summer with it's long warm days and mild nights would be the best time. Maybe Kira's mother would boil sap from maple trees, then let the pieces harden to become sweet sugary treats to be enjoyed on special occasions. At night, gathered around a fire, Kira would hear the tales of the young men who had traveled from the village to serve as guides for the white men. Other times she would listen to the elders espouse their wisdom and philosophies, helping her to understand the world she lived in. And then of course there would be the river and the Falls. There was always the river.

"Wherever the Iroquois went they carried the river and the Falls with them in their thoughts. It was the centerpiece of their lives. Their place of worship. Their temple of life. The Niagara spawned from the big pools of water to the north. One of the guides had talked of the lake known as Gitchee Gumee, then of the lake where the Erie tribe roamed. Out of the Erie's lake, the river ran wide and lazy. As the river narrowed, she gathered speed, rippling over the rocks. A little further on and the ripples became swells, flowing angrily, powerful and thick. Then came the white water where the canoes were never supposed to go. Here the water was wild, vicious, spinning, spitting white like the foam from a rabid dog."

"At the Falls clouds of mist billowed into the sky, as if from an eternal fire. Massive sheets of water poured over the edge in a furious rush to judgment on the crumbling rocks below. Out of the lower basin, most of her fury spent, the exhausted river somehow carried on through the cavernous walls of the canyon, walls 30-men high carved out of solid rock as testament to the incredible force and majesty that was Niagara. After a set of rapids and the whirlpool, the river finally broken, emptied placidly into the lake of the Ontarios. How could anyone explain such a force? It could only have come from the gods. The gods had chosen this place Niagara for their extraordinary display of sheer power and might. The Iroquois recognized the Niagara for what it was, a place where the gods had emblazoned their signature on the face of the earth. This was a temple and they were required to show the correct measure of humbleness and homage.

"Down in the river bed surrounded by the high walls of the gorge, Kira would know that no mortal could have created this. Why even if Loli, the strong one, and Tot, the wiry one, were harnessed to teams of ten horses each, they would not be able to move even one of the boulders along the gorge's edge. She would know that if one boulder presented such an impossible task, what about the thousands of boulders that littered the gorge? She would know that she was in the church of the thunder god. It would be the elders of the village who would choose Kira for her destiny.

"They would have noticed Kira's kind spirit, teaching the children of the village, helping her parents, her gentleness with the birds and small creatures of the forest. They would note her respect of the land, her many trips to the river to pay quiet reverence in the solitude of the night. They would conclude that she would be good company for the gods. Of course, innocence and purity would be taken into consideration.

"Usually when a previous season had been a season of plenty, the corn rising tall and strong, the fruit juicy and sweet, the vegetables full and leafy and the hunter's arrows guided to their marks so that plenty of meat hung smoked and stored for the winter, homage would be due. The gods had been extremely generous to the Iroquois and so the elders would have deemed someone like Kira to be a suitable offering. Soon winter would be upon them, and it was necessary to keep the gods favorable to their condition.

"Kira would have considered it a sacred honor to be able to give herself for the betterment of the people of the village that she loved so dearly. The previous evening she would be branded with the spiral sign of the Falls. The whole next day would be a day of feasting, dancing, and celebration devoted to the sacrificial ceremony. The time would draw near. She would not be afraid. If this were South America she might be administered a little curare in just the right dosage, to lessen pain. However this being the Great Lakes region of North America, a mixture of hemlock, possibly arsenic, and yohimbe may have been employed. Then it was over."

The conclusions that I drew from all of Rees's information did nothing to allay my growing suspicions.

"So contrary to what Indian myth would have us believe, maidens were not selected by the elders for sacrifice to their gods because they were judged to be the most beautiful in the tribe. Character and a kind heart were deemed to be more valuable and precious to the gods. Kira who was just average-looking but who was beloved by the tribe would have been a more suitable offering."

"That's correct," Rees said. Sometimes beauty and character would merge in a selection and some would erroneously assume that beauty was the dominant quality, when indeed it was just the opposite. But the real power of the sacrifice lay within the woman herself. Since nature was considered female a woman was the most powerful elixir there was."

Since I happened to know someone else who fit this criteria very well I was compelled to ask it. After hearing Rees' story I felt sure that had Sara lived back then she would have been a perfect candidate for sacrifice.

"Sara. I know that when we met that day in the gorge, I told you about my ancestry, but you never told me your background."

"Both my parents were English."

"Think back further, your grandparents, great grandparents. Is there anyone in your background with Indian blood?"

The answer came too quickly and too eagerly, as my stomach tightened.

"Sure, my grandmother was part Cherokee," she said, a puzzled little frown on her face.

I knew I was on the right track.

"Tell me, when Charlie Knowales interviewed you for this project, did the subject of your Indian heritage ever come up in the conversation?"

"Now that you mention it, it was one of the first questions that he asked."

I tried to keep a mounting sense of horror and fear from crawling out of my throat.

"What exactly are you driving at, Ro?" She asked. She must have read my face; I was never very good at poker.

"I'm not sure of all the implications yet, but don't you

see? They wanted you right from the beginning because of your Indian blood. The fact that you're a reporter from the Washington Post was the perfect cover. Listen, I've known Charlie Knowales all my life and it's not like him to show a lot of interest in dealing with a woman. That's what made me suspicious in the first place. Believe it's more than coincidence that you are the only woman to be associated with this project. And don't believe for a minute that it's equal opportunity employment in action. Knowales doesn't know the meaning of such things."

"What are you saying? That they chose me to be some kind of sacrificial lamb? This is the 21st century. People don't believe in old myths and legends, and even if they did how would they ever get away with something like that?"

The chanting grew louder, the dancing more frenetic, stick figures in rhythm with flame and fire.

"I'm not saying that exactly. I haven't figured it all out yet. Maybe they want you for some sort of protection, like a good luck charm. But if I know Charlie Knowales, you can bet it's a lot more than that. Those guys are obsessed to a point that they will let nothing get in the way of the success of this expedition. If I were you I'd give some serious thought about getting on that craft."

"Nonsense and miss out on the opportunity of a lifetime?"

I had to remember that this girl didn't scare easily with words. It was a quality the gods would have appreciated.

The dance ended with the abrupt cessation of drum and chant, the dancers freeze-framed in the light, and silence fell except for the crackling flames of the fire, piercing the dark void of night. A dog ran over to Sara and began licking the face of the boy asleep in arms. The boy woke up and hugged the dog with tears in his eyes. The people around the fire clapped at the joyous reunion.

Once again the light flickered favorably over Sara's features, and it was then that I realized that in the short space of a week I had grown to love her like a daughter and would give my life for her if necessary. Silently I prayed that it would never come to that. When it came to the river and rescues my batting average was not very high and that's what had me worried. My inexperience with smoking of any kind had left me kind of heady but I did not want to appear rude because the passing of the pipe was a custom of hospitality.

In that combination of haze and shadows it appeared to me as if a black rod on the ground had become animated. It slithered its way to Sara and any word of warning from me died in my throat. I was trying to speak but nothing came out. The snake crawled up behind Sara and wrapped itself around her neck and started to squeeze. I watched the expression on her face change from surprise to panic to horror. Why wasn't anybody doing anything to help her . Was I the only one who could see what was happening. Everyone else seemed to be preoccupied with watch the dance. Sara was being strangled to death right before my eyes and I could neither move or speak a word to help her. I was totally paralyzed. Frozen in place. She was alternately flailing her arms and clutching at the object around her throat. I could see the light glisten off the scales as the powerful muscles beneath constricted even tighter. When I saw Sara's eyes start to bulge, I opened mine, just as the dance was coming to an end. There was everybody, Sara included still around the fire clapping and smiling. There was no snake around anybody's neck. A black staff lay lifeless on the ground nearby. I shook my head as if to clear water from my ears. Apparently I had closed my eyes for a moment and drifted off. My dreams were bad enough but now I was having hallucinations. I forbade myself to devote one iota of thought to how much truth might be associated with the image I had just seen. But I knew one thing. I would never have to worry about seeing that image play out in real life because I would have been dead before allowing such a thing to happen. I politely declined any more partaking of the pipe for the rest of the evening.

Before we left the reservation, there was another matter that I had to discuss with Rees. "During your lecture you had mentioned that they branded the sacrifice. Could you elaborate?'

"You must be referring to the spiral brand that I mentioned. The spiral symbol was the sign of the waterfalls to the Iroquois. It signified the water spiraling downward, but it also signified the mist spiraling skyward into the heavens. It was the same journey one's soul who had been sacrificed would take."

"Could you draw me that symbol?"

Rees made the mark in the dirt by the campfire with a stick. It wasn't the spiral I was expecting, and in the final analysis

the symbol looked more like a helix, but I knew that I had seen such a marking before. This is what Rees drew:

It was the exact same marking that I had seen on the book on his desk out of the corner of my eye and I was compelled to ask him about it.

"There was a book on your desk that held a similar imprint and nothing else on it's cover that I found very intriguing and was meaning to ask you about it."

"Oh, yes, that book. That book is a very special book, indeed."

"Special how?"

"That book is not supposed to even exist."

"But it does exist. I saw it on your desk."

"I know it exists and now you do, but you are only one of a handful of people on this earth that have ever seen it. There are only two known copies of it, the original which you saw on my desk, and a copy which has disappeared. That book is an account of events there were not supposed to have occurred."

"Any chance I could take a look at it?"

"Normally I wouldn't let just anybody have access, but I like you Ro Patric and your young lady over there. Seems like we're all quite taken with her."

"Yea, she's quite a young woman, something special. I think she was quite taken with all of you also."

I made a silent vow that somehow, one day I would find a way to help these kind people. Good thing my wife wasn't here to remind me that talk is cheap and that up to now my record of 'one-day' promises was not very good.

"Then, in honor of our Indian heritage I'm going to let you read it, but I must warn you that the events which were recorded were not supposed to have occurred so take it with a grain of salt. And I have to tell you that the author of the book was a fourteen-year-old boy."

Rees retrieved the book out of his office and in the clear moonlight of that night I read the most amazing tale I have ever read of events that never happened on a similar clear night some 140 years ago.

In the year of our Lord, 1860, it was supposed to be a secret. I was only 14 years old when these events occurred. My name is Keaton and I am the only living witness. Canada was still seven years away from its own confederation and was largely under British control.

In America at this time many Indian tribes roamed freely, but in the Canadian territories the British had organized the tribes onto managed tracts of land known as reservations, a few years before. This loss of freedom was a sad and terrible time for many of the once proud Indian nations. The Huron nation was given a piece of land on the shore of Lake Huron while my tribe the Iroquois lived on a land grant here at Niagara.

By a sheer stroke of luck, the Hurons discovered gold on the land they had been relegated to. The gold strike would have paled in comparison to the gold rush in California, but still it represented a substantial amount of wealth. The Hurons secretly mined their strike for over a year when the deposit finally played out. The gold they had discovered was heavily imbedded in ore with a high content of iron, unusual in most gold strikes, but not uncommon for that part of the country.

The Hurons knew what they had was valuable but the did not have the equipment or the skills necessary to separate the gold from the iron. They were also cognizant of the fact that if the British found out about their cache of wealth, it would undoubtedly be confiscated much as their other freedoms had a scant two years previous.

In the United States at this time forces were mobilizing on either side of the issue of slavery and a struggle of epic proportions appeared imminent. It was in the midst of this impending chaos that the Hurons found a prospective partner or so they thought. Southern interests would purchase the raw gold ore from the Hurons, smelt it and use the considerable profits to finance their inevitable entanglement with the north. Secrecy was ultimate to sealing the bargain for the south as well as the Hurons. The South did not want to be caught in a deal that made them appear as if they were preparing for war.

A wooden ship, the Michigan, built on the upper Great Lakes would be sent to get the gold. Like many ships of that day she was a steamer but also had sail. She had a captain, skeleton crew, and two representatives from the Confederate government.

Over a period of three days (mostly at night) the ship was loaded to bursting with the ore.

On the fourth day she sailed for Buffalo N.Y. with her cargo and two representatives from the Huron nation. In Buffalo the gold would be transferred to rail for transportation south, at which time the Hurons would receive payment in US dollars.

The first mistake the southerners made was equating the Indians with their own slaves and assuming that since they had no rights, the gold was now property of the South.

The second mistake was killing the Huron representatives after only an hour out of port and dumping the bodies overboard. The current in this part of the lake is surprisingly strong and not to be underestimated, which would now bring the tally of miscues to three. The bodies washed up on the shore of the reservation even before the Michigan had crossed the lake. Thinking it would be days before the deed was discovered, the Michigan tied up in Buffalo and a keg of rum was tapped. At dawn the ship would be off loaded.

The gruesome discovery of their comrades on their beaches made the Hurons realize that all men of white skin were alike and not to be trusted. Quick action was needed or all would be lost. word was sent to their allies the Iroquois at Niagara to see if they could be of any assistance.

That was how my father got involved. He knew a little bit about boats. He and two others were selected for what was essentially an Indian commando mission. Even though I was only fourteen, I could tell by the way he kissed my mother and said goodbye to me and my younger brother, that he fully expected it to be the last time he would see any of us again. I was at that age where I was rebelling against authority and so when my mother told me to go to sleep, I ignored her and stole out after my father. I also loved my father very much.

I trailed the three of them as they ran down the path beside the river upstream to Buffalo. I was far back in the shadows.

When they reached the Michigan the sounds of drunken celebration came from below. One guard patrolled the deck. He was taken out by a silent arrow through the throat, dead before his weight hit the deck. The captain and the two southerners were surprised below and fell easy prey to the blade. At some point in the struggle for control of the ship an oil lamp was knocked over.

I watched from the darkness of the other side of the river as my father untied the mooring lines and cast off. I saw the flames flaring up in the lower portholes. They headed silently down river, tethered to the moon by a trail of gray smoke. I kept pace and followed on the riverbank. With the fire running out of control below and time at a premium, there could only be one destination.

Even before the fire, I'm not sure that my father and the others had not already predetermined their course of action. Returning the gold to the Huron reservation would have proven to be a futile endeavor. The white man would learn of its existence if he didn't already know about it and he would just take it away again.

The fire had escaped from the below decks and had its tongues out the lower portholes, lighting up the sides of the ship. I could see dark figures lowering the mainsail even as the Michigan fell into swifter waters. The engine and boiler would remain silent.

I thought that my father and the others would jump ship and make a swim for it, but once the wooden steamer hit the white water, I knew that saving themselves had never been their intention.

The fire now blazed onto the upper decks

illuminating this whole section of the river. I screamed to my father in the anguish of knowing that I was seeing him for the last time. He and his comrades had climbed into the rigging of the inferno when he heard my yell. Startled he turned and saw me on the shore. After his initial surprise a peaceful smile formed on his lips, then he turned and looked skyward, a faraway gaze in his eyes. Through my tears, that was what I remembered of my father's last moments: the ship teetering on the brink of the falls, the mainsail erupting in a glorious explosion of flame, and the three Iroquois warriors hanging from the cross of the mast with arms raised in tribute to the heavens. Heroic valkyries guiding their treasure to its final Valhalla. I felt as if I was witnessing a Viking funeral. Like a fiery comet, the Michigan dove and disappeared forever into the dark waters. My father and the others had taken the shipment of gold to the one place that they knew it would be safe; the watchful eyes of the thunder god. It was the ultimate gift of homage.

I had finished reading the account, and for a short time no words were able to pass my lips. Then I needed to speak as though words were in the saddles of wild horses.

"So that would mean that if this really happened the gold would still be in the plunge basin."

"I think that the original intention was that the gold would be recovered by Indians at some point, either the thunder god would release it somehow, or they would get it themselves. I don't think those who sunk it realized just how inaccessible a place the plunge basin would prove to be. So yes, to answer your question, I do believe the gold is still there," said Rees.

"So you believe then that this really happened?"

"Others have doubted it. The proponents are all dead. It was all so secret that there is very little evidence to prove it, but I have never disclaimed the validity of the document."

"What makes you different from the others?" I asked.

"The boy Keaton, the one who wrote the account. He was my great grandfather."

Amazing as it was, at the time I couldn't see how any of this would have any bearing on the Thrill expedition.

The call-board at the Niagara Falls police station on Dufferin was lighting up with incoming reports of an apparent suicide at the Falls. An unidentified man had leapt over the railing at Table Rock House. The Maid of the Mist had been sent out with searchlights blazing, even though the chances of a rescue were slim, even in the daylight and next to nothing at night. Nothing turned up. Normally Ro Patric would have been notified by now, but he was off this weekend due to events associated with the Thrill Expedition, so Phil Stinson filled in for him.

The investigation continued into the wee hours of the morning. A bystander had seen a man bolt from a cab on the Niagara Parkway. The cab driver had been taken to the hospital with an ear injury. This information eventually led police to the Welland cab company and the driver, Bart Fraser. Kane's description and erratic behavior were corroborated, although a positive identification could not be made because of Kane's facial paint.

"Yeah, it doesn't surprise me a bit. I knew that guy was trouble the minute I picked him up," said Fraser from his hospital bed after having his ear sewn back on. In a short while, there would be hordes of Ontario's finest combing the grounds of the farmhouse in Welland.

The only thing to do now was to wait and see if the river was willing to give up its dead.

At the same time that the police were conducting their investigation on the surface, something very strange was happening to Kane Rediens.

From the moment that he jumped over the railing to the time that he hit the water, everything went black. Everything but his sense of feeling. He felt the icy grip of the river water

– water released for journey from the northern lakes – render his torso numb and breathless. Then the mighty hand of the current, pushing, then pulling, then twisting him. He found himself powerless against its relentless force. He felt violent motion. He sensed the river's wrath. Then nothing. The grip was released. He was free. Floating. Weightless. Existing, but only in a void.

There was no sense of direction or position, and his equilibrium was distorted. He did not know if he was right side up or upside down .He could not even be certain that he was falling, but he knew that he was moving. Moving in some direction. He felt only a slight jerk as his numbed leg was sheared off above the knee by a rock; as cleanly as one might machete a stalk of corn.

Then WHAM.

A tremendous body slam jolted his frame, driving the air from his lungs and the consciousness from his brain. Kane was unaware that his body remained halted, suspended for a second, as another force grabbed him. It pounded on him with incredible weight, driving him down...down...down. The cascading weight drilled him deep into the depths of the plunge basin, and he found himself surrounded by rushing, violent, tugging, first one way, then the next.

Suddenly it was not as strong. The grip was again releasing. The turbulence was easing. He was still surrounded but he was drifting again. Floating endlessly. It was at this point that Kane regained control of his brain. It would have been wrong to say that he was conscious. He felt totally disconnected from the rest of this body. He was unaware that blood was flooding out of a stump where his leg had once been. There was no denying that the water in this area held an inordinate amount of oxygen-that turned the water into a frictionless, meatless gruel of the thinnest density. It would have made the task of trying to swim out of here tantamount to trying to climb a ladder constructed of Rice Crispies. Now the thought entered his mind that perhaps all this oxygen-rich water was meant to serve another purpose.

He did not know how long he remained in this state. He was not aware of any breathing that was taking place, so he assumed that he must be dead. But he couldn't be dead because he could still think. His brain was still functioning. Maybe he was in that gray area, where the breathing of his body had stopped, and now it was just a matter of time before his brain expended its oxygen and died also. Yeah, he thought that must be it, a kind of body death before brain death. He had never drowned before so he naturally assumed that this was the way it happened.

He waited patiently for death and its blackness. Then, slowly, he became aware of another feeling. It started out as faintly as the outer ripples of a water-tossed stone. It's presence grew stronger as he neared its center. He was being drawn to its vortex. It had locked onto him like some sort of tractor beam and was sucking him to its core. His sense told him that it was something ancient and salty, something from the beginning of time. Even through liquid it reeked of rotten eggs. And the putrid stench of death.

Rediens knew that he should have been dead long before now. He also knew that whatever was bringing him into its fold was terribly evil. Pure. Twenty-four carat unalloyed evil. The old master of the darkness was about to say hello to a new master. The hunter turned no one away from his gate.

Somewhere else, Charlie Knowales was screaming at the top of his lungs, waking from one of his worst nightmares yet.

CHAPTER THIRTEEN
INNOCENCE OF A CHILD
SUNDAY MORNING July 8th-

The Maid of the Mist had slipped its berthing ties and was easing out into the Niagara River, loaded with tourists for yet another pass at the great Falls. The touring vessel was eternally grateful to the Falls, for without one, there would be no reason for the other. However her gratitude was such that she would not allow herself to get close enough for an embrace and that was the secret of her success over many years. The Maid of the Mist knew enough of the Falls to show respect and keep her distance.

On board this day was a young girl by the name of Roxanne Watts, from the nearby Canadian town of Fort Erie, accompanied by her mother. Roxanne Watts was a victim of her own over active imagination, a characteristic that would not serve her well this day. She was as good as anyone her age at inventing imaginary friends and situations. Her frequent forays into the worlds of Oz and Wonderland had her mother worried enough that a psychologist was consulted. Roxanne was told that one could not always escape into fantasy but that life's problems had to be faced in the real world. Roxanne seemed to have responded. In fact, she was doing so well in therapy that her mother had decided to treat her with a ride on The Maid of the Mist.

The Maid of the Mist followed a time-tested route of her predecessors, and as the ship neared the Falls, Roxanne could feel the spray pit-pattering on her slicker. The mist hung heavy in front of the cataract like a low flying cloud that had lost its way. As the Falls loomed like a mountain up ahead the brave ship appeared to be getting smaller in its presence, and Roxanne squeezed tighter on her mother's hand.

Mist enveloped the craft and even when she was visible from above, she appeared as only a speck on the wake-tossed waters of the thunder god and his cavernous basin.

The boat was close now, and everyone on board stared up at the tonnage of water hurtling over the edge of what must have been Mt Olympus. The spectacle was breathtaking. Some passengers were unable to speak in the intimate presence of the watery giant. Slowly the tiny vessel was coming about. She was close enough. She would tempt fate no further. As she headed back down the river, many on board breathed a sigh of relief. Most still had their eyes riveted to the Falls.

Roxanne Watts, in a moment of shielding her eyes from the falling spray, glanced down into the foaming, seething river that boiled angrily around the retreating boat. Fifty yards from the hull, her eyes landed on something solid in the river. Something dark, floating against the backdrop of whitewater. The current was sucking it closer to the starboard side.

"Momma, Momma. Look it. Something funny is floating in the water. What is it?"

"Roxanne, please. No games today. You've been doing so well lately."

A bystander overheard the conversation

"No, ma'am, she's right. There is something out there. I see it too."

Finally, her mother saw it as well, and although she could not make out what it was either, there was something strangely familiar about it. Others began to crowd over to that side of the ship to get a look at the object, drifting as it was, almost within reach of the vessel. An attendant came starboard with a net, snared the object, and held it up out of the water. Whatever the object was, it was very puffy and black.

Everybody on deck continued to stare at it, trying to determine what it was. Young Roxanne then voiced an opinion, that would only occur to a ten-year-old.

"Momma, it's a leg!" It was a simple yet poignant observation of the truth. When this realization hit the other spectators, they gasped in horror and turned away in disgust. Mrs. Watts fainted.

The following week Roxanne was pulled out of reality

therapy. It was indeed a leg. A human leg, blackened and bloated by the water so that you could barely make out the toes.

It was Kane Rediens' leg. It was the only part of him that had made it to the surface. But that was okay with Lucky.

The rest of him was beginning to like it down there.

CHAPTER FOURTEEN
A MAN COMES BACK FROM THE DEAD

While Sara and Ro grappled with their dilemma, the only man alive who had an inkling of what was below the waters of Niagara Falls was making an astounding recovery in a Toronto hospital.

Laz Harrison, the diver who had been stricken while working for Sara, had stunned the doctors with his sudden turn of condition. His former state of mind had been a source of puzzlement to the doctor's in the psychiatric ward of Toronto General, where Harrison had been transferred. Toronto, a city of three million 90 miles north of Niagara Falls, was well known for its hospitals and doctors. However not even the highest degree of medical care had been able to determine what was wrong with Harrison.

Physically there wasn't a scratch on him, except for a spiral shaped scar on the diver's right had. At first it was believed that he had experienced an equipment malfunction in his breathing apparatus that may have resulted in a lack of oxygen. However the CAT scans revealed no evidence of brain damage. What the doctors did know was that the man was in a severe catatonic state introduced by some sort of trauma, a mental trauma so severe it had simply caused his mind to shut down. What could have induced such a shutdown? The only one with the answer to that question was Laz Harrison himself, and up until a few hours ago he was incapable of talking. The doctors had even tried hypnosis to no avail, thus abandoning hope for the man's recovery. Then everything changed.

"It's unprecedented. It's like the guy climbed back from the dead," remarked one of the doctors. "He's lucid. His reflexes are normal. He's made a complete recovery!"

"Has he given any indication as to what may have precipitated his condition?" another one asked.

"No , he's still not talking about it. It may take awhile."

In room 405, Laz Harrison was getting dressed as fast as he could.

"I must advise you against this, Mr. Harrison," one of his doctors warned. "You really shouldn't be up and about so soon, after what you've been through. You need more rest. Until a few hours ago, you were essentially brain dead."

Harrison continued as if he hadn't heard a word.

"Doc, have you heard anything about that Thrill Expedition going over the Falls? Is it still on do you know?"

"Why yes, I think I heard something about it on the radio this afternoon. That's all anybody's been talking about. As far as I know they're scheduled to go tomorrow. Why?"

"Good it's not too late. I have to get to Niagara Falls immediately," Harrison said in tone that silenced the doctor. Harrison was a man on a mission as he walked out of the doors of the hospital and down a block to the nearest car rental agency. Ten minutes later he drove out in a late model maroon Chrysler Le Baron convertible equipped with a full set of brand new Sears Roadhandlers freshly gassed, fully prepared to do road battle. He knew getting to the Falls wasn't going to be easy. He had two options. He could stay on the QEW through St. Catherines and right into the Falls. This was the more traveled route and likely to be the most congested. Or he could cut onto route 20 in Vineland and follow that through Fonthill and over the Port Robinson bridge and into the Falls. This route would lend itself more to the local traffic and those familiar with the roads, and the prospect of less traffic appealed to Harrison. The decision was made. Harrison calculated that he could cover the 90 miles to the Falls in about two hours, depending on traffic. It was early evening and with a little luck, he could be there before darkness.

"That's funny," he mused to himself, "why would that matter all of a sudden?'

He had grown up in Niagara-on-the-Lake, which was only a stone's throw from the Falls, so it wasn't like he didn't know the area. Besides he always considered himself to be a good driver and night driving had never bothered him before. Why was he suddenly so apprehensive about night and darkness? He didn't know why. He just knew that it bothered him to think about the night.

The drive on the QEW was uneventful, but Harrison was plagued with the thoughts of what he had witnessed under Niagara's surface and anxious to speak with someone from the Thrill Expedition while there was still time, Sara Wilson, Charlie Knowales, somebody. And that it was getting dark.

At the highway 20 cutoff, something about the impending darkness prompted Harrison to pull into a gas station where he called the Thrill complex in Chippewa village.

"Hello, Can I speak with Sara Wilson or Charlie Knowales? It's a matter of the greatest urgency."

"Neither one is here right now, can I take a message?" the voice on the other end of the line said.

"Who am I speaking with?"

"This is Judd Blackadder , engineer for the Thrill project."

"Mr. Blackadder, good. My name is Laz Harrison. I'm a diver and I have some information that you folks will be interested in. In fact, based on what I have to tell you, may I suggest that you make preparations to cancel the expedition?"

"Hold on a minute, Mr. Harrison. That's a pretty big undertaking to cancel on just the word of somebody we've never even met before. "

"I know it is, and I will explain but not over the phone. I'm on my way to the Falls now. I'll be there in less than two hours if everything holds up. But you must get a message to Miss Wilson and Mr. Knowales that I'm on my way with some vital information that places their expedition in extreme jeopardy. They must not get in that craft tomorrow under any circumstances."

"I'll see if I can reach them. By the way, what are you driving?"

"I'll be coming in a maroon late model Chrysler Le Baron."

"And how are you getting here?"

"I'm coming in by route 20."

That's the way I would have come, Blackadder thought to himself after hanging up.

Harrison made good time until the village of Fonthill. The shadows were growing longer as the sun prepared to make it's celestial adieu. He tried not to think about what he had seen under the Falls, but the images kept creeping back into his mind's eye. Such thoughts sent chills through his very core. A cold sweat broke over his brow, and the leather covering on the steering wheel suddenly got tighter.

At the main intersection in Fonthill a car cut right in front of Harrison. Brakes and horn galvanized simultaneously.

"Keep steady, keep steady," Harrison repeated this mantra to himself, trying to settle his nerves. It was then that it occurred to Harrison that he needed to be careful, not just for his own sake but for the sake of the others involved in the Niagara venture. The message he carried was a matter of life and death. He knew that they would never cancel the voyage based on words spoken on a telephone, but if they could see him face to face, if they could see that he had recovered from that day in the gorge, then the information that he had to convey would be that much more convincing. And it would take a lot of convincing, especially in light of his fantastic revelations. He knew Sara Wilson and Ro Patric to be rational reasonable people, but what he had to tell them would go beyond normal thinking. In the end, the final persuasion would be the scar he now rubbed on the back of his hand. The scar in the shape of a double helix had not been there before his dive into the Niagara plunge basin, and it was too organized, too deliberately formed to be a scrape from a rock. He wasn't exactly sure of its significance but he was sure it was related to the spectacle in the plunge basin. Anyway, all this made him realize that it was important that he stay in one piece.

Thankfully, he was almost there. He flicked on the

headlights. It struck him that he did this not so much as a safety precaution, but more as a maneuver to ward off the darkness.

The sun was setting and every degree it sank below the horizon another grain of sand slipped by to mark the time he had left to live.

The twin towers of the Port Robinson lift bridge loomed ahead in the dusky sky. St. Lawrence Seaway Authority bridge # 11 was one of many that had been built to span the Welland Ship canal. It was a genuine throwback to the past, a mechanical dinosaur. The bridge was constructed of all steel and painted a gun-metal gray. Two 130-foot towers anchored by concrete abutments in the canal loomed skyward at each end of the bridge. The two towers and the span itself were a framework puzzle of steel columns, cross supports, and steel ribbing. The towers dangled with steel cables and guy-wires.

Suspended from the top of each tower was a massive cement block twenty feet high, thirty feet across. These served as counterweights for the bridge and were raised and lowered by large linked chains, sort of like bicycle chains magnified a thousand times. When the weights were lowered to road level the bridge would be at the height of the towers and vice versa.

A small gray shack was perched on top of the lifting portion of the bridge where the bridge master once controlled its operation. Manual lifting was rarely required nowadays. Everything was controlled electronically and managed by computers. Now when a ship came down the canal, transponders fitted to the vessel would automatically trigger the lifting of a bridge as it was required. A single guard rail for each lane of traffic at either end of the bridge would be lowered to halt the oncoming traffic, prior to the raising of the bridge. All parts of the operation functioned in a perfectly computer timed sequence once a signal was received from an approaching ship.

The town of Welland, Ontario's sole claim to fame was

that by its particular geography it became a bypass. God, in his infinite wisdom had created one of the most dynamic and powerful pathways from the interior of the North American continent to the sea, except for one small glitch. That fly in the ointment turned out to be the impassable Falls at Niagara and the solution was to bypass the Falls with a man-made canal and set of locks through Welland.

In Welland, where the canal bisected the very heart of the city, waiting for the bridges had become an integral part of daily life, at least as long as the lakers were in operation. There were three bridges that spanned the canal in downtown Welland, each visible from one another. Sometimes, if you raced to beat the devil, you could beat the boat to one of the other bridges, but in most cases it wasn't worth the aggravation, so you just patiently waited for the boat's passage. If you were the type to develop boat rage or bridge rage you moved out of a town like Welland. Wellanders, such as Blackadder were adept at being patient. After all, life in small town Canada just wasn't that urgent and there was one thing that could not be denied—when it came to the art of waiting, Wellanders could wait with the best of them.

Just as the Harrison vehicle was almost through an intersection at Thorold Stone Road, a light blue Ford bearing Ontario plates wheeled in front of him, then puttered on down highway 20. The car was going considerably slower than the posted 65 mph, and Harrison was again forced to apply his brakes to avoid a collision. Most of the time it was the lost American tourists who were always getting in the way of the locals, but not in this instance.

"Damn it," Harrison muttered to himself. "You know what kills me about these guys? They're always in such a hurry and so quick to get in front of you and then they putt along, holding everyone else up, like they got all the time in the world."

Harrison leaned on his horn directing his anger at the crawling vehicle. The horn blasts did nothing, and the Ford continued its pace. Passing on the single lane highway was out of the question. In what seemed out of character, the blue Ford unexpectedly sped up then ducked down a side road about 100 yards from the Port Robinson bridge. Shortly thereafter, the road gates were beginning to go down signaling that a boat was coming and that the bridge was about to become airborne. All the gates went down except for the one that would have blocked the Harrison vehicle. For some reason that gate remained in the upright position.

When Laz Harrison saw the blue Ford turn off highway 20, he clenched his teeth and resumed muttering, "Damn it, the guy drives like a turtle and then he can't even put on a turn signal. Well, that's par for the course. Good riddance to him anyway." He stepped on the accelerator. By the time he approached the bridge he was going at a pretty good clip. And he was confused by the scenario that greeted him, all the road gates down except on his side.

"What the…?" was all that he could say before he realized what was going on. That momentary confusion was enough to delay his brain from sending the signal to his leg muscle to hit the brakes. Now the Le Baron went into a slide as the bridge began to rise. When the car hit the bridge, the jagged metal teeth where the bridge surface meshed with the permanent roadway had only risen about a foot. Even the new tires could not prevent the car from hitting the bridge with enough impetus to drive the front wheels onto the raised portion of the bridge, getting blown out in the process. The car's rear tires came to a halt against the jagged metal teeth, and one of those blew out as well. In all the confusion, all Laz Harrison could think about was that the new Sear's Roadhandlers were shot.

Now the bridge continued to rise, taking the car up with it, as only the rear wheels were hanging over the edge. In point of fact, as desperate as this situation looked, if one was able to keep his wits about him at time like this, there was no real danger of the car falling off the bridge because more than three-quarters of the vehicle was on the bridge, and the weight of the engine and the driver would have kept it there.

As the bridge gained height, Harrison's first impulse was to get the rest of the car up onto the bridge. In panic, he tramped on the accelerator, but with the flat tires hindering his progress, the new Roadhandlers were ripped to shreds on the jagged bridge facing, but not before a lot of squealing and burning of rubber. The bridge had now risen 40 feet.

On the ground Andy Miller pulled up to the bridge, annoyed that the delay was going to cause him to be late to work. He too was confused that the road gate on his side of the road was still up.

"Damn, that's dangerous. You'd think with all the taxes the government gets out of us they could make sure the roads are working right." His eyes were drawn to smoke up high in the bridge and he could not believe his eyes.

A car was stuck up on the bridge!

The whole scene was very bizarre to Andy Miller. Other drivers pulling up to wait at the bridge got out of the line to gawk at the drama playing out above them. As the bridge kept up its slow but steady ascent, the trapped car kept on spinning its rear wheels in futile desperation and began producing a sound of metal grinding against bridge steel, as the wheel hubs were stripped of their rubber. Some of the people in their cars started a cacophony of horn honking.

Then Miller noticed the massive descending, concrete counterweight, certain it would hit the car. He got out of his car and began yelling, "Get out of the car! Get out of the car!" Others saw this and did the same, a dozen people yelling, jumping, and pointing.

The logical thing was to get out of the car and ride up with the bridge. But Harrison could not see what was above him, and he would not have been able to hear Miller and the others above the din of the horns. He was too intent on getting the rest of the vehicle up onto the bridge. He and the Le Baron were up sixty feet, almost halfway, and neither the falling block nor the rising bridge showed any indication of slowing.

"They're gonna hit!" Andy Miller screamed, and he and others scrambled for cover inside their cars. The last thing Laz Harrison saw was the creeping shadow from the rear that blocked out what ever light of day was left The huge block of concrete caught the rear of the Le Baron flush on it's trunk deck and began crushing it like a sardine can. The front of the car was lifted high off its wheels like the high end of a see-saw The concrete compressed the rear end of the vehicle until it hit the heavier steel frame. The car, pinned between the two opposing forces, slammed violently, roof first, against the concrete slab. Somewhere in all the scrunching, squashing, and compressing of metal was a gas tank filled almost to capacity with a highly volatile fluid.

A tremendous explosion rocked the bridge tower and boomed through the darkening Canadian sky. Hot pieces of blackened steel and human tissue rained from above. Some of the gasoline covered fragments hit the ground and remained aflame. While Laz Harrison was no more, the bridge was not yet done with the ravaged carcass of the car. The concrete block, virtually unfazed by the explosion continued to squeeze the burned-out shell of the automobile like a tube of toothpaste, turning it into a wedge of scrap metal no more than a foot at its thickest.

Once the counterweight had scraped and screeched across the entire length of the car, there was nothing to hold it up, and so the blackened block of metal tumbled from seventy feet in the air, crashing on the pavement in front of the bridge and ricocheting into the canal. The hissing metal frame in the cool canal water served as a pathetic eulogy to this incredible and most improbable display of carnage. The onlookers were stunned into silence at the incredible sequence of events. So stunned, in fact, that no one noticed the light blue Ford heading down the side road parallel to the canal in the opposite direction as a laker would have come-its driver patiently guiding the vehicle as if to be in no hurry at all.

Few seemed to have realized that the bridge had gone up but that no boat came through, and even fewer realized that the only living person who could have warned the members of the Thrill Venture had died with the secret of the Falls on his lips.

Sunday Night, THE WALL OF WATER; WHERE DO THE BODIES GO? RESURRECTION

CHARLIE Knowales was at the railing by the Falls. He had been staring into its waters for the last thirty minutes, feeling tired and drained. He needed to think. In just over twelve hours he would be in the Hellion on its maiden voyage. He had expected Judd Blackadder to be at the Chippewa complex, going over charts or taking care of some last minute detail, especially so close to launch time, but Judd was nowhere to be found. With Judd mysteriously vanished Knowales ended up here with his thoughts. It had been a long time coming to get to this point, but it was finally going to happen. He thought about his brother Ryan and how much he still missed him. He thought about a life derailed in his youth, but he always attributed that to the fact that they had higher expectations of him than he had had and that was before the accident with his brother. But now he paid that no mind.

Even if he had cared, all that failure could be erased with the success of tomorrow. But it wasn't about that. It was about Ryan. He thought about all the characters that had come through his life, Judd Blackadder, Rediens, Ro Patric from the old neighbor hood. If tomorrow was a success he would probably be meeting a whole new class of people, interesting people, educated people, people with money that could grant him access to things he had only dreamed about so far, people who up to now wouldn't have given him the time of day.

And so when tomorrow was successful he would say screw them all. He would rather have Judd Blackadder around, someone who had been there through it all and had still remained loyal. As plodding, methodical, and offtimes downright boring as he was, Judd had been there for him then, and they would do this together now. Whatever was required, they would find a way to get it done. Judd was devoted to the project beyond question and that made his disappearance that much more puzzling.

"Want to take a ride, Charlie old boy? C'mon. The water is nice and cool. I'll give you a preview of what you can expect tomorrow. C'mon, Charlie. Ride me."

"Huh?" Knowales was startled. He turned around in the dark, but there was no one there. Knowales was sure he had heard voices coming from somewhere nearby. He strained his ears, listening. There was nothing. It was either in his head or on the night wind.

Maybe it was not a good idea for him to be at this spot. He was letting his imagination get the better of him. He continued to stare into the flow of water coming from upriver. Suddenly, he could not believe his eyes. It rose silently out of the black water 500 yards away. It rose up on its own, from nowhere, a wave forming and casting toward the railing he was leaning against. Knowales stared pop-eyed as the wave gained in strength, size, and speed. He gaped in utter disbelief as the wave swooped around the curve of the shoreline and took dead aim at him.

A fifteen foot wall of water was bearing down on him.

Knowales dove away from the railing as the mini-tsunami collided with the breakwall, the upper half of the wave crashing over the railing and sweeping anything in its grasp over the Falls. He hooked the head of his snake cane around a lamp post as the surge swept by. If Knowales had been standing at his original position at the railing the wave would have dragged him over. The excess water at his feet felt as if it were licking at him, hungrily licking and tasting him.

There was something else here in the water. A will. A presence. But then hadn't he really known that all along? What other explanation was there for Sara Wilson? He was up against some unexplainable power that had just created a wave out of nothing and sent it after him. Knowales pulled himself together and returned to the railing, sure now what had to be done. From the beginning, he had hoped that it would not come to this. He was going to have to play his trump card: Sara Wilson.

Suddenly overcome with vengeful passion, he spat into the black water and left.

If Knowales could have seen into the depths of the water at the base of the Falls at that moment something else was sensing him.

It was Kane Rediens.

Rediens was conscious to a degree, somewhere in that rock formation at the bottom of the plunge basin that was Niagara's dungeon. How or why he still existed he could not fathom. But it was known that in this region of any plunge basin there was an inordinate amount of oxygen in the water molecules. It gets trapped between the particles of falling water. Swirling, overturning, being driven down into the depths. There is probably as much oxygen down there as there is water.

Whatever the explanation, it didn't really matter.

What mattered to Kane was that he still existed in some form or another. All he could do was sense an ancient death. He could sense the evil. But that didn't matter to him now. He was being assimilated. He was a part of the evil. He was as much a part of the evil as it was him, and he reveled in it.

He was the evil.

What did matter to him was Charlie Knowales. Rediens had sensed Knowales's presence somewhere above. He still harbored his hatred for Knowales, but he never thought in his present condition he would ever get a chance to do something about it. But down here something helped nurture that hatred, helped it grow stronger. Something also told him that he would get the opportunity to exercise his hatred. In fact, it would be Rediens' crowning glory.

He had sensed Knowales up at the railing and could detect

his state of anxiety. Oh, how good it felt to see Knowales agitated. He wished Knowales could come closer and see what he was now. He would give him a show that would really make his eyes pop out. He wished he could get at Knowales. But his day was coming. He knew that Knowales was going to be coming even closer, very, very soon. And that was good because the big black cat would be ready.

Waiting. Waiting. Waiting. All good things come to those who wait. For Rediens was once a Wellander himself and everyone knows what they say about Wellanders.

If you could only see me now, good buddy. I finally found a place where I belong. Home. In the watery shadows of the "beast".

If you could only see how lucky I was now.

Where do bodies go? Sometimes the river never yields its dead.

CHAPTER FIFTEEN
A PLAN IS HATCHED
Sunday night, July 8th

By the eve of launch day, the world around Niagara had been most definitely knocked askew. The night was reasonably warm but unseasonably humid for that time of year, and. with most of the hotels filled, people set up camp where ever they could find an open space. Victoria Park, a huge tract of land, which dominated the Canadian side of the river from Clifton Hill to nearly the Falls itself, resembled something from a Civil War battleground. Tents, sleeping bags, blankets, and even campfires were permitted in designated areas. Many people milled around the fires discussing with great anticipation the long awaited events and how they would play out. Others tried to sleep, amongst the din of human activity and electronic gadgetry. Battery powered televisions, radios and cell phones buzzed cackled and flashed their images and messages, each contributing to the confliction and variety of noise. The Civil War had never seen anything quite like this and neither had Niagara Falls.

The roadways remained heavy with traffic, even though there was almost no place left to go. Foot patrols of police and now the National Guard worked diligently to keep the cars and the pedestrians flowing. Above, helicopters ferried those who could not afford to get caught in the delays on the ground.

While it continued to amaze me the lengths people would go to in death's shadow, I was on a mission in the waning hours of that night that I anticipated would not afford me much opportunity for sleep. I was in the bowels of the Niagara Falls Morgue, having been granted access to the microfiche library.

Except for the clicking of frames through the video machine, it was quiet and I was alone, unless you count the company of the dead. How much company, I'm not exactly sure. Because if there's one thing that can be said of the dead, you can't judge their numbers by the amount of noise they make. That was fine by me. I was always a big fan of peace and quiet and those things were at quite a premium these days.

The humidity seeped into the building and slowly descended until all levels of the structure were saturated. I wondered if that was how evil operated. Did it come upon you suddenly like a flash? Or did it take its time exposing itself in little digestible pieces, soaking the heart, section by section, until all was immersed.

I was worried about my cohorts, Knowales and Blackadder. I had known them since childhood, but lately it was as if I did not know them at all. Whenever I was around them, I felt their tension, and an uneasiness formed between us that I never thought was possible. Maybe the pressure of this expedition was more than they expected.

Maybe they would be all right when this was over with.

I wasn't exactly sure what I was hoping to find. Tom Rees' Iroquois spiral triggered something inside of me. Where had I seen that marking before? I could have sworn it was down by the river on one of the bodies. I thought it was the Simmon's suicide a few years back. I remember that it was one of the floaters taken out in the daylight. It had to be. I doubt if I would have seen such a marking at night and that seemed to be when most of my recoveries were made.

It would have been a remarkable discovery at any time of day considering the destruction the Falls and the river inflicted on human flesh. When you take into account the missing limbs, broken bones, massive bruising , open wounds, and discoloration, markings were almost imperceptible. However, once the bodies were cleaned and photographed under optimal lighting conditions, such markings should become more identifiable. At least that was what I was hoping.

Flipping back through the cases on the way to the Simmons file was like a gruesome tour in a museum of human sadness and devastation. I remembered most of them. In this business you might get used to some of the sights but you never forgot them. If I was present for the recovery, then I remembered it.

"Ah, here it was, Simmons. 1994. It was further back than I thought."

The heat from that hot sunny day in August came back to me. It was mid-afternoon when the head of the man drifted in first. The body came in about a half an hour later. I remembered thinking that except for the decapitation, the body was not that badly ravaged. I think they wired the head onto the body for the funeral. I looked closely at the photographs taken from every conceivable angle. If there was something to see, the microfiche would show it.

I found nothing in the first set of photos, but in the batch where the coroner had flipped the body on it's stomach, I noticed an unusual pattern of scrapes on the right shoulder blade. I zoomed in and sure enough there it was. It could have been accepted as a few random scratches, but, having seen the Iroquois symbol, I knew it matched.

I went to another case. With a little scrutiny, I found it again, this time on the victim's left calf. I looked at yet another file, and made yet another discovery.

How could this be, and what did it mean? I began looking at all the files that were on record. It wasn't until the wee hours of the morning when I reached my bleary-eyed conclusion. Every body that had been recovered from the plunge basin had the helix marking somewhere on it, as well as the death smile. If a victim came from another part of the river, I could not find either one on the body.

Judd Blackadder and Charlie Knowales were at the Chippewa boat complex, loosening bolts and hatching a late night plan that would seal the fate of their expedition over Niagara. Judd's conversation with Knowales ran to how fortunate he was to have had a father who worked at the Seaway Authority and gave him access to such equipment as canal bridge transponders. That and being a Wellander which imbued him with the patience of a monk in a monastery.

CHAPTER SIXTEEN
LAMENTATIONS

On the eve of the maiden voyage of the Thrill Expedition, I had my last nightmare. I just found it hard to put much stock in these things. In this particular sequence there was a scarecrow in a hot air balloon flying over the Falls. The day was beautiful, sunny, not a cloud in the sky. Suddenly without warning, the sky turned black. Out of nowhere thick clouds rolled in, accompanied by the rumbling of thunder. Lightening lanced from above, striking the balloon several times but with no apparent effect. Rain lashed at the balloon and high winds buffeted it about the skies above the Falls. The scarecrow and the balloon rode out the storm unscathed. As the sky began to lighten, another kind of darkness blocked out the light. Hundreds of black-winged creatures filled the sky and began to descend on the balloon. These creatures had the wings and head of a vulture and the black hairy body of a monkey, an auxiliary army for the Wicked Witch of the West. Several of the creatures landed on the balloon and began clawing at it but the balloon withstood this assault. Not until one of the vulture heads dived-bombed the balloon from high above, was the outer skin of the balloon finally breached by a vultures beak.

The leaking balloon sank slowly to the rocky shore of the river. Once it crashed on land the vultures and rats from among the rocks swarmed over the balloon and savaged the scarecrow. Clothing and straw was torn, shredded, and scattered about. The vultures flew off, the rats crawled back under the rocks, but the scarecrow was no more. It was Wizard of Oz on PCP.

ENTRY IN THE DIARY OF CHARLES KNOWALES -- NIGHT BEFORE LAUNCH DAY -- I am afraid.

As for myself nine had never been a favorable number in the

past and when I conferred with a text on numerology and the stars the message I got was-BEFORE THIS DAY'S JOURNEY ENDS THE OTHER SIDE WILL BECKON-whatever the hell that meant. Could that be right? It had to be a mistake. For the life of me I couldn't think of a single soul on either side of the river-American or Canadian who would need to get in touch with me. And even if there was I expected to be too busy in the next 24 hours to take their call.

ANCIENT IROQUOIS PROPHESY:
(translated)
On a day when salt air swallows the fresh air
The god of thunder will rise from its lair
A mortal soul on such a day in such a place
Will become one with the hunter and touch its face

TUNNEL INSCRIPTION
Amen evil from us deliver but temptation
not us lead and us against trespass who
those forgive we as trespasses our us
forgive and bread daily our day this us give,
heaven in is it as earth on done be will thy
come kingdom thy name thy be hallowed
heaven in art who Father our.

I saw the light
Burning me
By Farrenheit

CHAPTER SEVENTEEN
JUDGEMENT DAY
Monday July 9th

Launch day dawned sunny and bright, warm but low in humidity. It was the kind of day you took a deep breath of fresh air and felt glad to be alive. Puffy ships of white, propelled by heaven's gentle breath, sailed triumphantly on seas of sky, never richer in texture and color. I wondered what made a sky so blue anyway. Was it the angle of the sun or the amount of ozone or just the whim and will of God? Was there a scientific explanation of just the right mixture of CO^2 and O^2 or was that just the hue of the creator's brush on that particular day? Whatever the reason, it was a magnificent blue, a blue that soothed the soul, a blue the very color of life itself. The white fleecy clouds danced merrily to this backdrop like innocent lambs. What struck me the most about such a day- a day when it made you feel like shouting out loud because you felt so good to be alive that it was hard to imagine that on such a day blood would flow and people would die. Yet I was as sure of that feeling as I was the back of my hand. Unfortunately for someone my CYFIC radar was almost always on target.

Below the picturesque sky, the river flowed as it had for the last few thousand years or so. It lay tranquil for now. Seductive in its sereneness. It was a side of its personality that I new well enough to know that it was just lying in wait. Soon enough it would get its blood up and then the dark side of the river-some say the real side-will come frothing to the surface. This would be the stage to the unfolding drama with millions of witnesses present for a sight that few would forget. This river was not a stranger to drama, but never before to an audience of such magnitude. Seagulls screamed out as if in warning. It was the day that everybody was waiting for. The day. The big day. Crunch time, as they say.

It started off with the closing of the City of Niagara Falls at nine o' clock in the morning, three hours before the epic ride was to take place. The city was literally being bombarded by automobiles. So many people and cars had flooded into the city that by nine a.m. there was just no more room left to accommodate anyone. Streets were turned into massive parking lots, and roads for miles outside the city limits were in a state of gridlock. At 8:30 am, a meeting had taken place at city hall between the Mayor and Ontario Provincial Police officials to assess the situation.

Reports were patched into city hall from police helicopters surveying the traffic. The reports were all the same. Streets were clogged. Traffic was immobile and backed up. In some cases cars were driving on lawns and through people's yards. Pilots flying over the northern approaches to the city reported that Highway 20 was backed up to Fonthill, 15 miles away. From the east, the QEW was backing up to St. Catherines. To the west, the QEW was clogged from Fort Erie across the Peace Bridge and into Buffalo, New Knowales. Buffalo itself was a real mess, as well as Niagara Falls, New Knowales, coming over the Rainbow bridge in a southerly approach. Side streets and back roads, leading off the main arteries, were also barely moving. Dunn Street, McLeod Road, Morrison Street, Montrose Avenue, Dorchester Road, and Stanley Avenue, all at a dead halt.

"Well, that's it," said the mayor. "In another hour, everything will be paralyzed. Everything will be at a complete stand still. In the interests of safety, we have no choice but to shut her down."

Police cruisers were dispatched to set up roadblocks five miles outside the city in all directions. But this action could not stop people from walking into the city. A few foot blisters were not going to deter most of these people bearing witness to the spectacle that they had waited so long and had come so far to see.

Once people realized that no more cars were being allowed in, the word traveled down the long line of stalled vehicles. Many pulled over to the side of the road and begin spilling out of their vehicles. Many others just abandoned their cars right in the roadways. It was a bizarre scene to say the least. It was almost like some biblical exodus. Masses of people, families, kids, even the elderly, streamed down the sides of highways past the long lines of empty, stranded vehicles, and it was a classic policeman's nightmare. The roads would remain in this tangled state until the wee hours of Tuesday morning.

Inside the city limits, traffic hadn't moved an inch for quite some time. Along the Niagara Parkway, people were sitting or laying on the roofs and hoods of their entrapped cars. The best vantage points -- that of Table Rock on the Canadian side and Prospect point on the American side -- had been claimed long ago. People had secured their spots by camping there for the last couple of days, some even longer.

In the next few hours, the hordes of people on foot would fill every viewing space on both sides of the river from Chippewa to the whirlpool past the Falls. This stretch held the thickest concentration, and in certain spots the crowd would be estimated to be over 100 deep. In this five mile stretch of river it was estimated that there were 4 million spectators. From the whirlpool down to Queenston, the concentration was not as thick, but still, both sides of the gorge were lined with people.

Grand Island was jammed with another quarter of a million.

On the Rainbow bridge were perched another 100 to 200 thousand people along with about 30 stranded cars, and officials were beginning to worry if the span could take the weight. Just how much weight the could the bridge tolerate? Nobody seemed to know. A call was put in to the city engineer's office.

Thousands of sightseers crammed the tops of the two towers in the scenic area, filling them to capacity thirty minutes after they opened to the public. People climbed into any space that afforded so much as a glimpse of the Falls. Every roof top of every house and building, all the way up to Clifton Hill, became a viewing platform. The same situation existed on the factories and buildings near the river on the American side. People were climbing into the branches of trees. Up above the Falls, the Goodyear blimp and its Canadian counterpart, the Pioneer, drifted lazily about. They would be joined by a battery of tour helicopters come launch time at 12:00 p.m.

The best estimates available placed the live audience at the astronomical figure of 9 million and upwards. That was just the live audience, mind you. Television cameras had been set up at every conceivable location along the route and in the air. The event would be broadcast on the three major American stations ABC, NBC, and CBS as well as CBC in Canada, and also various cable and satellite concerns.

A tremendous display of fireworks from both sides of the river would accompany the Hellion on its history making journey. As far as everyone could tell everything was set to go.

Except me.

I was in a quandary. A part of me wanted to call Sara Wilson to tell her what I had discovered the night before and implore her not to get on the Hellion. Another part of me wanted to say I was nuts for allowing myself to believe something so fantastic. I had gotten up later than I had originally planned. I was to be at the Skycrane's helipad at 11 am. Phil Stinson and I would take her up and I was to monitor the Hellion's journey from the air.

Still torn about what to do and with time getting short, I showered and dressed and flipped open the morning paper. The Monday edition usually caught me up on the events of the weekend. This particular edition was especially chock full of gore.

MAN KILLED IN BIZARRE BRIDGE ACCIDENT

In a bizarre accident at the Port Robinson bridge a car was caught on the rising bridge and crushed by the bridge's counterweight causing a fatal explosion. One man, the driver of the vehicle, identified as Laz Harrison was killed instantly. Harrison was employed as a commercial diver and had recently been hospitalized in Toronto, following a diving accident at Niagara Falls.

It didn't make sense. The man had been brain dead. What was he doing on that bridge? I called the hospital in Toronto and was put in touch with the attending physician, who informed me of Harrison's miraculous recovery.

"Do you know what he was up to?"

"He was very determined to get to Niagara Falls, that's for sure. I think he mentioned the name Knowales, and Wilson, yea, Sara Wilson. Said he had some thing of vital importance to tell them. He didn't say what and then he was gone."

I thanked the doctor and hung up. That all too familiar CYFIC feeling was beginning to build up inside of me. A body goes into the plunge basin and if it doesn't come up right away, it either doesn't come up at all or it comes up within whiskers of 72 hours with a death smile and a helix scratched into the skin. A man dives into the plunge basin and surfaces with an expression of horror and the mentality of a turnip, unexpectedly regains his senses against all known medical knowledge, and his first instinct is to return to Niagara Falls. He had to be going there to warn them about what he knew or had seen. Nothing else made any sense. And what a way to die. How bizarre was that?

I gathered from the news article that there wasn't enough left of Laz Harrison to search for a helix. I remembered that Judd's father had worked for the authority that controlled those bridges. I had decided to call Sara at her hotel when I came across another article in the Niagara Falls Gazette.

TOWER JUMPER IDENTIFIED

The man who jumped to his death on the Skylon Tower

on Wednesday July 4th was identified as Bela Rediens of
Quaker Road in Welland. It is believed that he is related
to a man who jumped over Niagara Falls early Saturday
morning. Witnesses say at about 2 am a distressed man
dressed in black committed suicide . A leg recovered from
the river later on Sunday is believed to have come from the
victim Kane Rediens, according to Niagara parks employee
Phil Stinson.

This was almost too much for my mind to digest. I knew
that this was no coincidence. There had to be a connection
between all these incidents and the trip over the Falls. But
what? Was the whole world going insane? I had to get hold
of Sara.

I called her room at the Sheraton. No answer. Too late. She
had probably already left for the Chippewa complex. I looked
at the clock. 1030.a.m. I had to get to the helipad myself. I'd
try to reach her from there.

The trip to the helipad was an interminable battle through
stalled traffic on clogged roads. Even the breakdown lanes
were blocked with abandoned vehicles. Numerous times,
when the terrain allowed it, I found myself driving in ditches
along the side of the road. I finally had to abandon my vehicle
at the floral clock on the Niagara Parkway and proceed the
last mile on foot.

It gave me time to think. Time was running out, and I
still didn't know what to make of everything. I thought of
the diver. What was he trying to warn them about? Is Judd
Blackadder somehow connected with him at the bridge? I've
lived here all my life and I'd never heard of such a thing at a
bridge. I thought about Tom Rees and the information he had
about the Indian maidens. I wondered if Charlie Knowales
knew anything about the helix.

Something told me that Charlie Knowales knew all about
maidens and helixes. I had to get to the helipad and fast, so
I ran as much as my arthritis would allow for the last half

mile.

I was 15 minutes late but Stinson hardly noticed.

He was running behind himself, and he was in a panic.

"We had a problem with the rotor," he said. "Get in and get situated, Ro. We're gonna get this sucker airborne in a few minutes."

"Phil, I gotta ask you something."

"Shoot."

"You were on duty this week in the gorge when the guy jumped early Saturday morning. Did you make a recovery?"

"Only the leg. The rest of him is still down there."

"That's all I wanted to know. Whenever you're ready let's take her up." I logged in on the computer and punched in Conrad. As I suspected there never was a book called Hellion by Joseph Conrad. Charlie Knowales's big recruitment speech was a bunch of baloney.

I got on the walkie talkie and patched over to the Chippewa complex as Phil fired up the engines on the big steel bird.

Blackadder answered.

"I have to talk to Sara Wilson, Judd. It's urgent!"

"Is it as urgent as the message from Laz Harrison?"

"You bastard!" I screamed into the headset. I knew without a doubt that Blackadder had had something to do with the diver's death. I knew that the two of them were so consumed with this project that not even murder was above them. And I knew that they had something in mind for Sara and that she was in grave danger. All the pieces of the puzzle were coming together and it was not looking good in our favor.

"You'll never get away with this," I sputtered.

"You just do your job and we'll worry about the rest." He hung up.

"Phil, we have to get to the Chippewa complex, now!"

"You're the boss."

The copter rose into the air and wheeled in the direction of the rising mist. The time was 11:30. We had to stop them somehow, if it wasn't already too late. They were probably boarding the Hellion.

We reached the Falls and the wash from our huge rotors cleared a path through the mist as we headed upstream. A half a mile away I could see figures on the gangplank. Paul Martin and Mark Young were in the lead. They disappeared inside the craft. I pulled out the binoculars.

Sara was next, followed by Knowales and Blackadder dressed in silver jump suits. There was something very suspicious in Knowales mannerisms. It was almost as if he were stalking Sara. I saw something in Knowales's hand flash in the sunlight. It was the snake head cane. I wanted to scream, but it was futile. I saw with horror as he removed the gold tip to expose a stiletto-like blade. All I could do was watch as he grabbed Sara's arm from behind, and slashed at her leg with the sharp pointed business end, then pushed her against the railing of the gangplank.

The railing collapsed all too easily and Sara spilled into the water and was caught in the current of the Upper Niagara.

How could I have been so stupid? So that was it. They had been planning to use Sara as a sacrifice all along. She was chosen for the project because of her Indian blood and her womanhood and now they were sending her over the Falls as an offering so that the Hellion would be guaranteed safe passage.

It was my guess that the cane was used to put a helix sign of the Falls on Sara's leg. The snake cane had never been purchased as a symbol of the river but for its wound inflicting capabilities. A real student of Indian lore would have known that the head was too fierce to be a water symbol, a small detail that Knowales the man who tried to make it his business to know everything had somehow overlooked. Regardless the plan had been executed. Afterward they would deny everything and say it was an accident. A faulty gangplank. As long as the expedition was a success they would be allowed to continue. It was simple and brilliant. I had to find a way to stop them and save Sara. But how? We didn't have any rescue equipment on board. I thought about my body harness down at the shack. It was worth a shot.

"Phil, we gotta go back to the gorge and get the body harness from the shack."

"Roger."

I called ahead to have someone there to throw it to us.

The stealthy waters of Niagara had coaxed Sara into the middle of the river and now drew her downstream. I figured she had about six minutes to live.

Then it happened.

An event that would change the entire complexion of this day. A news copter with pontoons came out of nowhere from the American side and was attempting to rescue her. In the meantime we raced down river, descended into the gorge, and picked up the body harness. We headed back to the Falls but it was apparent that the news copter was going to have first crack at Sara, coming at her from upriver.

By now, Sara was less than a half mile from the Falls and losing ground rapidly. If anybody was going to do something it was going to have to be quick. Word had spread among the surprised spectators, and the television crews around the Falls were beginning to shoot. The major networks were now carrying the unexpected turn of events as millions watched with disbelief, astonishment, and fascination. The sky began to fill with helicopters but none would be able to get to her in time.

"Make your play or get out of the way," I muttered under my breath.

As if the news copter had heard my plea, it maneuvered itself ahead of Sara and went in low to the river. The pontoons would allow it to land right on the water. Apparently, this was its plan of action. The pilot maneuvered his chopper ahead of Sara's hurtling form and began to descend to the river. Both the craft and Sara were two hundred yards from the crest when one of the chopper's rotor blades caught the surface of the river. The remaining blades were deflected into the water, and the force snapped the whole rotary blade system off at its mast. The blades cartwheeled for a bit as they thrashed and slashed in the current. The body of the chopper, upended and slammed into the river. Just before impact, a crewman was tossed through the open door.

Sara went careening by the downed and sinking craft, her body hardly any drag at all in the swift current.

She was now one hundred and fifty yards from death and closing fast.

It was our turn and Sara's last chance as Stinson brought his craft down to river level, its whirling rotor blades whipping at the white foaming water. We would be coming at her from the Falls side of the river and that meant we had only one chance to snare her with the harness. If we missed her or she us, she was a goner. Millions of people watched the unbelievable scene with bated breath. By now Sara was turning over and over in the treacherous waters and looked more drowned than alive. We threw the harness out of the craft and dangled it at water level. I prayed silently that Sara would have the strength to grab the harness and hold on. So far she had battled valiantly in the rough waters and must be near exhaustion. *When the waves turn the minutes to hours. Only in this case it was more like when the waves turn the minutes to seconds.*

"C'mon, Sara. Show me some of that spunk. Just one time. That's all we ask."

She was thirty yards from the brink. We were ten yards beyond the edge coming at her. It was going to be close. We were going to have to time it perfectly. Stinson got even lower. He was only ten feet above the surging rapids.

Twenty yards for Sara.

We were at the edge, the harness dangled in the foaming water.

Ten yards for Sara.

I was close enough to see her eyes, frightened but still battling to the end. The odds were against her but I knew she would never quit.

"That's the spirit." I could only mouth the words; there was no voice left in me.

Five yards.

The Maid of the Mist had been alerted and was gently circling below the raging waters in case there were survivors.

Two yards.

Sara seemed too lethargic from the numbing cold or exhaustion to make a try.

"You can do it," I gasped.

Suddenly Sara snapped out of her paralysis and made a grab for the harness. She missed.

"C'mon, c'mon. Try again," Stinson urged under his breath.

I was desperate and all out of options and I couldn't face losing this woman. I would be *damned* if I was gonna lose her. And so I turned to the only place I could think of for help. I didn't know all of the words but I said what I could remember with a little improvising.

"The Lord is my shepherd,

He leadeth me beside the still waters

Oh God do we need still waters now

Yea, though I walk through the valley of the shadow of death

I will fear no evil

For though art with me"

That's all I could remember and I hoped it was enough to cement a pact between us.

On the second and what would have been her last attempt, Sara caught hold of the harness with one hand. Just as the current was about to sweep her over the brink, she grabbed hold with her other hand.

"She's got it!" I yelled.

Stinson eased back on the stick, putting his copter into hover. At the brink of the Falls, more than 180 feet above the surface of the deadly cauldron below, the craft hovered as I reeled her into the cargo bay. When she was safely inside, the crowd around the Falls gasped a sigh of relief, then let out a tremendous ovation. It was an incredible storybook rescue to the nth power. It was like hitting the home run in the ninth inning with the bases loaded and two out. Sara had been snatched from the jaws of death, and the Falls screamed in furious rage.

But there was still more to come. The downed copter and its two crewman clinging to its side was being swept towards impending doom. The crowd which had just had its nerves wrung dry like a twisted towel, was going to have to go through it again. Some in the crowd fainted from the nervous tension.

The helicopter was pushed on its side by the swift flow, but the copter was not sinking downward as fast as it was being dragged forward. None of the other copters were going to be in time to effect a rescue. There was not much anyone could do except watch as the chopper and its two riders was dragged the last thirty yards to the edge of the Falls, then dumped over.

The screams of the plunging men could be heard even above the thunder of the waters. No one else made a sound. The remains of the chopper, which had gone over in the dead center of the Horseshoe, stayed intact for the plunge until it hit granite at the foot of the Falls. A fiery conflagration echoed off the walls of the gorge, bouncing around the giant amphitheater. The exploding gas tank showered the plunge basin with bits of metal. It was all over in a second. No one at the Falls could move.

It was a tragedy that no words could adequately describe. Helicopters that had arrived too late to be of assistance now circled above the Falls like steel vultures over a dead animal. The vision of the screaming faces of the plunging men would always be engraved in the memories of those who had seen it. There was blood in the water and the sharks had gotten what they came for. It would always be a graphic tribute to the power and legacy of the beast. The Falls roared mightily in triumph.

On board the Skycrane, I hugged Sara out of sheer joy. She could hardly talk and when she did it was barely a squeak.

"You sure picked one hell of a time to finally save someone from this river, but I'm glad you did."

"You didn't think I was going to let an Indian blood sister down, now did you?"

Before I wrapped her up in the blanket, she showed me her leg where Knowales had slashed through her suit and crudely cut a helix into the skin.

I patched into Charlie Knowales on my headset. It was just him and me, one on one.

"I fell for your Hellion baloney but you're not gonna get away with this you know."

"Get away with what Ro? Sara was an accident, the railing was faulty. Accidents happen."

"What about the mark on her leg?"

"Must have been a scrape she received when she fell."

"Don't play games. You knew all along about her Indian blood and the sign of the Falls.

"I make it my business to know all kinds of things, especially when it's connected to this project. You should know that."

Well, your plan failed. There isn't going to be an Indian sacrifice to protect you. Sara, your sacrificial lamb, is aboard the Skycrane with me, safe and sound.

And here's a piece of information I'd be willing to bet you don't know. Kane Rediens jumped over the Falls two and a half days ago. His body still hasn't come up. He's down there in that plunge basin waiting for you."

Knowales' silence crackled with fear, and his voice was weak with it. "That's just conjecture on your part. You can't possibly know that."

"I guess you'll find out, won't you?" The headset went dead. I felt the back of my hand. CYFIC.

Pandemonium erupted at the Chippewa complex. The

engineers in the dock area had been watching the whole episode on a small portable television. They had cheered proudly and enthusiastically when their man Phil Stinson had executed a rescue of a dynamic magnitude, but they too were stunned and shocked at the following turn of events. The passengers in the Hellion had not had the benefit of a television screen but Blackadder had been in contact with ground control in the truck trailer at the Table Rock parking lot. The tragic news came filtering across the radio. An announcement came over the loudspeakers in the dock complex. "Attention all personnel, this trip is cancelled. I repeat, this trip is canceled. Abort all preparation procedures."

"The hell it is," yelled Blackadder. Blackadder was the only one in the craft not yet strapped into his seat, while all the others had been prepped and sealed for the expedition. Blackadder went over to the plexiglass hatch.

When he smelled the salt it came as no surprise. He had smelled it before. He knew what it meant. The Falls was waiting for them. It didn't matter. His blood was up. He closed the hatch screwing the turn-wheel on the inside tight.

"What are you doing?" Knowales exploded.

"What do you think?" said Blackadder.

"Didn't you hear what ground control said? Two people died up ahead. There's not going to be trip. They aborted it." The dynamics of this venture had changed for him because of Rediens. He realized that there was a real possibility that he might not survive this expedition and Knowales wanted to use the accident as a way to get out of this whole mess.

"What happened up ahead has nothing to do with us," Blackadder said. "We've come this far and were going all the way."

Blackadder raised Nate Kurtz at the Table Rock operations center. "Nate, stand by. Get in touch with the Maid of the Mist and tell her to clear away. We're coming over."

"Hey, I thought..." but Nate was talking into static.

"We're going as scheduled," Blackadder said with as

much emotion as a block of ice. Then, with a flick of his wrist, the engines roared to life. He had ripped out the communications so there would be no further attempts to stop the craft. Knowales unstrapped his seat belt and tried to get up. Blackadder pushed him back in his seat grabbed his cane and snapped it over his knee. Knowales was virtually helpless without it. Knowales's faithful servant had risen up and was taking control. The loyal lapdog was now the master. A momentum was driving him on. The patience of a Wellander had come to its end.

"Sit back and enjoy the ride Charlie. This isn't going to be like Jag Rock, There aren't going to be any ropes over the side," smirked Blackadder.

"What do you mean by that?" A stunned Knowales could barely spit out the words.

"You foolish, foolish man. All these years and you never knew the truth. You always thought Rediens had something to do with the accident and he always blamed you but it was me. I threw the rope over the side and it caused the Ark to flip that day at Jag Rock."

You but why? What did you hope to gain?"

"I guess I just hoped to shake things up a little, shuffle the deck if you will. We were all getting a little too comfortable with each other. Of course no one could have predicted the outcome. It was all a crap shoot Don't forget I was putting myself at risk, but I guess I thought it was worth the gamble. Anyway looks like the dice came up snake eyes because as things worked out, it got us here didn't it? To this day and place and that isn't so bad is it?

"All these years that I trusted you like a brother and you could look me in the eye knowing you were responsible for the death of my brother. You're insane...," Knowales tried once again to struggle to his feet to get to Blackadder, but again it was futile without the cane.

He was also met with a backhand across the face from Blackadder.

"If you don't want me to do that again I suggest you relax and buckle up."

Knowales, bleeding from the lip and where he had bit his tongue slumped back sullenly in his seat, eyes filled with hate and bewilderment.

"Besides who are you to pass judgment on me? You're the one that's crazy, pining away for your brother all these years, obsessed with revenge. Well it was that revenge that got us this far and after this voyage is over even you will think that it is worth a life, maybe even two or three. Besides, not a half an hour ago you were willing to trade Sara Wilson's life for your ambitions and two other people just died up there and you don't seem to be too concerned about that. So don't get all sanctimonious on me. You're only worried now because your skin is on the line."

"That's right didn't you hear? Rediens is down there in the plunge basin."

Well if Rediens is down there that means he is dead and I haven't seen the day yet when I was afraid of a ghost. Besides regardless of where Rediens is, the shine he's got is for you, not me."

"What about the ghost of C.J. Carpentier?"

The name was enough to produce a moment's hesitation but then Blackadder's mind seem to dismiss it equally as quickly. "That's long forgotten. That was twenty years ago.

"You didn't think I knew about that chapter of your life, did you?"

"Yea, yea, here's where you tell me you make it your business to know everything that concerns you. So what. It's ancient past. Dead and buried."

That's just it. It's not buried. The only thing in his grave is a foot. The body was never recovered. You might have known that if you had bothered to go to the funeral. And if he's down there, the only one he's got a shine for is you, my friend."

"Enough of this superstitious nonsense."

"You don't understand...."

Blackadder quickly cut him off, "Enough. We're going."
"Have it your way."
That's right it will be my way for the rest of this trip. You are no longer in control of what happens aboard this craft."

The Hellion eased from the dock and prepared to enter the river. A group of confused engineers raced to the end of the dock, waving for the craft to come back. I watched as Blackadder flashed them a thumbs up sign, accompanied by a big confident grin. It was unreal. Insanity. If it hadn't felt like it was all a bad dream, I would have found myself laughing hysterically at the whole chain of events. We couldn't believe it when we saw the Hellion leave from Chippewa, and decided we might as well accompany her.

But now it was time for serious business.

Blackadder began the regimen of activating the craft's mechanisms. He would be doing somewhat of a solo without the benefit of the now deposed communications. But everything else would be the same. He knew that all the tracking stations would continue to monitor him. He looked up, wondering where the Skycrane was. A loud thundering answered him. Phil Stinson had received a communique from the ground control that the mission was in progress against orders, but since no one could stop it now he might as well lend it his escort. When word spread that the Hellion was in the river, other helicopters fell behind.

"Pressurizing cabin and air channel. Lowering external outrigging, " came Blackadder's announcements from up front.

The crowd at the top of the river stared in disbelief as the Hellion made her appearance in the river, exactly on the scheduled time. After the disappointing news of the tragedy and a possible cancellation, the crowd surged forward and a tremendous cheer rose from both shores. The television people were having a field day. More drama would keep their audiences with their noses pressed to their televisions.

It was exactly 12 p.m. Time to go.

Blackadder aimed the craft down river and proceeded forward. The noisy airborne procession of helicopters rumbled forward, many with cameras mounted to film the action. The crowds on both sides of the river cheered wildly. On both sides of the river, the sea of humanity waved, rocked and swayed as the impressive procession thundered down the river to its appointment with destiny. The crowd was getting what it had come to see and more. Fireworks on both sides of the river exploded on cue as the Hellion passed by. It was a spellbinding sight, one that no one was likely to ever forget.

From inside of the copter, the spectacle of the masses was awe-inspiring. It was as if they were crusading knights, parading through the streets of a city on the way to do battle. Even I had to admit that I was caught up in the emotion of it all. So many people brought together at one time by one singular event. Everyone with the same thoughts on their mind, unified in emotion and anticipation. It was happening. It was really happening.

The craft pressed onward. The choppers marched behind. The crowd at the Falls waited. The electronically connected world waited. The Falls waited. Niagara always waited but when the time was right, she would strike with deadly venom like a coiled rattlesnake. *When the waves turn the minutes to hours.*

And Kane Rediens waited. He waited with the ancient evil that was all around him and in him. He could sense that his hated adversary was coming closer. Soon he would be within his reach. He would not escape Kane Rediens' wrath this time. Soon Knowales would be one with him. He was coming to join him in his world of unimaginable terror.

The craft continued to surge ahead. They were now encountering the fury of the rapids. The craft jostled like a piece of sea-tossed driftwood.

Paul Martin spoke into an onboard recorder "It is an incredible sight. We can barely hear ourselves think with all this noise. The roar of the water. The helicopters thundering overhead. The onboard engines. We see the multitudes on the side of the river, frenzied in their waving and exhortation, but we cannot hear them. The noise of all the engines drowns them out. But we know that they are cheering, which makes it all seem like some crazy kind of soundless pantomime. They have been incredible and have not let up for a minute since we left Chippewa. I can feel the power of the river now as we enter some rapids, and it tosses us about like we were riding the bucking of an untamed horse. I can feel a respect for this flow of water, and I am sure it has been instilled in all of my comrades. I also admit to a fear, a gnawing fear in the pit of my stomach, as I watch the skyscraper of mist ahead of us draw nearer and nearer, knowing that what lies ahead will be greater than anything I have experienced before. It is too late to turn back now, and I pray to God for deliverance."

More announcements from Blackadder. "Am shutting off the engines now and retracting the outrigging. I would suggest that you all check your seatbelts one last time to make sure everything is secure. Estimated time of arrival is about one minute."

The craft barreled forward. Her pace was unhesitating as she charged bravely ahead to meet the challenge of the "beast."

Knowales had been completely quiet for the duration of the trip but his brain was ticking away like a time bomb. Once Blackadder had shut off the engines, he could tell by the track the river was taking them on that they were headed for a point about one third the distance from the Canadian shore, which would ultimately take them to the deepest part of the plunge basin. It would be a smooth drop into the deep water. That much he knew. The rest was all a muddle. Thoughts of the past few days and even further back kept popping up in is head. Confused thoughts. Seemingly unconnected thoughts, but yet somehow all tied together by the thinnest of silk strands. His boyhood nightmares. His recent premonitions. The legends and curses of the Falls. The plunge basin formation.

That sometimes the river never yields its dead. Where do the bodies go? The mysterious wave. His boyhood accident. The enduring hatred it caused. And now the suicide, here at Niagara. No body was recovered. For all he knew, Kane Rediens was still under the Falls somewhere. His last thoughts were of his brother Ryan. What a waste. He should have let Ryan rest in peace, but he just couldn't. He missed him so much. Ryan had never done anything to hurt anybody in his entire life. He had never done anything but be a good kid and the best brother in the whole world. Why had God taken him, yet let Roger Woodward live. He should have let it go. He had let the vengeance over the memory of his brother turn him into a festering ball of poison and consume his life. Now, finally he was being forced to confront his demons. Now it was time to be done with it. There was no looking back now.

They were almost there. Ahead lay Niagara.

Niagara! They were about to enter the cathedral of the Thunder god.

Arguably Niagara Falls is the most visited and photographed natural phenomenon on the face of the earth. Fifteen million people a year come to gaze on her timeless torrential beauty. They come from every corner of the globe, twelve months of the year, to behold a visual panorama unparalleled by mortal architecture. Even God himself must have stood back and marveled at this breathtaking amphitheater, which only He could have designed.

The very brink of the Falls reaches almost a mile in width in a curved crescent of a horseshoe, the only one of its kind known to man, resulting in an omnipresent mist which towers skyward. It reaches 178 feet at its highest point, but its height is dwarfed by its immense width. Two hundred and fifty million cubic feet of water flow over its precipice in a single hour, every hour. It is this constant incredible volume that sets it apart from any other waterfall yet discovered and creates an illusion of a never-changing picture, the flow of water appearing as permanent columns. The effect of immobility produced by this vast flow is similar to the effect that the rapidly spinning spokes of a carriage or stagecoach wheel, makes the wheel appear to be going backward, even though you know the horses are drawing the coach forward.

Over the years, the action and force of the water have ripped through the slate and bedrock like a buzz saw, causing the actual Falls to recede at a rate of five feet a year and carving a gorge seven miles long in the earth's crust. Some of the water' s might has been harnessed to turbines, which ignite neon in New York City, some 700 miles away.

Long before you see it, you feel its dull, distant roar. Niagara is beckoning to come see. You can smell its soapy detergenty odor hanging in the air. Then the rising veil of the mist is visible, hovering above the Falls like a shroud. Then finally the deluge itself, cascading onto the depths below. It is said that the best place to truly appreciate the Falls is from the Table Rock venue, which abuts the Falls on the Canadian side. Here, one can get devastatingly close to the brink without actually going over, a mere guardrail between you and the unthinkable. You can see the violent surge of the upper river, right to the bottom of the striated riverbed below thirty feet of window clear water, and the plunge of the surf flying with white foam. The mist is as thick as rainfall and the roar, deafening.

To really know Niagara as the natives do, is to know its incredibly deadly power. And fear it.

There is a small photography booth on Clifton Hill where tourists can have a novelty picture taken of themselves going over a mock Niagara in a barrel. Naturally there is much joking and laughter as would-be conquerors mount the barrel for their snapshot. Yet if the scene were to actually come alive, I doubt that many would be quite so irreverent. The real Niagara would make them pay dearly for their mockery. In this booth an actual size barrel dominates the scaled-down backdrop of the Falls. These proportions could not be more opposite, for that barrel would be a mere buffalo on the vast plains of the real Falls.

Throughout history, men have dangled above Niagara on tightropes, sailed below her on boats, strode upon her frozen expanse in winter, and challenged the very teeth of her fury, by rafting her crest in all manner of jury-rigged contraptions.

Most of these men had no fear.

Most of these men died at Niagara.

"ETA. Twenty seconds," Blackadder yelled. The intense excitement had even infected his voice.

Paul Martin spoke into the recorder, his words choppy and breathless. "It's overwhelming. The fear mounts inside me by the second. The crowd at the brink resembles delirious pandemonium. The mist is getting thicker, but I can still see the two observation blimps hovering over the gorge…We are surrounded by a wall of noise…My heart is racing…I can see the brink now."

The fireworks climaxed with huge booms and flashes of color.

"We are going over!"

The craft teetered for a second at the brink, pointed her nose downward and was swallowed by a mouth of mist and spray. Inside the craft, the daylight was blotted out by the shadow of the enveloping Falls.

Martin made a silent sign of the cross.

Knowales'saw the malevolence in the mist and wondered what it would feel like to be dead. Blackadder also saw the image. No one else did.

Someone screamed.

The craft plunged downward.

Upon the violent jolting impact, the recorder failed. There would be no further record of what was to come. After the initial jarring, the craft sailed into the depths of the plunge basin, impelled by a heavy hand from above. This hand held the craft down deep in the depths and immobile.

Once the craft disappeared from sight, a hush of silence befell the onlookers. The copters whirled above, like seagulls waiting for the reappearance of a submerged whale. Every human and camera eye was focused on the waters below the Falls for a sign of life. The Maid of the Mist patrolled an area of the river, a couple hundred of yards away from the plunge basin, trying carefully to stay out of the way of the expected region of re-emergence. Still, she wanted to be in close proximity should she be called on in case of some emergency.

The watch and wait was on.

On the tracking monitors in the Skycrane and at Table Rock, the craft was being followed intensely. So far, all seemed well. One hundred and eighty feet under the surface, Knowales opened his eyes to more darkness. He was fooled by the darkness and his immediate impression was that he was dead, but he couldn't be. He didn't feel dead. He ran his hands over his face. He could feel it. He could feel it! He was alive! Incredulous as it had seemed to him, they had beaten the beast. Blackadder had been right. The nightmares. Everything. They didn't mean a thing. They had survived!

Blackadder switched on the interior lights. Unaccustomed to the sudden brightness, the passengers blinked in an effort to see. Each one surveyed the condition of the others.

"Everyone okay?" someone asked. Gradually the realization began to set in, the broad smiles beginning to crease the faces of the passengers.

"We did it!" they exalted. "We made it! We're alive!"

Up front Young and Martin shook hands and patted each other on the shoulders.

"It's not over yet," Blackadder warned, coldly. The water foamed and rushed around them. Blackadder snapped on the craft's underwater lights as the engines sputtered to life. The going would be slow, as they could only see but a few feet in front of them. Also it would take time for the engines to overcome the strong underwater current. Gradually the craft started to inch forward, breaking free of the grip that was holding it in place. The craft and crew had been submerged for seven minutes.

On the surface it seemed like seven hours. In the Skycrane Phil Stinson was cursing the fact that the communications had been severed.

"Those damn fools! At least we would be able to determine if they were okay. Now all we can do is wait. Hold on, what's this?" The stationary green dot on his monitor screen began to move slightly. "They're moving! Cliff are you picking it up? I detect some movement! I think they might be okay! Judd is probably firing up the engines."

"Roger, I got some movement too," replied Nate Kurtz from Table Rock. "If all goes well, they should be up in about five or six minutes."

But all would not go well.

It was a strange new world that the crew of the Hellion was witnessing underneath the Falls. The swift current and the forever crushing columns of water, which had hewn the massive cavern out of the granite, also prevented any growth of plant life. One look at this realm of the subterranean and there was no doubt that one was in the lair of the god of thunder. This was where the unknowing crossed the Iroquois river of Styx. Most species of aquatic life that could live in these waters chose more peaceful domains. It was like being in a giant rock-floored void. In many places the action of the water had worn the granite surface smooth, but in others, there were jagged juttings of rock, still waiting for nature to apply its knife. At one juncture there appeared to be the remains of a boiler, probably from a ship and around it butterflies of light. As the Hellion passed over, Blackadder flicked a switch on the console, but only after he'd made sure that no one was looking. Spirits on the craft were running high as the engines gunned away from the Falls. The craft seemed to be moving easier now as it put some distance between it and the base of the Falls.

Then the engines died.

"I've lost power," shouted Blackadder. " The engines just

quit on me. I can't believe it." Blackadder repeatedly tried the engine switch. No response. The engines were completely dead. Snuffed out like a candle. A sick feeling began to grow in the pit of his stomach.

"No matter," said Blackadder, " there's no reason to panic. We're beyond most of the pull of the plunge basin and the craft will drift to the surface on its own. So let's just stay calm and wait it out."

But instead of rising, the craft continued to move forward. She had no power but something was causing it to move forward. It was not an aimless current because it seemed to have a sense of direction. Now, Blackadder regretted smashing the communication system. The lights continued to play on the rocky river floor as streams of bubbles and pockets of air floated by. Nervous anticipation and fear began to infect the crew. The air inside the cabin was heavy with the smell of salt.

The lights fell on an uprising rock. It was surprisingly large as compared to the relative barrenness of the rest of the river bed. But it wasn't just a mass of rock.

"It looks like a cave of some sort," Knowales blurted. The craft continued to be drawn through the mouth of the sepulcher. What happened next was a blur of reality. An aberration of the explainable. A journey into insanity. The lights began to play on images of dead bodies in various stages of decay. There was bone and skulls and rotting skin, somehow all attached in a oneness. It was an inferno on a scale not even the imagination of Dante could have conjured.

Whatever it was, it was alive and it was coming at them. The crew stood frozen by the sight of it, the blood in their veins running to ice. The conglomeration of decomposed tissue, bone, and fungus all fused together, surrounded the craft in its lair and tried to attack it. Hundreds of bodies and body parts, melded together by a fungus, converged on the craft.

Now Knowales knew where all of the unrecovered bodies

went. They became part of this organism of death. In fact, the hunter thrived as it preyed on the endless supply of victims sent its way by the cataract. The cold temperatures at this depth were responsible for slowing the rate of degeneration of the bodies. But still, the organism was always in a state of decay. Time and water tended to erode it. That is why it needed to seek new material to renew itself.

The entity assimilated the bodies into its being, as it was now trying to do with the craft. A kaleidoscope of cadaverous faces from the beginning of time paraded before the craft's plexiglas windows. Each visage was a gruesome contortion of features, reflecting the agony and horror that the victim had felt at the time of his death. Many faces were frozen in a soundless scream. Others had hideous smiles of death ingrained. Some were clothed, some were in rags, others were completely naked. There were even some carcasses of dogs, cats, and other animals in the melange. Somewhere in the mix was the remains of C. J. Carpentier. Blackadder may have been a Wellander but so were Carpentier and Kane Rediens-a fact that may have escaped him until now and they were about to reap the rewards of their patience.

The whole scene was more than human sanity could withstand. Most of the crew could only manage to gape in utter terror, before their retinas detached and they were rendered blind. When the entity sensed that it could not penetrate the highly developed materials of the Hellion, it issued an unearthly shriek from its ancient soul, so low and guttural that it could have come from hell itself. It was enough to suck the breath out of any living lung, to penetrate and shatter the hearts of everyone onboard the Hellion much like the correct frequency of a tuning fork can shatter glass.

But before he died, Knowales saw the distorted face of Kane Rediens. It was also the face of the "beast" eye to eye. Even though he tried desperately not to look he was riveted to the sight of Rediens.

Kane was smiling at him with taunt lips over a toothless

grin and looking at him with eyeless sockets. The horns on the sides of his head were more prominently featured than they had ever been before.

Loose strands of optic nerve floated in the pits of the empty sockets. The smile was an evil smile of triumph.

It was a smile of death. It was a perfect Dr. Sardonicus smile. Oh, if only the neighborhood kids could have seen this. It was the perfect horror story ending. Knowales took that final image with him to his grave. Once again Lucky had had the last laugh.

Phil Stinson, up in the Skycrane, was getting impatient, along with the rest of the world. The green blip on his tracking monitor had stopped moving.

"They should have been up by now. What are they doing anyway? What's going on down there?" Frustration and worry in his voice was plainly evident. His thoughts were interrupted by Nate Kurtz. "They're rising now! They're coming up!"

In a short two minutes that played like an eternity, the Hellion and its crew broke the surface and bobbed languidly on the water. It was the ascension everyone had waited so long for.

And still there was no movement from inside.

The craft slowly drifted downstream. The Maid of the Mist nosed in to intercept her. The craft was brought alongside the Mist and a couple of crewmen boarded the floating capsule. They had to cut their way through the top hatch. A man entered with a walkie-talkie. The next transmission was agonizing to Phil Stinson's ears.

"They're gone! They're all gone."

There were no bodies in the craft . Only a couple piles of salt on the floor. Had they been DNA tested which they never were, they would have matched the genetic material of Young and Martin.

Knowales and Blackadder had vanished completely. The chaff from the wheat had been harvested.

CHAPTER EIGHTEEN
AFTERMATH

Seventy two hours after he had jumped over Niagara Falls, the blackened severed body of Kane Rediens resurfaced. Entangled with him were the missing bodies of Charlie Knowales and Judd Blackadder. Their bodies were also blackened but, except for the death smile and some spiral scratches, they were untouched. Before the bodies were taken out of the river, they bobbed together on the surface of the water as though they were all dancing one last jig.

The funerals were closed-casket. Not even the coroner could fix the faces. The Niagara death smile can't be erased, even by modern science. No autopsy was ever able to determine what caused the deaths. There were only the exploded hearts, the horror-contorted faces of the dead, and the shattered dreams. Later it was decided that Knowales' body would burn in the fires of cremation. Blackadder and Rediens were buried in Niagara Falls cemetery in separate locations.

Long ago I learned that you have to accept what the river gives you. It was my grandfather's credo, "Work hard, take what the river gives you, and make the best of it." By that token, I don't consider myself to be a hero although Sara might tend to disagree. I was just in the right place when the river and, ultimately, it's creator decided not to take a life.

In the end Charlie Knowales never did leave his mark as he intended. The world doesn't much recognize second place finishes never mind outright failure. His desperate attempt to catch lightening by the tail burned both his dreams and his life in its backflash. Ironically the name he had chosen for his craft Hellion actually meant to stir up trouble and he certainly did that and more. He challenged the heavens by waving his red flag in the face of God and he paid the price for doing so. Charlie Knowales would also be the first to tell you that the old Indian saying was right. You can't legislate life's heroics, they just kind of happen on their own. Besides the reality of it is that most of us do our living and dying in relative obscurity anyway. And what's so bad about that. Sometimes I think that maybe the simple way is the best way to go. There's a lot to be said for the uncomplicated joy of a bright summer morning or the love of a good woman.

I learned that perhaps Sara is right. You can't escape your destiny no matter how many tricks you try to employ . Our fate is in the hands of some power so great we mortals can't even begin to fathom its greatness. Evil and goodness come in many shapes and forms and in Sara Wilson I certainly came in contact with the essence of goodness. I have no doubt when her time comes (thank God it didn't come on my watch) flowers will grow on her grave (the sign of a good soul). By the way one month after they were buried weeds appeared on the graves of both Blackadder and Rediens even though they were in different parts of the cemetery. Even Sara had to concede that maybe there was something more to this than mere superstition. And although I have adopted more of Sara's point of view I still carry my four leaf clover. What the hell – I'm part Irish and sometimes old habits just die hard. But I'm not one to go back on my promises either. I'll always keep the bond I forged in those desperate moments above the Falls when Sara's life hung in the balance and I will never forget who really saved her that day but the way I figure it; these days have got to be pretty busy ones even for Him – He's got plenty of other sheep to look after and since I'm already back in the fold maybe I can help Him out a little by throwing a bit of luck His way.

The river also taught me to accept the mystery of the plunge basin, although that's as far as I ever took it. The secret will not pass my lips. In the end no one ever thought to look under the Falls for the answer. That's the trouble with the world today, no one takes the time to look below the surface. No one believed that there was anything under there. As far as you or I know, the horror still exists. It lies waiting…waiting… waiting…

POSTSCRIPT

Three weeks after the tragedy of the Thrill Expedition, I was feeling a little depressed and went down to the river to think. I was down by my hut where everything that passes over the Falls usually ends up when, lo and behold, what comes floating by but a black book with the helix symbol on the cover, just like the one in Tom Rees' office. So I fished it out all soggy and dripping wet, careful not to damage it, treating it just like it was a body.

It was the missing copy of the account from Rees grandfather, describing the lost Huron gold. In the back were handwritten notes that I recognized immediately.

Judd Blackadder's.

Suddenly, I realized a lot of things. Blackadder knew about the gold all along. His father worked for the Seaway Authority and was always coming into possession of unique nautical articles. I can only speculate that is how Judd came by a copy of the Indian gold. It also explains his obsession with the Thrill venture. Most people, myself included, thought that it was his loyalty to Charlie Knowales. Knowales was driven by his obsession to avenge his brother, but now, as it turns out, Blackadder had his own agenda all along. It was his greed that drove him to mutiny and finally murder, to prevent any disruption of the Thrill expedition.

You see, Blackadder had a plan to recover the gold at the bottom of the plunge basin using the Hellion. He had a powerful electromagnet installed under the belly of the Hellion. That was the stainless steel panel we had all seen in the drydock before the test run. As indicated by his notes, every time the Hellion went into the plunge basin he would energize the electromagnet, and it would attract some of the gold because of its high iron ore content. As the Hellion progressed down river, Blackadder would take it by the Maid of the Mist dock to an area where a rock shelf protruded out into the river. In these shallow waters he had installed an electronic sensor system.

When the Hellion passed over, a sensor in the river would trigger a sensor on the electromagnet, releasing whatever gold had been picked up on that run. Later Blackadder would recover it from the shallower waters of the shelf. It was simple yet beautiful in its simplicity.

So as always, I decided to take what the river would give to me. I decided that fishing would be a great hobby in my retirement. I bought a heavy duty fishing rig, like the kind they use to take marlin and other deep sea species out of the ocean. No one seemed to notice that instead of a hook and bait I dropped line with a small but powerful magnet. Over the next four months, I could be found fishing in the gorge.

A lot.

And always at the same spot.

Sometimes the Maid of the Mist would go by loaded with passengers and I would smile and wave and go back to my fishing. I blended right in with the whole facade of Niagara as far as anyone was concerned. To the tourists I was just a guy fishing on the river, as long as you didn't look below the surface and see what was really going on, or realize that at the end of the day there was never any fish in my catch basket, only a few strange looking black rocks. In four months time, I figured I pulled out close to a half a million dollars, which was returned to Tom Rees and the Iroquois on the reservation, which they used to fund their social skills integration center.

Of that I received a twenty percent finders fee. Near the end of my fishing, I snagged a rather unusual object. It was the top half of Knowales' golden snake headed cane. Now it was just a symbol of failure. I held a little private service.

"Now I commit thee to the deep. Ashes to ashes, dust to dust."

Then I threw the instrument back into the river where it belonged.

On the battlefield of good and evil. Armageddon.

Like I said it was getting cold, so I thought I'd take the wife up on my years of promises and head south.

"One day" finally came for us.

And go, we did. Where time and the weather were never relative. In the end there were plenty of rescues to go around. The Iroquois would get their social center and there was no telling how many lives that would salvage. My wife was rescued from a life of worrying about me on the treacherous waters of the Niagara River.

We threw away our watches bought a boat in the Florida Keys, christened her The Ark Angel, stocked her with a couple bottles of Niagara's Icewine and just basked in the warmth of an embracing sun, toasting all the while to being alive. And I rescued myself from the cold northern winters and the insanity of a maelstrom that swirled around a waterfall.

In the end I was right, the whole thing had been one helluva ride indeed.

To those of you who still remain in the valley of the river of the snake. CYFIC.

THE END

One's purpose on earth is not to own or control the natural world but to deepen one's character and to realize spiritual truth in one's own life.

Arthur Versluis - Sacred Earth

GENESIS: IN THE BEGINNING

A waterfall. One of the most powerful forces on the face of our planet and ironically it all starts with a single drop of water. It is a miracle that is conceived of the smallest of elements in the same way that human conception is forged from a single cell. It would have started like many of life's odysseys, innocent, pure and simple as the untainted mind of a baby. Its evolution into the complex entity of the present would have been gradual but no less dramatic than a theory of a Big Bang.

Two parts hydrogen and one part oxygen. Water. At first, a single droplet, either from on high or from below the ground. Whatever its origination, its destination was always the same: the vast eternal sea.

That first drop would have been particularly ambitious. Using elevation and gravity it would have needed to be extremely discerning in choosing a path of least resistance, lest it run dry before joining up with others of a like mind. This coagulation was the key to survival because there was strength in numbers. A successful marshaling of forces produced trickles, rivulets and springlets. As more water was collected ponds were established and the overflow became streams; all the while striving to create a main flow in the direction of the ocean. Stragglers in the near proximity seemed to detect the determination of this main flow and melded with it.

As the welding of droplets continued, reinforced from ground and sky, the scale of the entity created grew to the form of river and lake. A river's purpose was to be the highway between lakes, filling some and draining the excess of others but always advancing to the sea. Usually the initial overflow from a lake is gentle and meandering not unlike the slow tentative first steps of a toddler. Its progress is a match for the terrain that runs in its proximity. But as a river's accompanying terrain turns more confident so does the pace of both river and toddler. Soon both find the need to stretch their wings and test their limits. A steeper track equals an all-out run.

Then for no apparent reason like a youngster's temper tantrum, the terrain turns angry. So does the water. Steep and rocky begat swift and turbulent. The water starts to growl and snarl and spit white foam voicing its disposition as a young man asserts his independence. And much like a man, the older it gets and the longer it goes, the grumpier it's demeanor is likely to be.

If this is allowed to continue, violence is on the horizon. The conspiracy of swift current and gravity is now wild, bloodthirsty and out of control. It does not think or sympathize or respect but sweeps everything within its grasp regardless of stature or reputation to a humble inevitability.

Before that it explodes in a conflagration of sunlight, mist, air and descent. A final cannon blast from the heights into the deepest recesses of an apocalypse. At Niagara, this is where evil's seed germinates. Darkness. Undercurrent. Destruction. Followed by a period of peace, tranquillity and transcendation. Then rebirth, resurrection and immortality when the droplet finally reaches the great expanse of the sea.

CHRONOLOGY OF HIGHLIGHTS AT NIAGARA FALLS

11,000 B.C. - The Falls is formed at the Lewiston-Queenston site.

1500 - The Falls carves its way upriver to its present location.

1570 - The Iriquois have established permanent settlements in the Niagara region.

1615 - Etienne Brule is believed to be the first white man to view the Falls, although he leaves no written account.

1678 - Father Louis Hennepin describes the Falls in the first published record.

1753 - The Cave of the Winds is discovered behind the Falls.

1763 - The Senaca Indians under Chief Pontiac, ambush British soldiers at Devil's Hole, a few miles from Lewiston. Ninety soldiers are thrown to their deaths over the gorge.

1812 - During the War of 1812, American forces are repelled in the Battle of Lundy's Lane.

1825 - The Erie canal is built.

1827 - Niagara Falls museum is founded.

1827 - The first stunt is performed at the Falls as the Michigan is sent over with animals aboard.

1832 - The Welland canal which allows ships to bypass Niagara Falls is completed.
1833 - The Terrapin tower is built on Goat Island.

1837 - The American paddle steamer, the Caroline is attacked and sent burning over the Falls.

1838 - The first steam powered railway is in operation on the American side of the gorge.

1841 - The first railway on the Canadian side is built from Queenston to Chippewa.

1844 - Niagara's water power is utilized by Joseph Schoellkopf's plant.

1846 - The first Maid of the Mist is launched.

1848 - An ice jam causes the Falls to go dry for a day.

1841 - The first bridge built across the Niagara River is located at the whirlpool rapids, constructed by Charles Ellet.

1850 - The Table Rock overhang crashes into the river.

1855 - John Roebling constructs the first railway bridge across the river.

1859 - Blondin arrives at the Falls for a series of tightrope stunts.

1861 - The Maid of the Mist with Captain Joel Robinson, successfully navigate the whirlpool rapids.

1867 - The first Falls View Bridge is constructed.

1873 - Terrapin tower is pulled down.
1881 - Electric carbon arc lights are installed at Niagara by Charles Brush.

1883 - Matthew Webb dies trying to swim the whirlpool rapids.

1886 - William Kendall, a Boston policeman, swims the whirlpool rapids.

1886 - Carlisle Graham navigates the whirlpool rapids in a barrel.

1887 - Robert Flack killed trying to skirt the rapids in a boat.

1887 - The second Falls View Bridge is in place.

1889 - A storm collapses the Falls View Bridge.

1896 - Electricity is transmitted from the Falls to Buffalo N.Y.

1898 - The Falls View Bridge is replaced by the Upper Steel Arch Bridge, later know as the Honeymoon Bridge.

1899 - An ice bridge breaks loose with 150 people on it; everyone escapes.

1901 - Martha Wagenfuhrer becomes the first woman to successfully navigate the whirlpool rapids in a barrel .

1901 - Maude Williard dies in a barrel at the rapids.

1901 - Anna Edson Taylor becomes the first person to go over the Falls and survive.

1911 - Bobby Leach goes over the Falls in a barrel and survives.

1911 - Lincoln Beachy, the first pilot at Niagara, flies over the Falls and under the Upper Steel Arch Bridge.

1912 - An ice bridge breaks free and three people are killed.

1915 - Thirteen school children are killed in a gorge railway derailment on the Canadian side.

1917 - Fourteen people are thrown into the river and die when a gorge railway train is derailed on the American side.

1918 - An iron scow gets stranded above the falls. Two men are rescued.

1921 - The Adam Beck power station comes on line.

1923 - The American sub-chaser, the Sunbeam breaks free from its moorings and capsizes above the Falls.

1928 - Jean Lussier successfully goes over the Falls in a rubber ball.

1930 - Charles Stephens dies attempting to go over the Falls.

1930 - George Stathakis dies attempting to go over the Falls.

1938 - An ice floe causes the collapse of the Honeymoon Bridge.

1950 - The floral clock is built.

1951 - Red Hill Jr., dies attempting to go over the Falls.

1953 - The movie Niagara! Is filmed starring Joseph Cotton and Marilyn Monroe.

1954 - A large section of Prospect Point crumbles into the river.

1956 - The Schoelkopf plant collapses into the Niagara River.

1960 - Roger Woodward becomes the first and only person to date to survive after going over the Falls unprotected, in what would become known as the Miracle of Niagara.

1961 - Nathan Boya successfully goes over the Falls in a ball.

1975 - A whitewater raft overturns in the whirlpool rapids and three people are killed.

1984 - Karel Soucek successfully navigates the Falls in a barrel only to be killed later in another stunt.

1985 - Steve Trotter survives the Falls in a homemade barrel.

1985 - Dave Munday survives the falls in a barrel.

1989 - Peter DeBernardi and Jeff Petkovich survive together. First team stunt.

1990 - Jessie Sharp dies in an attempt in a kayak.

1993 - Dave Munday becomes first person to go over twice.

1995 - Steve Trotter and Lori Martin survive.

1995 - Robert "Firecracker" Overacker dies on a jet ski.

*2003 - Kirk Jones survives

OVER THE FALLS

1901 - Anna Edson Taylor - survived with cuts and bruises - used a wooden barrel with an anvil for weight-later died in poverty.

1911 - Bobby Leach - survived, broke both keecaps and jaw - used a steel barrel-went on lecture circuit-died after slipping on an orage peel, breaking his leg an incurring an infection.

1928 - Jean Lussier - survived unscathed - used a large rubber ball contraption.

1930 - Charles Stephens - died - used an oak barrel with an anvil tied to his feet-he was ripped apart in the descent-left 11 children fatherless.

1930 - George Stathakis - died - survived plunge but was trapped underneath the Falls for 22 hours and suffocated.

1951 - Red Hill Jr. - died - used a contraption of inner tubes strapped together-was ripped apart in the upper rapids.

1961 - Nathan Boya - survived unscathed - used a rubber ball called the Plunge-O-Sphere-disappeared into anonymity.

1984 - Karel Soucek - survived - used an aluminum barrel-communicated from inside and filmed his journey-later died from barrel stunt in Houston, Texas.

1985 - Steve Trotter - survived in a homemade barrel of tubes and plastic.

1985 - Dave Munday - survived in the most highly sophisticated barrel that cost 16,000 dollars to construct.

1989 - Peter DeBernardi and Jeff Petkovich are the first two person team to go over. They employ a 12 ft. steel-reinforced tank.

1990 - Jessie Sharp plunges to his death while attempting the stunt in a 12 ftt. red kayak. His body is never recovered.

1993 - Dave Munday becomes the first person to complete a second ride over the Falls.

1995 - Steve Trotter goes over the Falls for a second time with partner Lori Martin. Martin is the second woman ever to perform the feat successfully.

1995 - Robert "Firecracker" Overacker plunges to his death while trying to go over the Falls on a jet ski.

*2003 - Kirk Jones survives a plunge over the Falls wearing only his clothes. There is controversy whether this was a stunt or a failed suicide attempt.

*On Monday October 20, 2003 an unemployed man from Canton Michigan became the only person known to have survived a plunge over the Falls without a safety device. Witnesses said they saw Kirk Jones, 40 go over the Falls feet first and was miraculously spared.
AUTHOR'S NOTE

This is a work of fiction. The plot and the characters-in-action are a product of the author's imagination. Where real persons, places, or institutions have been used for background to create the illusion of authenticity; they are used fictitiously. Facts have been altered if necessary for the purpose of the story.

BIBLIOGRAPHY

Berton,Pierre. *NIAGARA , A HISTORY OF THE FALLS.*
Donaldson,Gordon. *NIAGARA THE ETERNAL CIRCUS.*
Hubert, Archer Butler. *THE NIAGARA RIVER.*

Mason,Phillip. *NIAGARA AND THE DAREDEVILS.*
NIAGARA FALLS REVIEW.
Siebel, George A. *NIAGARA RIVER OF FAME.*

FINAL NOTE

In researching this book I was required to go over hundreds of old photographs and pages of history. Since I grew up near the Falls and have always found it fascinating, this was a labor of extreme interest and love. As I walked the hallowed and often checkered halls of Niagara's past, more and more I was drawn into the emotion of the events surrounding this cataract. I found myself exulting with the few who had triumphed and suffering with the many who had failed. I was left with the overall impression of sadness. There was just so much tragedy . Each page I turned was steeped in someone's blood.

An old photograph from 1912 was particularly striking. It depicted a doomed ice floe heading into the rapids with Burrel Heacock and the newlywed Stanton couple aboard. In the frame you can actually see Heacock kneeling in prayer and the Stantons embracing, moments before they met their deaths in the merciless rush of waters. Such a scene even in the black and white of many years hence, plucked poignantly at my heartstrings.

I can still see in my mind's eye the horrified face of Deanne Woodward as she was swept hopelessly along the shore of Goat Island towards the brink. I can almost hear the screams of a little 11 year old boy who was carried over in a raft accident in 1970. His terror must have been unfathomable and not a thing could be done to help him.

Finally I can see Red Hill Jr.'s dog Pal, whimpering pitifully for a fallen master who would never return, somehow innately knowing that his disappearance had something to do with the thundering noise of water in his ears. These were my inspirations and as a result I have been told this novel is on the dark side. Then so be it, but I had to remain true to the real heroes who fought in the trenches of Niagara. If it causes the reader to see Niagara Falls in a new light then all the lives that have been spent there can claim the credit. For those who have never been to Niagara Falls I highly recommend a visit. And always CYFIC.

Robert Sneider

Printed in the United States
76108LV00004B/7